LAST CALL

A TEMPLEVERSE ANTHOLOGY BOOK 1

SHAYNE SILVERS
CAMERON O'CONNELL

ARGENTO PUBLISHING

CONTENTS

Shayne Silvers & Cameron O'Connell

Last Call

A TempleVerse Anthology Book 1

A TempleVerse Series

ISBN 13: 978-1-947709-19-5

© 2018, Shayne Silvers / Argento Publishing, LLC

info@shaynesilvers.com

PART I

MOTHERLUCKER

Feathers and Fire #4.5 / Phantom Queen Diaries #3.5

Coming-of-age can be an awkward time in any young person's life. Hormones flair. Hair grows in weird places. Wrestling becomes foreplay. But at no point in any would-be adult's life is the transition more obvious than the 21st birthday—an American tradition as rich as drinking to celebrate other cultures. But for some, this transcendent experience is rockier than others.

For Aria and Sonya, weredragon sisters and birthday girls, it's about to be downright turbulent.

Head out for a night out on the town with Callie Penrose, Quinn MacKenna, Othello, and the Reds as they do their best to break the "what happens in Vegas, stays in Vegas" adage by taking on the leprechaun mafia, hitting on Johnson Beaver, avoiding were-strippers, donning Dorian Gray's clothing line, robbing a bank, and drinking everything they can get their hands on, of course. If these girls thought Lady Luck was on their side, they should have known better.

Because in Vegas, the House always wins...

CHAPTER 1 — QUINN MACKENNA, BOSTON

They came for me in the middle of the night.

I felt them the instant they entered the room, my hard-won instincts jerking me from an already troubled sleep. A pair of dainty hands snatched my wrists, and another set grabbed my ankles. Or they would have, were I not already drawing them towards my stomach, coiling into a defensive ball. I lashed out with one foot, catching the figure at the base of my bed—little more than a feminine silhouette in the dim light of my bedroom—squarely in the face. She, whoever she was, yelped in pain and fell away.

"Aria!" the woman reaching for my forearms yelled. She didn't get to say much more than that, however, because I used the momentum of my kick to spin away from those hands. I came up swinging, firing off a left jab, then a right cross that made my knuckles sting like hell.

"Damn! That hurt!" the other woman said, clutching her face.

"Sonia!" Aria cried, struggling to her feet on the other side of the room. "What happened?"

"She punched me in the eye! I think she knocked out my contact!"

I rolled off the bed, putting it between me and the would-be assailants, and snatched up the Sig Sauer P226 on my nightstand. I raised it and adjusted into a shooting stance but didn't flick the safety off. Usually, I'd have shot first and asked questions later, but something held me back. For one, if one of my many enemies wanted to jump me in the middle of the night, they'd have hired professionals. These two sounded young and had so far been anything but professional. For another, they clearly had no idea who they were dealing with, or they would have brought at least a few more thugs; two-against-one odds rarely guaranteed a flawless victory.

"Who are ye?" I asked, my Irish brogue cutting in sharply through their muttered curses.

"Is that a gun?" Aria asked, crouching down. At first, I thought she was trying to avoid me aiming at her, but then I realized she was scouring the carpet for the contact lens I'd knocked loose.

Definitely not professionals.

"It is, so don't try anythin' stupid," I said, sounding cliché even to myself.

Sonia perked up, and—even in the darkness—I could tell the pupil of one eye was not only a different color, but a different shape. A horizontal slit like a goat's eye. And the iris was blood red. Well, *that* was entirely new to me. "Cool. Almost none of our friends use guns. I've always wanted one, but Nate never lets me touch his thing."

"That's what she said," the other assailant muttered. Before I could ask the half dozen or so questions this exchange prompted, she spoke up again. "Who the hell keeps a loaded gun next to them in bed?"

"Someone who doesn't like to be woken up in the middle of the night," I replied. "I'm not exactly a mornin' person. Now, tell me who ye are, or I'm goin' to shoot ye on principle." I left out the fact that—now that the adrenaline had worn off—the hangover from the drinks I'd had only a few hours before was making it harder and harder not to shoot them and be done with it.

I could always clean up the mess in the morning.

But then, before they could respond to my ultimatum, a series of knocks sounded at my door, making my shoulders twitch. The two girls exchanged looks in the dark, their faces unreadable. As I considered my options, wondering whether it was merely coincidence that someone was at my door in the middle of the night or whether this was some elaborate scheme, the theme song of "From Russia with Love" began playing on the nightstand on the opposite side of my bed, the light from my phone illuminating the room.

Now that I could see them more clearly, I realized I was looking at a pair of nearly identical girls, each with red hair remarkably similar to my own. They were stunning. Not simply because they were attractive—though they were—but because they were ridiculously dolled up in a pair of cocktail dresses and heels that added five inches to their height at least. How they'd managed to stay upright in those things, let alone sneak into my room, was beyond me.

"Do you want me to get that?" Sonia asked, inching towards the nightstand.

"No, stay right where ye are," I growled.

"I'm just going to get it," she said, stepping forward to flick her finger across the screen with inhuman quickness before returning to where she'd stood only a second before, simultaneously accepting the call and revealing her true nature.

So not professionals, but definitely not human, either.

I snarled and flipped the safety off, overly cautious despite the fact that my own supernatural ability routinely rendered all magic obsolete in close quarters, including superhuman speed. "One more move like that, and I'll put enough silver inside ye to make ye worth sellin' at an antiquary."

"Did she say silver?" Aria asked, hands suddenly raised in surrender.

A voice I recognized echoed throughout my bedroom, emitting from both the phone and outside my door at different speeds. "Quinn, don't shoot them!" Othello urged. "Reds, what did I say?!"

I froze. Othello, a Russian hacker and businesswoman who also happened to be one of my very few friends, was apparently standing outside my apartment, telling me not to gun down the girls who'd broken in to abduct me. "Someone tell me what the fuck is goin' on," I growled. "Now."

"We were just trying to have some fun," Aria whined.

"It's not our fault she fisted us," Sonia added.

"*Punched*," Aria corrected. "She punched us. Well, you. She *kicked* me."

"Girls, what did I tell you?" Othello hissed.

Aria hung her head, her red hair falling forward over her face. "That kidnapping Miss MacKenna was a terrible idea."

"And?" Othello said.

"And," Sonia replied, "very dangerous."

"She still didn't have to kick me in the face," Aria muttered under her breath.

I took a deep, calming breath and flicked the safety back on. "Othello," I said, finally, "what the fuck is goin' on?"

"Oh! Right. Are you busy this weekend?" Othello asked.

I blinked, too thrown by the question to function, my hangover making it nearly impossible to figure out what I'd done in my past life to deserve this shit. Kicked a baby, maybe? Hunted an endangered species into extinction? "Why?" I asked, hesitantly.

"We're going to Vegas," Aria said. Her grin was easy to see in the light provided by my phone. She was no longer the least bit remorseful.

"For our birthdays," Sonia said, hopping up and down, her skintight dress barely holding everything in.

"And we wanted to see if you'd like to come," Othello chimed in, her voice still echoing from the corridor.

I lowered my gun, eyeing the two girls, each of whom looked like a kid who'd been given a Golden Ticket to Willy Wonka's Chocolate factory. I could tell they desperately wanted me to say yes, despite the swelling settling in along Sonia's raptorial eye and along Aria's cheek. Had it been anyone but me they'd come for, it was entirely possible that these two—with their frightening speed and supreme recklessness—would have succeeded in kidnapping them, whisking them off into the night. I set the gun down on the mattress and began massaging my aching temples.

Jesus Christ, a night in Vegas with two would-be kidnappers and a Russian hacker.

Sure, why not? What could go wrong?

CHAPTER 2 — CALLIE PENROSE. KANSAS CITY

I stepped out of the darkened alley, scanning the streets for any sign of danger. My tight jeans and tank were casual, but the cleavage factor was a ten, and the sporty short black coat dressed up my outfit enough to hopefully gain me entrance into the club across the street.

Regulars—humans without any flavor of magic about them—formed a line waiting to get in, but I knew the bouncer was something else entirely, a shifter cat of some sort, one of many supernatural creatures we called Freaks. The unsuspecting humans, of course, had no idea they were so close to danger, probably assuming the bouncer was nothing more than a strong, handsome Hispanic man. But like knew like, which meant he would probably recognize me—Callie Penrose, the wizard who hunted monsters for the Vatican—in an instant. He might even wonder if I was here to ruin his day.

Luckily for him, I wasn't. I had a friend waiting inside. Well, *friend* might be pushing it. More like a business acquaintance. As per usual, Dorian Gray only held business meetings in less than reputable places. Hence the night club.

I walked up to the bouncer, making sure to not look threatening or aggressive, in case he'd heard of me. As expected, he marked me before I made it even halfway across the street, and his eyes narrowed instinctively.

He wasn't challenging me. It was more like he was asking a silent question. *Are you going to be trouble tonight, Miss?*

I smiled innocently, lifting my palms as I continued to walk, shaking my head as I neared. "I'm here to meet a friend. Mr. Gray."

A trio of curvy brunettes at the front of the line tittered upon hearing what sounded like a *Fifty Shades of Grey* reference. More giggles followed as they openly judged my casual attire, obviously a few levels below what they deemed club appropriate. I didn't really care about their fashion opinions or what deep-seated fantasies they held about a billionaire bondage relationship. I wasn't that kind of girl.

The laughter continued longer than I decided I wanted to tolerate, so I glanced over at the instigator of the group, meeting her mahogany eyes. I pointedly studied her up and down, from cleavage to caboose. If her top had been any lower or her shorts any shorter she could have auditioned for a job at a strip club. Her friends weren't dressed any classier. They hadn't learned that a girl could still look sexy without baring it all.

"If you keep giving away the popsicles for free, no one's going to want to buy the ice cream truck," I told the three of them with a full-faced smile.

Their laughter cut off as cleanly as if I had used a cleaver on a slab of meat, but the rest of the line burst out laughing and clapping. I dipped my chin at them in proud acknowledgment.

"Mr. Gray will see you now," the bouncer said hurriedly, unclipping the velvet rope. The gang of harlots quickly realized that not only had I embarrassed them, but that I really did have some kind of VIP connection.

I shot them a smirk. "See?" I took a step forward.

"Callie!" a seemingly familiar pair of voices shrieked from behind me. I spun reflexively, the sheer volume of their combined shouts enough to set my every sense on alert. The bouncer's shoulders tightened, and his jaw clenched as we both looked across the street.

I relaxed somewhat upon seeing the Reds—two sister shifter dragons, named Sonia and Aria, who looked almost identical to each other with shimmering red hair—marching across the street, dressed to the nines in high heels and classily-revealing club clothes. I blinked once, twice, and then held out my hand to the bouncer. "I know them," I murmured, before realizing the Reds were not alone. Othello—a hacker extraordinaire and friend of mine—who pretty much ran Nate Temple's billion-dollar tech company—was also with them. Taking up the rear was a third woman I did not recognize—a very tall, blade-thin, red-haired stunner. Except, at the moment, her striking features were molded into an angry mask, reminding me of a Catholic after last call. I considered telling the bouncer I didn't know her, but Othello was waving excitedly just as the Reds skidded up beside me, and I decided not to split hairs.

"Where have you been all my life, Muscles?" Sonia asked to the bouncer, lightly flicking his nipple where a barbell piercing could be seen poking from beneath his shirt.

He had been sniffing the air absently, likely sensing she was a dragon shifter, but her question caught him up short and he blinked incredulously. He burst out laughing. "Evening."

"You can't let them cut in line!" one of the girls in the crowd complained in a whining tone. "It's not—"

"Can it, skankbitch, the women are talking," Aria snarled.

I arched an eyebrow at her, ignoring the indignant squawks from the Kansas City socialites. "I'm pretty sure they're older than you," I offered, still wondering what the hell the Reds were doing here. They lived in St. Louis, after all, and hadn't told me they would be visiting.

Sonia glanced past me at the still-whining woman, eyeing her pointedly from heel to hair. "You're right," she murmured. Then she cleared her throat. "I'm sorry for my sister's rude comment. We were taught better than to disrespect our elders. But should someone your age really be going to places like this?" she asked, too sweetly. "And in your lingerie, no less?"

The woman shrieked, extending her fingers out like claws. Luckily—because Sonia and Aria were suddenly grinning in anticipation—the bouncer knew how to spot potential trainwrecks before they happened. "Now, now. No fighting. Since Callie is holding up the line, you and your friends can go on in," he told them.

The woman sniffed disdainfully in our direction and gave the bouncer a cool look, as if he was merely doing as he should and not granting them a favor. Then they were walking past him before he could call them on their shitty attitudes.

"Be sure to give them the old-bird special!" Sonia called out, loud enough for everyone to hear, igniting an encore of laughter and claps from the crowd.

The brunette socialite's shoulders stiffened, but she jerkily made her way closer to the door.

"I think you mean the early bird special. For the senior citizens," Aria corrected. Again, loud enough for all to hear.

The brunette socialite turned back with a snarl, and Othello suddenly latched onto the Reds' shoulders with her hands. "Time to go! Callie, can we talk to you for a minute?"

"Is it important? Because I have a meeting inside," I said, pointing my thumb at the club.

"No offense, but I'd rather not break up a girl-on-girl mosh pit," the bouncer said meaningfully. "I hate seeing pretty things destroy each other."

Sonia sniffed in disapproval. "You should try *everything* once, Muscles."

He grinned before Othello jerked them back across the street. With a regretful sigh, I shot the bouncer an apologetic look. "I didn't know they were coming here, but I'll take care of them."

He nodded. "You are welcome to come back, but as much fun as those two are, they look too young, and hotheads cause problems when the alcohol flows."

"Thanks," I said, turning to jog after Othello, who was pigeon-walking the Reds back across the street. The red-headed stranger looked annoyed, leaning back against the brick wall with the flat of one boot propped against it so her knee was bent out ahead of her.

"I'm goin' to need a fuckin' drink soon if I'm goin' to chase away me hangover," she said in an Irish brogue thick enough for me to chew on, by way of introduction.

"There are drinks right there," Sonia pointed back at the club.

I shook my head. "Not a chance. Bouncer shut us down."

I studied the unknown red-headed woman, who had arched a brow at Othello. "Can ye explain to me why we aren't in Vegas already?" she asked. "Ye know I don't like bein' this close to St. Louis."

I frowned at that—as did the Reds—but Othello seemed to dismiss both the comment and the woman as she turned to me. "It's their twenty-first birthday," she explained, pointing a thumb at the Reds. The two dragons were bouncing on their toes, nodding their heads.

"We want to go get drunk," Sonia said eagerly.

"Really drunk," Aria clarified.

"Jesus. Was I ever that young?" the redhead muttered, staring up at the sky as if she were actually talking to God.

Othello noticed my frown. "Oh, this is Quinn. She works in the antiquities business in Boston."

Quinn snorted. "That's a fancy way to put it." She met my eyes. "I'm an arms dealer."

I nodded as if that made perfect sense.

"Don't worry. Her face doesn't always look like that," Sonia said, studying Quinn. "She said it gets more pleasant with alcohol."

Quinn shrugged, but nodded. "Doesn't everyone's?"

"Vegas," I breathed, thinking. My appointment with Dorian wasn't particularly important, more of a catch-up and hang out than anything. However, if I skipped our meeting he was liable to show up at my apartment in the middle of the night to ask why I had stood him up, ignoring my demands about how he had broken in, why he was naked, or why he had brought two lovers with him. Dorian was unashamed about any deviant act he chose to participate in, so I could wake up to find him napping next to me naked—all because he hadn't wanted to wait to call me about it in the morning. So, if I did skip my meeting with him, I really did need to get out of town.

"Fine. I'll just wear this."

The Reds clapped eagerly.

"To Vegas?" Quinn asked, looking me up and down. "Whatever does it for ye, I guess."

Thus began the most bizarre night of my life. I waited for a few seconds, but no one moved.

Finally, Othello turned to me. "Um... could you make us a Gateway to the Bellagio? I used the last of Nate's tiny balls to get us here." I smirked at the nickname for the magic traveling devices he had created—able to transport you from one place to another across the globe with a single step. Great for those non-wizards who couldn't use magic to make their own Gateways.

"Nate's what?" Quinn asked, thrown by the reference to Nate's genitalia.

Othello waved that away. "So, how about it?" she asked me.

"Alright," I said, realizing I had no way to get out of it. They wouldn't leave me alone until I agreed. This way I could hold onto at least a sliver of my dignity.

CHAPTER 3 — QUINN MACKENNA, VEGAS

My hangover had gone from bad to abysmal the instant we left my apartment. Maybe it was something about traveling via Gateway, but I was quickly learning that defying the laws of physics by traveling from place-to-place instantaneously came with some serious physical repercussions. Or maybe I was just that hungover. Either way, I hadn't exactly been up for easy-going banter with Othello, or able to handle the manic energy the Reds exuded at all times. If anything, I felt like I enjoyed the company of our newest member—Callie Penrose—best of all.

And by that I meant we'd hardly exchanged more than a few words since we met. She'd guided us to a church where she said she could make a Gateway undetected. Something about a guy in the club being the kind of person who might track her down if she used magic too close to where we had met her.

To be honest, I still wasn't sure what to make of Callie. I'd picked at her a little every so often, trying to get under her skin, but with little result. It wasn't personal, not really. But there was something about her, something dangerous and calculating, which simultaneously attracted and repelled me. Her long snow-white hair was as silky and thick as fresh powder on a mountain. Then again, maybe it was her getup; who wears jeans and a tank top to go out in Vegas, for Christ's sakes? Only someone that gorgeous with that much cleavage, I decided.

Cocky bitch.

"Now what?" I asked, almost the instant we stepped through the Gateway into an abandoned stairwell. I spun in a slow circle. "This is not a bar. Ye promised me a bar," I said, arching an eyebrow at Othello.

"You can't go around creating Gateways in public places," Othello said, as if that were obvious.

"The Bellagio is through there," Callie said, pointing towards a sign that said exactly that, indicating we would find a door two floors down. Now that I thought about it, I could make out the whirr and chimes which could only have represented one thing: a casino floor. And, where there are gamblers, there are drinks; it's easier to lose a shit ton of money if you're too drunk to care.

"I could kiss ye," I said, smirking.

Now it was Callie's turn to raise an eyebrow. "I would rather you didn't."

"Ooh, cat fight," Aria teased.

"Knock it off you two," Othello interjected.

I considered ignoring her, wondering if this was my chance to test the white-haired woman's patience. Sure, she looked dangerous enough, but she was also some type of wizard—at least that's what the Gateway suggested. And wizards, in my experience, were a bunch of pansy-asses who relied entirely too much on their magic. Callie looked plenty fit, but it's hard to tell how much of her muscle was for function and how much for show. Ultimately, though, a fight wouldn't be in my favor; I'd gone with a pair of black suede pants, stylish black leather boots, and a black bustier that left my chest and arms bare. It was a ridiculously severe, monochrome look, but I'd dressed in a hurry with the Reds literally breathing down my neck. On the other hand, in jeans and a tank top, Callie could wrestle me to her heart's content without screwing up her outfit.

Which meant I needed a different approach.

"D'ye have a problem with me?" I asked, planting both hands on my hips and squaring off my body. I watched Callie slide her foot back, centering herself in case things got aggressive. So, a fighter. Good.

"I don't know you," Callie replied calmly.

I grinned. She'd taken the bait. "Well, where I come from there's only one way to fix that." I turned my body slightly and adjusted my feet, letting her see that she wasn't the only one who knew how to size up an opponent.

The Reds, I noticed, licked their lips in anticipation at almost the exact same moment. "Hold up! This is going on Instagram!" Aria grinned, snapping a picture of the two of us with her phone before I could slap it from her hands. I sighed, wondering what batshit crazy hashtag she'd throw on the description. Regardless, it was obvious the Reds were eager to have some entertainment on their birthday. I hoped not to disappoint. Callie's eyes were no longer cool and rational. In fact, something lurked behind them, something that had nothing to do with reason or fear. Something predatory. "And what's that?" she asked in a too cool tone.

I grinned, turned, and began descending the stairs. "We drink, ye daft t'ing! Bet ye can't stay upright longer than I can, Callie Penrose." I glanced up at them all from a few steps down. Othello looked appropriately mortified, although a little relieved, as well. The Reds seemed to waver between disappointment and excitement; they were going to get a show alright, just not the one they'd anticipated. Callie, on the other hand, seemed entirely sure of herself. She approached the rail and leaned forward, chest on display.

"You're on, Quinn MacKenna." And her eyes glittered like an impending avalanche.

CHAPTER 4 — CALLIE PENROSE, VEGAS

My phone began ringing, so I slowed my walk to bring up the rear of our ragtag crew. "Hello?" I asked without looking, focused instead on my companions because between the massive crowd in the lobby of the hotel and Quinn's brisk pace, I couldn't afford to lose them. Especially not with all the wealthy men nearby taking far too much interest in me now that I was lagging behind. My pale hair drew looks wherever I went, but their attention was even more pronounced now that I trailed behind the three redheads and stunning brunette who looked suspiciously like one of those kindergarten teachers who may or may not strip on the side.

As a whole, we were figuratively snapping necks of any hungry male within eyesight. But it was likely any one of us drifting from the group would earn more male attention than we'd bargained for. Which meant I had to speak loudly into the phone, using it as a shield whenever a guy got too close. "Hasn't anyone ever told you foreplay without climax is pure torture?" a man's voice asked.

I found myself rolling my eyes and smiling. "You're welcome, Dorian."

He sighed. "You pick a fight outside the club and then leave? You could have at least finished it and started a girl fight inside," Dorian complained.

I shook my head. "Sorry. I had a last-minute emergency."

"Where? I'll meet you. This place is a bore. There are hardly any naked people here."

I snorted. "I can't. I'm actually in Vegas."

"Oh, *really*?" Dorian replied, sounding suddenly very interested, as if he was leaning over his phone and drooling. "Do tell."

"Last minute birthday party for a few friends."

There was a pregnant pause. "Friends... but you only just now learned it was their birthday?" he said doubtfully.

"Maybe close acquaintances would be more accurate," I admitted. Sensing he wasn't buying it, I pressed on. "*Twenty-first* birthday."

"Ahhhh..." Dorian replied. "Those are sacred events for the virginal."

I spotted the Reds dancing past a section of slot machines and towards what looked like a bar on the opposite side of the casino. I ignored the glazed looks from those unfortunate souls who lived and breathed the casino atmosphere. It wasn't my cup of tea. The dichotomy of the uber rich and those desperately hoping and praying for a big score to pay back their debts always rubbed me the wrong way.

"Hello?" Dorian asked, sensing my distraction. I'd been too focused on making sure all four of my party were in fact heading in the same general direction, in pursuit of the giggling, skipping, hand-holding weredragons. Their boobs were going to be on full display at some point, I just knew it. There was simply no way around it the way they frolicked around like drunk puppies.

"Yes. Sorry, Dorian. I need to go. You know how new drinkers can get. Like herding cats."

"Because you are such a seasoned drinker..." Dorian said dryly.

"Hey! I know how to drink!" I argued. "It's just not a major hobby of mine."

"You won't get better without practice. Where are you anyway?"

"The Bellagio," I said, before I could consider lying. Shit. I didn't want Dorian Gray showing up to this soirée. That had been the entire point of making my Gateway far away from the club. "Promise you won't coincidentally appear at the same bar as us. It's a girls' night."

He sighed. "But I love girls' nights," he said in a pouty voice.

"I'm sure you'll manage. But you still haven't promised."

He let out an impatient sigh. "Fine. I promise. We will reschedule our meeting, party pooper. Don't do anything I wouldn't do," he teased.

"That's a very short list, Dorian." I could hear him chuckling in agreement. "I need to go before I lose them."

"One more thing," he said. "Consider it very friendly fashion advice from Dorian Gray. Leather is a girl's best friend." He hung up before I could reply with a response. I glared down at my phone before slipping it into my coat pocket. The bastard.

I saw Othello glancing back at me, having slowed down enough to make sure I didn't lose them. She matched my stride, pointing towards the bar. Quinn was right behind the Reds, far ahead of us, and I saw them enter the bar on the other side of the casino floor.

Othello noticed my attention on Quinn. "She really is a nice girl," she said.

"God save us from nice girls," I murmured, studying the tall redhead. With a face and legs like hers, I secretly hoped to catch her stumbling around like a baby deer, but so far, no such luck.

"Fine. She's an ice-cold bitch. But I like her, so play nice," Othello said firmly.

I met her eyes and finally let out a breath, nodding apologetically. "I'll try." Othello seemed pleased enough with my response, because she gave me a warm smile as we continued on.

She flicked my braid with a finger, leaning close. "Not a fan of the short hair?" she asked. "I think it makes you look smoking hot. I can think of someone else who agrees, but then I'm pretty sure he likes both styles. Maybe you've met him..."

I slapped at her hand. "I *do* like the short hair, but the legend of the long white hair saves me from a lot of unwanted attention in Kansas City. Both from fights and men."

"Maybe it would help if you made some new legends with your short hair."

"Maybe..." Truthfully, I'd been looking into growing my hair back out. I missed it. Surprisingly, short hair was harder for me to style, and with the Midwest's humidity it usually turned into a puffy bob, which I definitely didn't like. I decided to change topics. "So, the ice-cold bitch. What's her story?" I asked, discreetly jerking my chin towards Quinn.

Othello grinned. "Sooo cold. I love her. She's got that Catholic upbringing and the same devil-may-care attitude as you, but she's rougher around the edges. You two really would get along quite well if you got out of your own way. She's helped me acquire a thing or two for Grimm Tech recently. Quite the thief. But, even better, she's one hell of a negotiator."

I watched Quinn slip into the bar after she glanced back at us suspiciously. I tried to smile, but from the look on Quinn's face, I wasn't that successful.

Othello sighed. "I'll talk to her, don't worry. She's cagey around new people. Especially girls."

"I can drink to that," I said, smiling as I let out a breath. This was supposed to be a fun night for the Reds. I wondered if their mother knew about our little adventure, or if Othello had kidnapped them. Thinking about that further, I probably didn't want to know.

Plausible deniability.

"She looks ready for a fight. No, not just ready. It's like she *wants* to fight," I clarified.

Othello nodded. "She's like that. But she's handy in a pinch."

I glanced over at her. "We aren't planning on getting in a *pinch* tonight, right?"

Othello gave me a crooked smile. "Right," she said in a way that gave me zero confidence.

We entered the bar to find the Reds already seated on two stools at the far end of the bar. Quinn took a stool near the corner, letting her face the room, leaving her back open to no one. I sighed, brushing my braid back over my shoulder, and put a happy smile on my face as the Reds motioned us over with gleeful smiles of their own.

I joined them, sitting next to Quinn. Othello walked up to the center of the bar and slapped a stack of cash onto the counter, leaning close to speak with the bartender. "How are we doing this?" the Reds asked excitedly, leaning far enough forward that their breasts might as well have had a spotlight trained on them. Several men in the bar took notice, but Othello snapped something at them and they cowered under her motherly glare. I grinned and heard Quinn chuckle beside me.

I turned back to the Reds, an idea coming to mind. "Let's play Never Have I Ever," I told them. This could break the ice that was—for some reason—

growing between me and Quinn. It could also give me an opportunity to put her in her place. Because, without knowing it, Othello had let a few things slip about our black magic arms dealer friend which I could use to my advantage.

"How do you play?" Aria asked, grinning at me with her dazzling white teeth.

"We take turns making statements like this: *Never have I ever robbed a bank.* The person speaking can't have done whatever it is, and anyone else who has done it puts one of their ten fingers down, then drinks. A drink for each finger."

"Can we say something we *have* done and then drink, anyway?" Aria asked, licking her lips.

I shook my head. "That would defeat the purpose. You want to find out what you haven't done that the other people have."

Quinn studied me suspiciously. "Good way to learn some secrets about each other."

I shrugged. "Everyone gets a turn."

Othello suddenly sat down beside me, interrupting the tension. "Drinks inbound, but before we get started, we need to have a toast to Aria and Sonia. If we save it for later, you bitches might be too drunk to remember it."

Quinn snorted. "Aye."

As if on cue, the bartender brought over a fucking castle of shots. Literally. A pyramid of shots was divided among us—except Othello only got one. I arched a brow at her. "Oh, really?" I said, eyeing her solo drink.

She shrugged. "I'm playing mother hen." She pointed at the Reds. "Their mom's orders."

The Reds exchanged perplexed glances.

I arched a brow. "I'm not sure she chose very wisely," I teased. "Nate's told me stories about you."

She stiffened momentarily at my comment, but when I didn't speak she simply picked up her drink. "Toast," she demanded. What had I said to elicit *that* kind of reaction? I'd have to ask Nate. Othello cleared her throat as we each grabbed one of our eleven shots. I took a calming breath. Eleven shots were going to kill us. Some mother hen she was.

Othello lifted her glass and we all followed suit, smiling as we realized this signaled the beginning of the fun night ahead. A peaceful night in the bar was doable. Then we could stumble up to our hotel rooms and pass out to sleep it off.

"Here's to the nights we'll never remember with the friends we'll never forget." Othello said.

"Awww…" the Reds said in unison, blowing kisses at Othello. Quinn had a decidedly awkward smile on her face, as if pretending to like the meal her mother had just made her.

We all grinned madly as our attention turned to our drinks, and we downed the shot.

My eyes widened as I stared down at my empty glass. "What in the hell was *that*?" I asked in disbelief. It tasted delicious, but I still sensed the heavy, heavy, *heavy* amount of alcohol within.

Othello grinned, tipping her shot glass in an educational display for the Reds, setting it down in front of her upside down. "It's called a Fairy Bomb. And no, I won't tell you what's in it."

Quinn looked like she had tasted Heaven for a moment, and I found myself grinning. The Reds' entire understanding of life was about to change. In fact, Sonia was licking the rim of her glass. Aria elbowed her gently, glancing at a pair of older men down the bar who were eyeing her sister with entirely too much interest. Sonia slowly looked up and locked eyes with the men in such a fashion that they instantly averted their eyes. Content, they both tipped their shot glasses before them, duplicating Othello's movements, and then turned to me expectantly.

Wanting to take advantage of their attention and to take the first question, I spoke. "Never have I ever—"

"Hold on," Othello quickly interrupted. "I think it's safer if I start this one off," she said, eyeing Quinn and me—we were both leaning forward, I noticed. The feisty redhead was just as competitive as me, and she masked a faint blush as she came to the same realization. I shot her a guilty smile and forcefully relaxed my shoulders before turning to Othello. "Fine, Mommy."

"I'm ready whenever ye are, Othello," Quinn said, hands splayed. "As long as it's *now*."

Othello sneered triumphantly. "Never have I ever…assaulted a priest."

There was a brittle silence. "Well, fuck," Quinn said, looking amused as she gripped a new shot glass. "See if I ever tell ye any more stories from me childhood." She pounded her shot but set it down with a smile.

I grinned at her and took one of my own shots. "The Antipope in Rome," I shrugged with a smug grin. "Beat the living shit out of him after he turned into a werewolf." I mimed a punch to the jaw.

Quinn chuckled and propped one foot up on the bar of her stool. "Callie, I t'ink this may be the beginnin' of a beautiful friendship." Othello and the Reds seemed pleased by the exchange, but I noticed the Reds looked disappointed to have avoided a shot of their own.

Guess we'd have to fix that.

CHAPTER 5 — QUINN MACKENNA, VEGAS

I cradled my chin in my hands, two digits outstretched to represent the two shots remaining in front of me. Nine empty glasses and most of my sobriety had already been swiped off the bar top by the industrious bartender, who'd poured our squad forty-four shots, plus one for Othello. I had no idea what was in the damn things, but their name I would never forget: Fairy Bombs. The delicious taste masked the intensity of the alcohol content and made me wonder just what Othello's goal here was; if she wanted us all loosened up, she'd done her job. If she wanted us even remotely sober, she was totally fired.

"Never have I ever," Callie began, sitting firmly upright as if trying to fend of the alcohol's effects, "hit a god. Little g," she added, with a giggle and a slight hiccup. She glared down at her only remaining finger, as if it was somehow responsible for the slip in her stoic demeanor.

Othello sighed and dropped to one finger, as well, even though she wasn't actually drinking. "I hit one last night." Then she, too, giggled.

Callie rolled her eyes. "The Horseman of Death is not a *god.*"

"Weird, since he makes me say it so often. *Oh god, oh god, oh god,*" Othello moaned, doing her best impersonation of Meg Ryan in *When Harry Met Sally.*

The Reds, who'd given up playing the game in favor of simply drinking the shots, spat out the contents of their final glass onto the bar at the same time, choking with laughter. Meanwhile, I surreptitiously downed my own. I wasn't sure how many of the creatures I'd put down qualified as gods, but I was betting the cumulative karmic result of beating a demonic fox spirit to death, taking down a millennia-old monster, and smacking around a pinhead of angels was the same.

Basically, I'd been a bad, bad girl.

I watched as the Reds lapped the spilled liquor off the sticky bar top with excessively long, forked tongues, clearly too hammered to fret over things like hygiene, social etiquette, or partially shifting. I didn't know what kind they were, but the forked tongues gave me a pretty good guess. "Can't leave this stuff lying around," Sonia explained, half to herself, half to us.

Aria nodded, her own voice slurred. "Alcohol abuse. Not cool."

"What are you two doing?" Othello hissed. "This is a casino full of Regulars. And since when can you two partially shift?"

"Oh, the things we can do that you don't know about," Aria began.

"Would blow you," Sonia finished.

"Your *minds*," Aria amended. "Blow your *minds*."

The sisters glanced at each other and began to cackle. Yes, cackle. Then, before any of us could respond, they plopped off their stools and began wobbling away, skittering across the casino floor on their freakishly tall heels. Othello's eyes narrowed as she saw them leaving. "Hey, where are you two going?"

"Ladies' room," Sonia yelled.

"Or the men's room, if the lines are too long," Aria added, loud enough to draw stares.

"How are they walkin' straight?" I wondered aloud.

"Shifter constitution?" Othello suggested.

"I'm surprised their mom let you take them out," Callie said, watching the girls as they left, then the men who were doing the same.

Othello groaned and set her head down on her forearm. "I didn't tell her. Quinn, I think it's your turn."

I coughed to cover up a laugh and glanced down at my lone finger, then at the two women sitting before me. Callie and I were drunk. The signs were obvious, no matter how tall Callie held herself. I operated in a perpetually tipsy state a vast majority of the time when I wasn't working or training, which meant I had the edge when it came to endurance. But soon, I knew, I'd collide with that fuzzy wall we all hit eventually. The wall which knocks our memories loose and sends us careening into a night we can't forget no matter how hard we try.

"Never have I ever..." I said, drawing out the last word like Squints from *Sandlot*, "wanted to sleep with Nate Temple." I watched in grim amusement as the heads of both women jerked up. Their eyes widened in surprise, then narrowed in suspicion.

"Who told you?" Callie hissed.

"What she said," Othello added.

I grinned and waggled my finger. "A lady never tells." The truth—that it had been a blind shot in the dark which I'd hoped might nail at least one of them—wasn't particularly relevant. What *was* relevant was the fact that I'd won. I'd emerged victorious. Queen Quinn.

"Wait, you mean you really didn't want to sleep with him when you first met him?" Othello asked, as if the thought of that were like passing on your birthday for no reason.

"The dickhead who hijacked me Uber? No t'anks," I replied.

"Wait? That was you?" Callie said, liquid dribbling all over her hand from her shot glass that was poised mere inches from her lips. But before I could reply, Othello's phone rang. The Russian woman snatched the device up and slid her finger across the screen, then hit the speakerphone option.

"Where are you two?" she barked.

A cacophony of noise spewed out from the tiny phone—more noise than I'd thought possible. Mostly cheers and jeers, but also funky, twangy music that might have been bluegrass or old country. "We got lost!" Aria shouted.

"But we found nice people who helped us take our clothes off!" Sonia yelled.

"You *what*?!" Othello asked, mouth agape. "You've only been gone a few *minutes!*"

The line went dead and the three of us stared at one another, wondering how in the world we'd let the birthday girls get abducted in the first few hours. In Vegas. Competitiveness, maybe? Cattiness? Either way, we had to table our Nate Temple discussion for later. Not that I minded.

That guy was a prick.

CHAPTER 6 — CALLIE PENROSE, VEGAS

I slipped off the barstool faster than I had intended, but Quinn had done the same, and we ended up leaning so that we essentially caught each other in one of those typically awkward stranger hugs. We both froze like startled deer, laughed uncomfortably, straightened, and took unsteady steps back. Othello was frantically punching her screen with her thumbs, muttering under her breath.

"Got them!" she snapped, using her thumb and forefinger to rotate something on her phone's screen. I shambled closer, learning to work with my new tipsy equilibrium since I wasn't used to getting drunk very often. I squinted down at Othello's phone to find a bizarre version of a map that had a lot of numbers, coordinates, and strange icons on it. It looked suspiciously illegal, and there were two flashing red circles surprisingly far away. I squinted closer. No. They weren't far away. They were in the same building, but a few floors down—apparently Othello's phone showed vertical, in addition to lateral, distances.

I cocked my head, sensing Quinn doing the same. She even had one of her eyes closed, as if that could help. "That doesn't make any sense," I said slowly. "I can't tell if that's the same building or not..."

Othello looked concerned. "I think it's a secret area..." She tapped her screen a few times, pulling up a different angle. She suddenly had a second phone in her hand, revealing…

"Fuck me!" Quinn hissed. "Is that a blueprint for the Bellagio?" she hissed.

Many in the bar glanced over at us, including a trio of young, baby-faced guys sporting the confident look of men who thought they stood a chance with any of us. They were rocking that wealthy, homeless look that was popular with a subgroup of hipsters these days. Strangely enough, I noticed three other men spread about the bar, eyes fixated on the trio—but not in a way that seemed threatening. They were ridiculously well-muscled and had ear pieces in. Shit, building security? No, *personal* security. Quinn followed my gaze, noticed the men, and instantly set her shoulders, squaring off with all of them.

Not the hipsters or the security personnel.

All of them.

Before I realized it, I was standing beside her, glaring down the security detail—who suddenly looked very interested in us.

"Fuck ye lookin' at, One Erection?" Quinn spat, eyeing the would-be boy band.

"What did you call us?" the guy in the middle said, sliding a hand along his pompadour as if he were practicing for a shampoo commercial. He stared at us with a crooked smile, cocking his head.

"Ye heard me. And I don't like to repeat meself," Quinn warned. "Keep your eyes to yourself, ye hear?"

His smile faltered, and he shot incredulous glances at his pals. "You don't know who he is?" the bleached blonde kid on the left said, jerking a thumb towards the guy in the middle, his arm layered with a full sleeve of tattoos.

"Of course we don't know ye. I don't make a habit of poundin' 'em back with high-schoolers," Quinn replied.

The three stiffened as one, but the one in the center looked especially offended. The security detail began angling towards us like sharks. I flicked my hair over my shoulder, smirking darkly at the three. "And how are you supposed to protect your boss' son if I send you to the hospital for disrespecting two young women?" I called out, loud enough for everyone in the bar to hear.

I may as well have chucked a full bottle of top shelf liquor to the floor for the reaction it got. Silence fell, and a few of the older men stood from their barstools, slowly making as if to enter the fray.

"Six on two..." I tapped my lower lip and glanced over to Quinn. "I think we're sober enough for that warm up."

Quinn grinned, her eyes twinkling. "Eeny, meeny—"

Othello suddenly clapped her hands on our shoulders, spinning us around and pushing us in the opposite direction. "I think we've had enough of this bar," Othello told the men, shoving us again and essentially marching us away before we could respond. "That was Johnson fucking Beaver, you drunkasses!" she hissed into our ears.

"Who the fuck is Johnson Beaver?" Quinn asked, incredulous.

"We could have taken them," I growled under my breath.

"Not the point! He's a celebrity. It would be *bad* if you beat his ass. We'd go straight to jail, no questions asked. And we would be on the news for ruining his concert tonight."

"Concert?" I asked, frowning. Then the rest of her words hit me. "Wait. He's that Johnson Beaver? The singer?"

"Looked more like a drug dealer," Quinn said.

I agreed loudly, hoping they might overhear. "I didn't even see them enter the bar! Didn't Nate have a run in with him at a concert?"

Othello met my eyes very intently, holding up two fingers. "Firstly, we aren't allowed to talk about that alleged event. Secondly, it doesn't *matter*." Othello growled. "The Reds, remember?"

"Oh..." I said sheepishly. "Did you, *hiccup*, find them?" I asked.

She took the lead, calling over her shoulder. "Stay close or I will blame this all on you two."

Quinn muttered something about putting Beaver on the endangered species list where he could remain safe, but she did shoot me a conspiratorial grin when Othello wasn't looking. I found myself grinning right back.

I realized, in hindsight, that I had acted unusually courageous. Well, fearless. Reckless. But the lights here were bright and pretty, the sounds like a piano solo designed just for me, and I felt light on my feet, no longer burdened with stress. I couldn't really remember the last time I'd been drunk, now that I thought about it.

I'd been missing out on life.

I was no longer a wobbly mess, and I'd kind of found my stride. Maybe the brief adrenaline rush with the security had sobered me up a little. Or redirected my focus. I also realized that whether intentional or not, Quinn and I had bonded. Friendship forged in a near bar fight.

Stranger things...

CHAPTER 7 — QUINN MACKENNA, VEGAS

You know when you meet someone you're determined not to like, but then you find out you have a singular crazy, obscure thing in common that could potentially bind you together as friends forever? Well, that was Callie and I after we stood up to our newfound acquaintances—the punk ass hipsters and their hired muscle. At least until we found the Reds in a hidden pocket of the Bellagio compound and realized we had one other mutual acquaintance whose legendary charm was highly debatable: Dorian fucking Gray.

"I'm not surprised, but I am appalled," Callie said between the bout of hiccups she'd picked up on our mad dash chasing after Othello. She was staring up at the graffiti which marred the nearest wall. A ten-foot mural of Dorian Gray, so pretty it almost hurt, had been rendered lovingly along this side of the alley, revealing far too much of his anatomy for my liking, but stopping mercifully short of gratuitousness. Below one of his nipples hung a blocky sign with two words branded into the wood: *Rassle Tassel*. Massive double doors took up space beneath and were manned by two beefy bouncers dressed only in leather chaps. Classy. Super classy.

"So you think this is one of Dorian's clubs?" Othello asked, looking skeptical.

"I mean..." Callie replied, waving a vague hand at the mural as if that was all that needed to be said.

She was right. It was a tasteless display, but definitely consistent with Dorian's gaudy style. Of course, I was determined not to like it; the last time I'd seen the bastard he'd been producing a fight-to-the-death, no-holds-barred tournament on a lawn in upstate New York. And yours truly had been on the fight card. "Fuck that guy," I said. "Next time I see him, I'm goin' to shove me foot up his ass and see how he likes it."

Callie snorted, then covered her mouth, then snorted again. "I think he'd like it a lot."

Othello was nodding as if that made perfect sense.

I frowned, then realized what she was saying. "Oh, gross. I didn't mean that literally."

"Still, it's true," Callie grinned.

"Come on," Othello said, wearing her sobriety like a shawl; she'd been casually bumping into us whenever we threatened to wobble off like a mother duck pecking at her chicks. I'd allowed it only because I was pretty sure I'd have careened into strangers, otherwise, and I hated strangers on principle. Occupational hazard, you might say.

Callie trudged after her as she headed towards the door, and I followed. The bouncers took one look at us—Othello with her sexy librarian look, me in my skin-tight leathers, and Callie in her form-fitting street clothes—and parted without a word, pulling the double doors open as they went. Noise burst from within, shockingly loud, a combination of country music and catcalls. One voice, however, rose above the din. A recognizable voice, though deeper and fiercer than I thought could possibly emerge from her pale, dainty throat.

"We are the mudpackers!" Sonia roared. She wore a red leather bondage outfit that reminded me a lot of Leeloo's initial getup in *Fifth Element*. It trapped and hid the parts of her that needed to be trapped and hidden, but little else. Of course, she was also covered in a film of mud that oozed along her skin. Dirt caked her arms and legs, even her hair. She looked like a cross between a science fiction dominatrix and a Neanderthal.

"The mud-*slingers*!" Aria corrected in a primal roar of her own, wearing a nearly identical outfit, although her straps ran diagonal rather than horizontal. She thrust her fist into the air triumphantly and suffered a wardrobe malfunction she didn't seem to notice.

The crowd went wild.

Othello, Callie, and I looked at each other. I couldn't read their expressions. Horror, maybe? Shock? Amusement? Either way, we were going in. We stepped through the double doors and waded into a crowd of spectators. Most were dressed country in various forms of denim and flannel, but a few wore significantly less—men in ragged jean shorts that hugged their groins and women in skimpy bikinis. All were covered in mud. A few looked battered, maybe even a little dazed.

Othello got there first. "Girls! What are you doing?!"

Aria spotted us and ran over. Well, I say ran. In reality, she marched over, yanking her legs free from the mud pit in which she and Sonia stood. Each step revealed parts of her to the crowd that sent salacious jeers throughout the club. "We're tournament champions!" Aria crowed.

"You're flashin' the crowd," I commented, nodding towards a group of men and women who'd dropped into squats to get a better angle. I sneered at their shamelessness; if anyone ogled me like that, I'd have to beat them all to a pulp on principle.

"Please, they aren't seeing anything they wouldn't see if we were in bathing suits." Aria grinned and twerked a little for them, propping herself up on the rails that formed the boundary of the pit.

Othello snatched the girl by the arm. "If your mother finds out about this —" she began.

Aria pulled back and put her hands on her hips. "They don't allow people to take pictures here. She won't find out. Unless we tell her." Her eyes narrowed. Sonia, who'd been busy rubbing herself down with more mud, finally came to join the conversation.

"We can't leave until someone spanks us," she said.

"Does *what* now?" I asked, eyebrows raised.

"Spanks us," Sonia replied, adamantly. "You know, until we lose."

I sighed. Trust the two redheads who'd tried to kidnap me in the middle of the night to become mudwrestling champions in a bar in Vegas run by Dorian Gray. Was this real life? I shook my head. "Who are ye fightin' next?" I asked.

"They have beaten all challengers," a man said, to our right. He was conspicuously dressed in a frock coat, complete with tails and white gloves. He looked like he belonged in a mansion in Europe, proffering a tray of tea and biscuits, not hosting at a Vegas nightclub.

"And who are you?" Callie asked, looking suspicious.

"I'm a representative of Mr. Gray. He sent me to speak with you on his behalf. He said, and I quote, 'Well, darlings, I really wish I could be there, but a promise is a promise. I'm glad you took my advice, Callie. Hopefully these will be to your liking.'"

The man offered two piles of clothing to each of us. If you could *call* the leather outfits clothing. One was a green so vibrant it looked like St. Patrick himself had painted it, while the other glittered silver. At best, I'd say—combined—they'd cover maybe a quarter of my body.

And, even then, not entirely the quarter I'd have chosen.

I glanced over at Callie. "Seriously? D'ye plan this whole t'ing with Dorian from the get-go?"

Callie raised her hands in surrender. "I swear this was not my idea. Is not my idea." She glared at the messenger. "You can tell Dorian that—"

"I'm sorry," he interrupted. "The message was one-way, only. I'm afraid Mr. Gray is indisposed, at the moment." He draped the mounds of leather on the rail, the various straps and buckles swinging. "If you wish to challenge our young champions, we'd be honored to help. These are two of the newest pieces of Mr. Gray's Fetush Clothing Line. They are incredibly rare and highly sought after, if I must say so myself."

"This is Hell," I replied, rubbing my forehead. "I've drank too much, died, and gone to Hell."

Callie shook her head. "Hell is way worse than this. But I'm still not wearing those."

The messenger dipped his head. "As you like. But if the ladies wish to challenge, it might be wise to have another outfit on hand." He eyed our current attire critically, as if wondering how it would hold up in the mud. Sadly, his point was valid; we'd end up caked in dirt for the rest of the night at this rate, and I hadn't packed a change of clothes.

Callie and I exchanged glances.

"No way," she said.

"I say we go in there and drag 'em out," I said. "Or I can shoot 'em? Just a flesh wound?"

The Reds snorted, drawing our attention back to them. "I think they're scared of us," Aria said, flashing her teeth.

Sonia nodded. "They know we'll spank them."

Callie and I exchanged glances once more.

"Fuck it," I said.

"We're in," Callie said.

CHAPTER 8 — CALLIE PENROSE, VEGAS

Since there were no changing rooms, and the line to the bathrooms was —as usual in a bar full of women—infinitely long, Quinn and I backed into a corner near a broken down rodeo bull which wouldn't be fixed anytime soon. The head was completely detached from what looked like a swipe of massive claws. Quinn turned herself into a tall, skinny wall while I changed into my new outfit, my blush matching the shade of her hair. Since she was lean and thin, it didn't afford me much protection, but in the end, I realized I may as well have gone in nude for all the cover the outfit provided.

Finished dressing, I glanced down, stumbling slightly from the effects of the alcohol. I was essentially wearing silver tinsel, like the kind you put on a Christmas tree.

And it fucking fit *perfectly*. Dorian was going to pay for this. Then again...

I briefly imagined a certain someone catching an eyeful of me right now and my blush instantly turned purple, my cheeks on fire. The alcohol was definitely impairing my judgment for me to entertain that errant thought.

Still, I kind of wished at least someone had brought a camera. For posterity. They could have taken the picture at an angle so as not to reveal too much of my assets. Glancing down at my attire, I realized there was no appropriate angle that could make me look like anything remotely PG.

Quinn didn't bother hiding her outburst of laughter when I tapped her on the shoulder to let her know I was finished. I glared in her general direction, having a hard time focusing accurately. "Your turn, Lucky Charms," I deadpanned.

That shut Quinn up.

But she handled it like a champ. I made like a swaying tree, trying to block Quinn's pale skin from prying eyeballs. I caught a quick glimpse of old scars and ridiculously toned muscle. She wasn't as curvy as me, but she was banging in her own way.

"Excuse me?" Quinn demanded, when I mentioned it without thinking.

My eyes widened. "Just a compliment," I murmured, cursing myself for having spoken out loud. She finally got ready and tapped me on the shoulder. I glanced back at her, my jaws dropping as I struggled against my grin. "Jesus..."

"I would leave him out of this. I'd rather not be smited in this outfit," Quinn joked. She gave me an appraising once over before checking herself out, turning this way and that. "I wish I had your curves. I'm afraid this t'ing will fall off if I'm not careful."

I giggle snorted at the comment. "Whatever," I said, smiling in spite of myself. "You look great. Like a stripper on St. Patrick's Day." I flicked the emerald tassel hanging from the leather where her nipple would be and burst out laughing. "Rassle Tassel. I get it now," I managed between giggles. It was just so damned ridiculous.

Surprisingly, she didn't deck me. She let out a resigned sigh, but her lips did curve into a faint smile. "Might as well give 'em a good show."

"Agreed. Let's go teach these girls a lesson," I said, storming off towards the ring. I took several breaths—not too deep, obviously—and shoved my clothes into Othello's hands, ignoring the look on her face while simultaneously interrupting whatever she had been about to say.

Before she could recover, Quinn did the same.

Without hesitation, I hopped over the wall leading to the ring, landing in the wide mud-pit. The mud was warm and squelched beneath my feet and between my toes. Quinn landed beside me, her lip curling up instinctively as globs of mud splattered her legs.

The Reds catcalled us from across the ring like sexy mud golems. Sonia shook her shoulders, her breasts wobbling back and forth in Quinn's direction, and Aria turned to twerk her ass at me.

I shot a look at Quinn over my shoulder. "I'm feelin' like letting off some steam from the bar. I didn't get to play with those boys. This is going to end badly for them. I promise."

"Fuckin' right it is," Quinn snarled through bared teeth.

Without any warning, the bell rang, and the match began. Apparently, it was a winner-take-all match. I didn't care. It was better than standing around ninety-five percent naked while Quinn fought Sonia. I sprinted at Aria—or more of a drunken forward fall, really—but I threw down a ball of ice in front of her to slow her down. She was a shifter, after all, and would outclass me in the physical strength department. I might be a better fighter, but she could easily handle anything I threw at her outside of magic.

Aria reared back from my magic, knowing she would slip and fall face-first into the mud if she didn't—which was exactly what I had hoped for. I dove, tackling her at full speed. I heard her grunt as my shoulders slammed into her muddy flesh, and I rode her to the ground where we splashed into a great puddle of mud, rolling and slipping for a good ten feet.

I'm pretty sure I lost my hair-clip in the tumble, but I soon realized I was cackling as the mud covered my bare skin. I gripped Aria by the hair and shoved her down into a puddle. "Mudsling this!" I hooted, waiting until she tapped out by slapping one of her hands into the mud.

I threw my hands up to the screams of the crowd. That's when she lurched to her feet, sending me cartwheeling to the side where I slipped, slid, and rolled through what seemed like never-ending mud. I clawed at the slick filth, embedding it under my fingernails, but I didn't care so long as I could get back up. I climbed to my feet to see her spitting out mud and wiping scoops of it from her eyes. She stared at me, breasts heaving, an odd look on her face. Then she curtsied, lost her balance, and fell on her ass. I burst out laughing and walked up to offer her a hand.

She was laughing as she stared up at me. "Even covered in mud, you look like fucking Xena the Warrior Princess," she said, grinning. She clasped hands with me, but right as I was preparing to pull her up, my feet slipped and I fell down right beside her.

I wiped the mud from my face, giggling at her as the crowd roared.

"Happy fucking birthday," I said, slapping a handful of mud onto her back. I wondered if Quinn had been victorious. I doubted it, considering she was up against a shifter dragon. Unless she had a few tricks up her corset.

CHAPTER 9 — QUINN MACKENNA, VEGAS

I didn't have time to watch Callie's fight with Aria, though I think I'd have thoroughly enjoyed watching the older woman put the young upstart in her place. But the match wasn't tag team, it was a free-for-all; the instant the bell rang, Sonia started stalking me, wading through the mud with surprising quickness, as though it were water and not something much thicker. I lowered my stance, arms out wide for balance, feeling absolutely ridiculous in the skimpy, green leather corset with emerald tassels and boy shorts, both of which were tied together loose enough to expose an uncomfortable amount of skin. Ordinarily, I'd have gladly waded in and knocked her silly—if only to get out of the outfit—but I didn't want the girl spending her birthday in the hospital. This was a wrestling match, pure and simple, which meant I had to rely on my grappling skills, my reach, and my luck.

Of course, I had one other advantage: Sonia's overconfidence. Ever since I'd seen her exposed eye and the forked tongue, I'd suspected she was something other than human. Some form of reptile shifter. Which meant the mud was probably her element. What she didn't know—that I had the innate ability to negate all forms of magic, including the perks of being a shapeshifter—was about to hurt her. Well, *I* was about to hurt her. But you know what I mean.

Sonia came at me, pressing her shoulder into my stomach as if she might tackle me to the ground. I was already braced for the impact, however, and didn't fall. Sonia, still determined to take me down, began plowing forward, putting her legs into it. I laughed a little, struck by the idea that Sonia was acting like a toddler trying to take down a full-grown adult. Sonia must have heard my laughter because she fell back, panting, her chest heaving with exertion.

"What are you?" she asked. "There's no way you should have been able to stop me."

"Not sure," I replied honestly, "but I'm definitely *not* a mudpacker."

Sonia mocked a sumo wrestler by throwing her legs wide and slapping her knees one after the other. "Well, this time, I'm definitely going down on you."

"Takin' me down, ye mean?" I asked, hopeful.

"Whichever," Sonia said, charging once more. I waited for her to come to me. With mud up to my shins, I knew it would be hard to maneuver; I was as likely to fall walking as I was fighting Sonia. Which meant I had one sure shot at winning. The moment Sonia stepped within arm's reach, I sidestepped in a lunge that left one leg extended like a tripwire. Sonia toppled over it as if it were a log, falling flat on her face with a squawk. That's when I pounced, landing on her back with my legs on either side, as if she were a horse. I spanked her, playfully. "Giddyup!" I yelled, my accent making the phrase sound extra absurd.

Sonia lifted her face out of the mud and spit out a gob of gunk. "Has anyone ever told you that you suck, hard?" she muttered.

I leaned forward. "Only the boys I didn't like," I whispered.

Sonia began to laugh.

A moment later, I joined in.

CHAPTER 10 — CALLIE PENROSE, VEGAS

We sat around the bar, cackling over the highlights of our mudwrestling. The host had come by to offer us free drinks on the house and to let us know that our names would be added to the Wall of Shame where they had placards for all the winners. The Reds would also be added since they had been undefeated rookies before we broke their streak. I leaned in close to the waiter and ordered drinks, careful to make sure he heard my order. "Water means vodka," I whispered to him before anyone could interrupt.

"Don't even think about it, Callie," Othello warned. "Water for me."

"Ye can have one drink!" Quinn complained. "Ye owe me that, at least."

Othello shook her head. "One drink brought us to *this*," she said, smiling in amusement. "I shudder to think of what a second drink would do to us."

I shrugged at the waiter. "You heard the woman..." No one but him caught my wink. His poker face was flawless as he dipped his chin and left.

I clapped my hands, now at least somewhat clean thanks to the steamed towels they had brought us. The host had generously offered us the option to use the shower in the corner of the bar—the one with glass walls in full-view of every customer. We'd given them enough of a show already, and so had declined the offer at further embarrassment.

Surprisingly, not a single face was leering. They were appreciative, sure, but they looked at us more like we were celebrities rather than pieces of attractive woman meat like most men did at bars. A quartet of leather-faced cowboys even offered to buy us a pitcher, tipping their gallon-sized cowboy hats at us. But they hadn't tried to approach or anything, just told the bartender they would like to sport us a round.

The bartender had informed them that our drinks were on Dorian Gray's tab for the duration of the night. Which was probably the only reason I hadn't made a Gateway to track the bastard down and toss him into the ring for a fight of his own.

As mad and embarrassed as we had been, I was kind of glad we had gone through with it. The experience had been oddly...therapeutic.

"I'm growin' older and sober over here," Quinn said, and I realized everyone was staring at me since I had clapped my hands to get their attention.

"Oh, right. A drinking game. We have to chug the drinks they bring us. Once your hand touches the glass, you have to pound it in one go. No matter what." Othello began to argue, and I held up a hand, rolling my eyes. "Don't worry, you heard me order your water. But you still have to chug it or you will ruin their birthday," I said, pointing at the Reds—who instantly put on mock pouting faces. "It's no fun unless everyone plays."

Othello sighed and finally nodded. I kept the easy smile on my face. Just because Othello had heard me order water didn't mean I hadn't made a prior arrangement with the bartender.

The waiter returned with a tall glass of chilled water for Othello, and a bottle of *Don Julio 1942* with a small bowl of limes for the rest of us. I motioned for him to set the glasses before us and pour our drinks with three fingers each—easily triple shots, since we couldn't touch the glasses without having to chug them, thanks to my stated rules. Othello eyed the tall glass of clear liquid in front of her, then met my eyes warily, searching for deception. I pretended not to notice, leaning forward to grin at the Reds. "To the Mudpackers," I grinned. Even Quinn was grinning, now. "Ready?" I asked, my hand hovering near my glass.

"Three, two, ONE!" Aria cried out, snatching up her drink.

We all pounded our triple-shot of tequila, but my eyes were locked on Othello's face.

Her expression was pained and she was glaring at me from the rim of her glass, realizing that her water tasted suspiciously like pure vodka. But she had to finish it. After all, without rules, we were little better than Neanderthals.

Quinn caught on quickly, noticing the strain in Othello's eyes and shot me an approving smirk. The Reds, on the other hand, were licking their lips and staring at the bottle wonderingly. "I want that in my mouth again," Sonia said in a serious tone. Aria shrugged and began pouring a fresh drink for the two of them. Quinn slid our glasses over for a refill as well before I could stop her. But, to be honest, I wanted more as well. It was ridiculously good tequila. Nothing like the cheap stuff I was used to.

Othello finished her drink and slammed the glass down, glaring at me, but I could tell she was fighting a smile of her own.

I batted my eyelashes innocently. "I ordered Russian water. Honest mistake."

She sighed, shaking her head. Then she rolled her shoulders and let out a long, pleased breath. "I think I actually needed that." She eyed the bottle of tequila thoughtfully. "Is that any good? Nate only ever has whiskey or absinthe on hand."

Quinn was already pouring a healthy glass for the hacker. "It's terrible, really. Ye have to try it."

CHAPTER 11 — QUINN MACKENNA, VEGAS

I wasn't sure how much time passed, and I'd lost track of how many more drinks we'd consumed, but I figured we'd been at it for a solid hour at least. The buzz that had faded leading up to my match with Sonia was back in full force, threatening to brim over into true inebriation. Othello had a rosy glow to her cheeks, and the Reds were hooked arm-in-arm, singing along with Johnny Cash's "Ring of Fire" as they tossed back their glasses. We'd had to bribe the waiter to bring them flavored water after the first few drinks, which they'd been fortunately too drunk to notice thus far.

I wasn't sure about the resilience of shifter constitutions, but if they ended up upchucking on their twenty-first, it'd be a shame to do so in public. At least this way they could stay on their feet a bit longer. I half-turned towards Callie, thinking to ask her about herself—maybe get to know her a little better now that we weren't in a pissing contest—when I overheard a man at the bar. He was practically yelling in his attempt to be heard over the Reds, who were singing alternative lyrics like "they fell into burning rings of fire" and "they burned, burned, burned."

"I'm looking for a Russian woman! She'd be in her early thirties, medium height. Our facial recognition software flagged someone who came into your bar," he said. I glanced at him out of the corner of my eye. Red jacket.

Earpiece. Black t-shirt and slacks. Casino security, no doubt about it. And not just any security because this was a place for Freaks, so he had to have some awareness of the supernatural, which meant he would have a way to deal with us.

The bartender kept pouring drinks like he was barely listening, his face an expressionless mask as he shook a cocktail. "What did she do?" he called back distractedly.

I nudged Othello. "Security at the bar. 9 o'clock."

She grinned, then caught my expression and frowned. She leaned back, peering past me at the guy before plopping forward. "What about him?"

I tugged my earlobe. "Listen."

"More like what *didn't* she do. Arson, extortion, defacing public property...the list goes on and on. We have her on video taking winnings from every hotel on the strip in one weekend. Never caught her."

Othello snorted. "Good times," she chuckled.

"They've got ye on facial recognition software," I whispered.

"From when I was sixteen?" Othello asked, eyebrow raised. She looked impressed, although her smile was way too wide for my liking. "The statute of limitations has passed on most things I did back then in Vegas, but I'd probably vomit in the interrogation room. Cover me for a minute." She ducked her head down while I turned my back to shield her from sight. The bartender, meanwhile, was pointing towards us.

Shit.

"Excuse me, ladies, but can I see your IDs?" the man asked. I noticed two other flunkies were standing nearby, scanning the crowd as professionally as one can when people are half-naked and covered in mud.

The Reds giggled and hurriedly yanked their IDs out from beneath their leather straps, although I had absolutely no idea how they'd managed to conceal the damn things. "This is the first time anyone has asked us for them!" Sonia said, excitedly.

"We just turned 21," Aria explained, happily.

The man's eyes narrowed, and he flashed the bartender a very pointed look that said they'd be having a talk later. He shrugged dismissively and walked off towards other thirsty patrons. "Well, these look in order," he said, staring at the licenses. They were Missouri issue, a bland shade of khaki, and displayed the Reds as I'd never seen them: tame, well-kempt, and wholesome. Lies.

He passed them back after shining a penlight on them, then looked expectantly at me. I sighed, then fetched my own license from my back pocket. My Massachusetts ID was equally as bland, underwhelming next to Callie's bright Kansas license. "Showoff," I said, nudging her. She nudged me back, harder, and we glared at each other.

"And you, miss?" the man said, staring at Othello's back. She'd refused to turn around, and I could see his suspicions flaring. But before he could say more, she spun around. Her brunette hair spilled around her shoulders in a wave, and for a moment I wasn't sure what I was seeing. Then I realized whose face I was looking at: my own. My features, drawn slightly smaller, where Othello's should have been. My slightly dimpled chin and broad cheekbones. My lips. My nose. My eyes, but brown, not green.

"Sorry, laddie," Othello said in an Irish accent that made me want to cringe, "but I t'ink I left it in the ladies' room at some point. Me sister here," she clapped me on the back, "was supposed to go with me, but got distracted. She likes men with muscles, ye see." Othello eyed the man up and down with my face, and it looked positively rife with promise.

Jesus, did I really smolder like that?

The man grinned in response, but then shook his head. "Well you'll have to go find it," he said. "Otherwise I'll have to escort you off the Bellagio premises. You have to be of age and able to prove it to be here."

Othello pouted, drawing my lips down like a bow, looking like a child. But before I could swat her off her stool for making ridiculous faces, Dorian's messenger slid up alongside us. The would-be butler held out a hand. "If you ladies would be so kind as to follow me, there is a gentleman in the back room who would like to have a word."

I frowned at him while the Reds ogled Othello's new face, pointing and giggling so hard I was sure we were busted. But the security guard seemed unconcerned with them, focusing instead on the newcomer. "I'm afraid the women won't be leaving until I check this woman's identification," he said, sounding a little hostile.

The messenger leaned in, looking far less harmless than I would have given him credit for. "This establishment is outside the jurisdiction of Nevada's Gaming Commission, sir. I suggest you remember that." He teetered back. "Now, if you would follow me," he said, herding us towards the back of the club. "I will be sure to have the lady's identification sent along momentarily, sir," he called to the security officer, whose fists were balled in anger.

Once we were out of earshot, he urged us to huddle around him, still escorting us towards the back. "We saw what was happening on the cameras," he said.

"Wait, there were cameras?" Callie asked, sounding mortified.

He waved that away. "Private use only. Mr. Gray suggests you make use of his private entrance. Come along." the man strode off, and we followed, exchanging looks. Othello had yet to remove my face, and seeing it was starting to give me a headache; seeing double had never been a literal experience up to this point, no matter how much I drank.

Finally, the messenger pulled aside a curtain and waved us through. "Here we are," he said. "The back door."

"Dorian's private entrance?" I asked, incredulously.

Callie was shaking her head, massaging her temples.

Othello was grinning with her teeth.

The Reds were running their hands along the velvet curtain making cooing noises.

"He calls it the BackDorian, yes," the messenger replied, without even a hint of a smile.

Of course he did.

CHAPTER 12 — CALLIE PENROSE, VEGAS

We exited Dorian's back door—yes, I know how it sounds—with a sigh of relief as the door closed behind us. We were in a wide, long, empty hallway full of painted portraits of Dorian Gray in different levels of both dress and undress. It was wide enough to drive a fucking SUV through. As I scanned the life-sized portraits, I realized he had one for pretty much every culture in the world, from every time period. Even one where he was dressed like Cleopatra.

As per his usual vanity, the Marc Antony standing beside Cleopatra in the painting was *also* Dorian Gray. And the two were making out violently. Dorian was literally molesting himself.

I knew where he had hidden the real picture of Dorian Gray—the one that made him immortal—the one that showed the results of all of his depraved hobbies, leaving his physical person flawless and beautiful. In a way, it was very clever to have so many paintings of himself. Seeds of misdirect to keep the real painting safe, because if anyone ever got their hands on it and destroyed it, he would finally face death. I knew this because I had held a butane torch close to the real painting in order to bully him into helping me with a demon problem back in Kansas City.

We'd been pals ever since.

The fact that Dorian had a hallway of beautiful pictures of himself leading to his private entrance into his own club did not surprise me in the least. It didn't even faze me at this point. Still, I wasn't up to finding out where it led. Likely some wildly unbelievable orgy in the Library of Congress, knowing Dorian's penchant for the outlandish. Also, I didn't feel up to dealing with Dorian right now. He was quick on his feet and the grand champion at enabling or coercing his acquaintances to make the worst kind of decisions. Like a puppet master of sin. Or *fun*, as he would call it.

None of us could match wits with him in our present drunken state. This thought was confirmed when I caught Othello snapping pictures of the Reds posing before a portrait of Dorian dressed in full drag.

Quinn met my eyes, looking desperate. "I don't t'ink I'm drunk enough for this," she admitted, jerking her chin at the portraits.

I snorted, wobbling slightly. "You haven't even considered what horrors might be at the end of the hall. If it's tame, it's probably like the mud pits back there, but with KY Jelly, zero clothing, fog machines, cocaine, and *The Mighty Morphin Power Rangers* playing on a big screen on the back wall."

Quinn's eyes widened incredulously. "Well...I wouldn't turn down the Power Rangers marathon. But the rest..." she trailed off thoughtfully, and I began cackling. She scowled at me. "Don't judge me."

I nodded, grinned, and opened a Gateway, seeing as our party were the only ones present in the long hallway. Quinn didn't even hesitate, jumping through to escape the paintings' leering eyes. They really did seem to follow you, I realized with a shiver.

"Let's go, bitches!" I called out. And we all jumped through the Gateway after Quinn.

Just in time to hear her shout in horror.

We were in a large hotel suite, and two men and one woman in Ninja Turtle masks—complete with appropriately colored armbands to match their flavor of mask—were unashamedly ruining my childhood memories with their naked, adult-themed remake of the classic.

Othello grinned wickedly, not an ounce of surprise on her face. "Go ninja, go ninja, go!" she hooted in a sing-song voice.

Quinn pointed a warning finger at them, shaking her head in mock horror. "Splinter would be ashamed," she chided.

The three turtles turned to look at each other. "We have another mask..." one of the men said suggestively, lifting the mask for Donatello. Quinn made a face, disgusted, but Sonia snatched it before I could say anything, and then Aria and Sonia began fighting over it, bitching at each other the way only sisters could.

"Don't touch that," Quinn hissed. "D'ye want to catch syphilis?"

"We just bought it," Leonardo's mask owner insisted.

"If ye don't get us out of here, I'm goin' to go Shredder on them," Quinn said to me, matter-of-factly. I nodded woodenly, not really sure what else there was to say, and ripped open another Gateway, not even caring where it led. Anywhere was better than this. Hell, maybe Dorian's swank party at the Library of Congress would have been better. At least there my childhood wouldn't have been irreparably ruined.

Othello herded the Reds through the Gateway, but not before Quinn yanked the mask from the Reds hands with a scowl. I hopped through the Gateway into darkness, ignoring the sounds from behind me.

CHAPTER 13 — QUINN MACKENNA, VEGAS

I stepped into the incredibly dark room only a few feet behind the others, taking up the rear to make sure we weren't followed by teenage mutant nympho-turtles; I wasn't super eager to turn my back on the threesome, but I suddenly felt the desperate need to wash my hands. And maybe my brain. Was it possible to scrub your brain clean? I cringed as I moved forward. Now that I'd changed back into my normal clothes and was moving around, I could practically feel the dirt clinging to my body, and it made even the simplest movements aggravating. Between that and the burning sensation in my gut from the last drink I'd taken, I was too busy fussing to realize the others had stopped. I bumped into Callie, and the Gateway snapped shut, leaving the room in total darkness.

"Watch it," Callie said, cursing while the Reds giggled like schoolgirls. They'd decided to stay in their leather outfits, which had begun to creak as they walked. Before I could tell them to pipe down, however, Othello held up a light attached to her briefcase.

"Where d'ye hide that this whole time?" I asked, frowning.

"Wouldn't you like to know?" Othello said, sticking out her tongue. "I'll tell you, but it's worth..." she trailed off, scrunching her nose as if she were trying to do advanced calculus in her head. "Ummm...a fuckload of Rubles," she finally said. She let out an eruptive snort of laughter. The extra drinks must have brought her to our level, I realized. I wondered if she was drunk enough to give me a peek of what all lay inside the briefcase—fancy gadgets from Grimm Tech, if I had to guess. Fancy, *expensive* gadgets. The kind warlords pay a lot for.

I tried to glower at her, but she was being too goofy, so I let it go. When Othello answered questions with another question, it usually meant I was never going to get a straight answer, no matter how many Rubles were involved. "Fine," I said, crossing my arms over my chest.

"Where are we?" Aria asked, drawing our attention to our surroundings. Beneath the glow of Othello's flashlight, steel gleamed. Steel, and something else, something that glistened under a heavy tarp. Gold. Thick gold bricks piled waist high in the center of the room. I took a long, slow look around. Bank vault. We were in a fucking bank vault.

"Callie..." I said, her name echoing in the tiny space. "I t'ink ye need to work on your aim."

Callie glared at me. "Backseat Gateway driver."

"That's enough, ladies. You're both pretty," Othello said. She grinned and shined the flashlight at us. "Let's just go before we get caught."

"Oh, it feels so good..." Sonia whispered reverently.

"So good," Aria echoed as if on the verge of climax, causing all three of us to turn.

The two young women were rubbing themselves up against the stack of gold like cats rolling in catnip, sliding their hands up and down the metal bars in a very erotic fashion. It was excessively carnal, and vaguely masturbatory, given the gold couldn't touch them back. And yet, the gold didn't seem entirely unaffected. As I watched, the metal seemed to brighten, gaining more luster with each caress. Any other time, I would have been weirded out enough to demand an explanation, but I was too focused on the room itself to do so. Have you ever accidentally wandered onto someone's property without realizing it? No trespassing sign to warn you away, and yet you know you don't belong? That's how this vault felt. It sent shivers up my spine.

"Get a room, for Christ's sakes," I said, finally. "Or better yet, knock it off. We have to go."

Simultaneously, the two shifters snatched at the bars, yanking one apiece off the platform and cradling it to their chests like children refusing to give up their teddy bears. "Ours!" they cried in unison.

And that's when the alarms went off.

The sound was a claxon scream that pealed through the room. The decibel level was so high that it made my eyes water and my chest ache, like when you stand next to a subwoofer at a rock concert. Lights came on in the vault, showing all of us cradling our ears, though the Reds did so by pressing one ear to their shoulder and a hand to the other; they still held the bars.

"Put those down! We need to run!" Callie yelled. She held out a hand and another Gateway appeared, only this time it did so in a shower of angry, violent white sparks, much larger than the other one had been. White flame licked the edges of the portal, wild enough that I was suddenly glad to be surrounded by so much steel—adding arson to our growing list of felonies sounded like a bad idea. I stared at the flames for a moment longer than I should have, too entranced to move, body listing to the left unconsciously before I stumbled and caught myself.

Damn I was drunk.

"Never!" Aria was shouting. She'd clutched her bar of gold to her gut like a fullback and was running past us through the portal at full speed, followed quickly by her sister. Othello, laughing wildly ever since the alarms began going off, trailed by only a few feet. I glanced over at Callie, then down at the mask in my hands, which I'd forgotten to discard. Donatello's hollow eyes stared up at me, his goofy grin leering and strange.

Fuck it.

If we were going to rob a bank, I might as well have a mask.

Callie threw her hands up anxiously as I slid the plastic disguise over my face. "Why do you get a mask and I don't?" she asked.

I flashed her a hang loose sign and cackled. She responded with sign language of her own, and then together we followed our entourage, bursting through yet another physics-defying hole in space...

Onto a harshly lit stage of a live concert performance. Tens of thousands of concert-goers were singing, dancing, and repetitively chanting a name. *Beaver* something. *Johnson Beaver*, that was it. Son of a bitch, that douche again?

"Alright, now I t'ink your doin' it on purpose," I yelled at Callie's back, but my words were lost in the clamor of the crowd. We'd kept running, the Reds a good ten feet in front of us, trying our best not to lose them. The Gateway closed, mercifully out of sight behind a curtain on the far side of the stage, and the alarm bells—audible even over the roar of the crowd— stopped clanging.

"Am not!" Callie snapped, sounding a little embarrassed. So she *had* heard me.

Then Othello, whose run had turned into something of a skip, bumped into one of the speakers. It was taller than her and fell amidst a shower of sparks. Since there were about a dozen more, the show continued, but it drew unwanted attention. Rather than stop to assess the situation or apologize, Othello scrambled to her feet and continued after the Reds who were now passing the center of the stage.

Where they found Beaver himself. To his credit, he didn't stop singing, although his eyes did widen in surprise the moment he saw the two redheads barreling towards him wearing skimpy leather outfits and caked in dirt. He seemed to take it in stride—scantily clad women were probably part of his show, after all—at least until he saw us. His mouth turned down, and I knew he recognized us.

Despite being well and truly drunk, I tried to think of how we appeared in his eyes: two mud-covered redheads in hardcore leather lingerie clutching gold bars and sprinting as if their lives depended on it, followed by three women who'd verbally threatened him in a public place not a few hours before. Not good, I decided. Definitely not good.

Apparently Beaver's security team agreed, because they were now rushing towards us from the way we'd come, resulting in an almost comical *Scooby Doo* chase montage. Still, if we hurried we could make it to the other side, I knew, before they caught up to us. That was, of course, until Sonia dropped her precious gold bar not three feet in front of Beaver. I groaned and, before I could think about what I was doing, dropped to one knee and slid across the stage, planning to scoop the damn thing up and make our escape.

And maybe, just maybe, survive the night.

CHAPTER 14 — CALLIE PENROSE, VEGAS

I sprinted past Johnson Beaver, flashing him a sultry grin in hopes that a quick smile would distract him long enough for us to make it across the stage. Sonia was just ahead of me, so when she dropped her bar of gold it almost crushed my foot. I leapt instinctively, flinging out a hand to slam my palm into Sonia's back since she was trying to stop so she could retrieve her treasure. "Keep going!" I snapped. "If security catches us, none of it will matter!" Sonia snarled savagely, pouring on the heat. I glanced over my shoulder to see Othello had hopped over the golden bar without concern.

She was too busy waving animatedly at the crowd.

But my heart skipped a beat, and I almost tripped when I saw Quinn— her face concealed by a Donatello mask—sliding across the stage like she was stealing a base in a company's drunken softball tournament. She skated on her side—thankfully no longer wearing lingerie, which would have hurt like a motherfucker—with one hand reaching for the gold bar, and the other stiff-arming towards Johnson Beaver, who was leaning down as if intending to scoop up the gold.

Her extended arm hit him like a battering ram, folding him in half, her balled fist colliding with his groin. Beaver managed to squeal a very unmanly sound into his microphone before dropping it and falling backwards into another speaker. Quinn retrieved the microphone on reflex as she climbed to her feet, gold bar in her other hand, and the music cut off.

The crowd was silent as she stared down at it for a moment, her red hair poking out of the mask in all directions. Then she looked out at them and held the microphone to the place where her lips would have been beneath the mask. "Turtle Power," she said, before extending the microphone, straightening her arm.

And dropping the mic.

She didn't wait for a response, merely resumed her sprint after us. I hadn't realized I had slowed, or that Othello had sprinted past me to catch up to the Reds. I matched pace with Quinn and we exited stage left, cackling like a gaggle of crazy bitches.

We were far from safe, but at least we no longer had thirty-thousand witnesses for the prosecution to call.

I focused intently as I skidded up to Othello and the Reds, finding the magic easier to call now that my blood was up. I ripped open a Gateway, the adrenaline rush making my magic flare wildly. The Reds made as if to jump through, but I held out a hand to stop them, and got a palm full of were-dragon boob for my effort. I poked my head through the Gateway to see a hotel room, blessedly vacant.

"Okay, hurry! Before security catches up to us!"

We jumped through the Gateway. I immediately let the Gateway wink out and let out a long, exhausted sigh before collapsing onto one of the beds, panting and laughing at the ridiculousness of it all.

"One out of four," I giggled. "Could have been worse." I still wasn't sure if it was the alcohol that had affected my Gateway destinations, or just me not paying as much attention as I should have. Either way, it had finally worked. We were safe. As I lay on the bed, my head resting in someone's lap, I realized the room was spinning slightly. I flung up my hand to instinctively flip my hair and suddenly began cursing.

"Damn it! My extension is gone!"

"We know, Callie," Othello said with a resigned chuckle. "You've mentioned that three times already, tonight."

"Oh..." I said, frowning. "Well, it's still a travesty," I muttered.

CHAPTER 15 — QUINN MACKENNA, VEGAS

I took off my mask, tossing it to the floor, and patted Callie's head, which had conspicuously ended up in my lap. "Vanity, thy name is Callie Penrose," I teased. Othello grunted and rolled over, upending Aria and sending her careening off the bed with a thunk. Her gold bar never left her arms. I glanced down, realizing the gold bar I'd retrieved had mysteriously disappeared, only to find Sonia rubbing it against her face.

"What the hell is their deal?" I asked, baffled.

Othello waved a hand. "Weredragons. They can't help it. Gold is like crack to them. But here, Callie, I have something for you."

"A present?" Callie asked, hopeful, though she didn't seem inclined to move. Not for the first time, I wondered what the side effects of using magic were. Were there physical consequences? Before I could ask, Othello popped open her briefcase, reached inside, and withdrew a hair straightener.

"I don't know if I have enough hair to need that," Callie said, drily.

Othello rolled her eyes. "Well fine, then I guess I'll leave it up to you to figure out how to stimulate hair growth magically, and I'll just take this back home with me..."

Callie sat up so fast she almost clocked me in the face with her forehead. "Wait, what does it do?"

Othello grinned. "The science would fry all your puny Freaky brains, so let's just say it'll make your hair grow as long as you want it to be. Just use it like you would a flat iron and run each strand down as long as you want it to go."

Callie reached out and cradled the hair straightener in her hands as if she were holding the Holy Grail. In a way, I suppose she was. Inventions like that could revolutionize the hair industry. "I don't know what to say," Callie said, sounding choked up.

Othello laughed and plumped her hair with one hand. "Don't worry about it, I've got two more at home." She snapped the briefcase shut and I found myself wondering, yet again, what else lay inside. Callie curled around her newest accessory and practically purred, which meant we had three women fondling objects at this point. After a few seconds of silence, I began to hear snores drifting up from the ground where Aria lay. Sonia was next, then Callie.

"Oy, Othello," I whispered, deciding to go for it. "What else d'ye have in there?"

Othello's eyes narrowed suspiciously. "Nothing."

"Aw, come on. Tell me!" I insisted. "Or was that all ye had and you're afraid to admit it?"

Othello sniffed. "Please, what I have in here could take out a whole wing of this hotel, if I wanted it to."

"Likely story," I said, grinning, sensing my opening. Othello was a genius, but she had her flaws: like wanting to prove how brilliant she was whenever possible. Honestly, I doubted she'd have bothered around normal people, but around Freaks with insane abilities she could never hope to gain herself? Well, let's just say she'd finally found some worthy competition.

"The Galvinator would drop you like a—" Othello began, hackles rising.

But just then there was a knock at the door.

Othello and I exchanged startled looks. No one should have known we were in here. Hell, we didn't even know where we were. A hotel room, sure, but which hotel? Which floor? I slid off the edge of the bed, careful not to disturb Callie, who'd begun stroking her hair straightener in her sleep, and padded towards the door.

Another series of knocks sounded, though louder and more insistent. I waited for the telltale cry of "housekeeping," wondering if we'd be forced to wake Callie up and move rooms, but it never came. Instead, a rough baritone echoed from the other side of the door in a snarl, the man's accent so thick it made my own sound tame by comparison. "C'mon now, ladies, I know you're in thurr. Open up and let's have us a wee chat, alright?"

I frowned and glanced back at Othello, who'd reached into her briefcase once more, still rosy-cheeked, but grim. "Do it," she whispered.

I wasn't sure how I felt about our only weapon being a device that could destroy half the hotel, but I trusted Othello to make sure we didn't all end up dead. I considered waking the girls up, but at this point the five of us were too messed up to make sound judgment calls—assuming the Reds ever were. If I shook them awake and said we had company, it was entirely possible they'd end up running again, or shifting into dragons. I shook my head, chasing away the image of twin red dragons descending on the crowds along the strip, and opened the door to an empty hallway.

"Down here, ye damn giant of a woman," the man said, startling me. I lowered my gaze to stare down at the man in shock. He wore green the way some people wear black, in layers so thick his body was swaddled in shades of emerald. He was also bald with brown eyes and a grizzly ginger beard the color of ripe mandarins. He bowed a little, though he never took his eyes off my face. "Pleased to meet ye," he said.

"And who the hell are ye?" I asked, my own accent flaring as if our voices were two flames meeting up in the middle.

His eyebrows shot up. "Don't tell me our gold was swiped by one of our own? No self-respectin' Irish woman would do such a t'ing."

I frowned down at him. "Ye didn't answer me question."

He ducked his head. "Aye, you're right about that. The name is Paddy. Paddy McKnob. And ye are?"

"Quinn," I replied. "Quinn MacKenna." I wasn't sure why I told him my full name, except that he'd offered his, absurd though it sounded. I wasn't exactly rude by nature, after all; people just typically rubbed me the wrong way.

"Pleased to make your acquaintance," he said, with another slight bow. "So, now that we have the formalities out o' the way, can ye tell me why ye stole our gold?"

"*Your* gold?" I asked, emphasizing the word.

"Aye, 'tis ours. The Little People's."

My mouth hung open. I couldn't help it. "Wait, ye mean *the* Little People? Like, leprechauns?"

He shot me a dirty look. "Didn't anyone ever teach ye not to call us that? I don't care if ye are Irish, I won't tolerate ye usin' a racial slur to demean me fine race."

I held a hand to my mouth to stop myself from giggling, and glanced back at Othello, who shrugged. "Alright, so why are ye here again, Paddy?" I asked.

"That's Mr. McKnob to ye, young lady. And I'm here for our gold."

"What makes ye t'ink we have it?" I asked, coyly.

Paddy grunted and withdrew a tablet from his jacket pocket, the device comically large in his hands. He tapped it a couple times and held it up for me to see. There, in black and white video, was the vault. I watched with a bird's eye view as we entered through Callie's Gateway, piddled around in the dark, and eventually realized where we were. There was no sound on the video, but the instant the alarms went off, I cringed, remembering the awful noise they'd made.

"We got Banshees to install the alarm system," Paddy said, proudly.

I handed the tablet back to him. "To be honest, I'd be more than happy to give ye back your gold," I admitted. "T'was an accident we ended up with it in the first place."

Paddy looked skeptical. "Well then, pass 'em along, and we'll be on our way."

I frowned, then glanced on either side of the hallway. Where before there had only been plush carpet and tasteful wallpaper, there were now a small army of leprechauns holding shealeighs and brass knuckles made out of gold. The Little People Mafia.

Not good.

"Tell them to go to Hell, Quinn!" Aria shouted from behind us, apparently awake enough to have heard at least the part of the conversation where her gold was going to get taken away.

"Yeah, tell him!" Sonia echoed.

Well, shit.

Paddy's eyes narrowed as his mob took a collective step forward, brandishing their weapons. I glanced back to see Othello shaking Callie awake, demanding she make a Gateway in a hushed whisper.

I sighed and turned to Paddy and his army. "How fast can Little People run?" I asked. Then, without waiting for a response, I slammed the door in his face and took off towards the bedroom, praying we'd have enough time to escape.

CHAPTER 16 — CALLIE PENROSE, VEGAS

I wiped the sleep from my eyes, still slightly drunk, but finally snapped to the present with Othello pushing me, insisting I make a Gateway. The sound of Quinn slamming the door on a leprechaun brought me fully to my senses. "You want a Gateway, I'll give you a goddamned Gateway," I muttered. Only three things would make me feel better. More alcohol, sleep, or my fist grazing some unlucky bastard's teeth.

I wasn't sure which would be more satisfying, even though the rational side of me informed me it was sleep, water, and a fistful of vitamins.

But I'd settle for a fistful of Lucky Charms.

I flung my hand out and a Gateway erupted a few inches off the floor so as not to scorch the nice carpet. None of us were drunk enough to jump through without looking this time. I was also careful to control it better so as not to let errant sparks start a fire. We'd committed enough felonies tonight. I didn't want to burn down a hotel.

Unless I had to.

The Gateway opened up to reveal a bizarre mass of gyrating flesh, fragrant smoke, black lights, velvet lounging couches, and the throbbing pulse of deep, steady bass.

No treble.

I shrugged at my party and stepped through, sensing them following me.

I closed the Gateway and scanned our surroundings, somewhat taken aback. "I t'ink ye may be broken inside, Callie Penrose," Quinn murmured. "Ye took us to a God-forsaken strip club, because, what? Ye didn't t'ink we'd seen enough already?"

"It is Vegas," I muttered defensively.

"Boobies!" Sonia blurted, only just now realizing that it wasn't a dance club, and that their horizons had just been unexpectedly expanded with the addition of pay-to-see nudity.

"Good talent, though," Othello said, smiling. "Real skill over there," she said, pointing at a particular stripper hanging upside down on the pole, her breasts covered in glitter and reflecting the flashing lights like two perfect disco balls. "Welcome to the Jungle" by Guns N' Roses was blaring, and the surprisingly young crowd were going wild as they threw money at the chee-tah-thong-wearing stripper.

"Is this what adults do when kids aren't around?" Aria whispered in awe.

"Adulting is amazing," Sonia agreed in a hungry whisper. We'd begun to attract some attention since we were just standing around ogling. Thankfully, our Gateway hadn't attracted any attention, what with all the strobing lights and loud music. They probably thought we had just left an uber-VIP lap dance chamber.

One of the dancers walked up to us, entirely topless and perky—both physically and with her personality. "My name's Lucky. How y'all doin' tonight?" she asked in a syrupy Southern drawl. "Which one of y'all want a dance?"

Sonia raised a hand, but Othello slapped it down. "Thanks, Lucky," Othello said, turning to smile at the dancer. "But we're just looking for a place to sit down for now. We've had a wild night and need to take a breather. Maybe later?"

Lucky smiled with her luminescent white teeth and winked. "Y'all want to get Lucky later, you just let me know." She eyed the rest of us, especially the Reds, who were openly admiring her toned body, still clutching their gold bars. "I do group specials," she added with a purr, eyes locked on the hunks of precious metal. Then she spun, skipping away from us with a perfectly cute rear end, and glided down the stairs.

I shook my head in disbelief as I motioned everyone to follow me to a circular couch with a round table before it. "You weren't kidding about a breather. I feel like my brain needs a reboot."

We sat down with different flavors of sighs—mine was tired, Othello and Quinn's sounded comfortably at home, and the Reds' were positively eager.

I glanced over at Lucky, who was eyeing our table suggestively, no one else around her for the moment, although eyes tracked her from different tables, looking forlorn that they didn't have her attention thanks to our arrival.

Quinn spoke up. "Ye know, we should have asked for drinks—"

A sudden rainbow laser beam twice as wide as my waist interrupted her by blasting down from the ceiling of the strip club and slicing entirely through Lucky, surgically cutting her in half. Her startled expression will be stuck in my mind forever as what remained of her collapsed to either side of the new...

Rainbow slide.

One particularly gothic looking stripper rushed over to her friend's dismembered body, ignoring the shimmering rainbow laser slide. After a few seconds, she stood, forearms covered in blood, and she was shaking.

"They killed Lucky!" she snarled in a feral tone, panting. Strippers from every corner of the room were suddenly sprinting over, as were a half-dozen beefy security members.

We all watched as dozens of tiny leprechauns brandishing gold knuckle-dusters or shillelaghs—basically canes with fist-sized mallets on the end—rode down the slide with horrible laughter. Basically, envision the gnarled staffs one always thought of when imagining a leprechaun. Then add blood, a few spikes, or a brass finish to the tip. That was the end intended for your face.

They swarmed the strip club like an army of those St. Patrick's Day Troll toys, their fiery red hair enhanced by the blacklight decor. Their devious little eyes scanned the room, obviously in search of us.

Surprisingly, a squad of strippers were lined up at the base of the rainbow between us and the leprechauns, lips curled back, and fingers extended like claws. No, wait. They *were* claws! Upon closer inspection, I realized they weren't just great at angry faces, they were all fucking shifters. This was noticeably obvious with each passing second as fur began to sprout over their skin and they burst into different flavors of shifter.

"Me name is Paddy McKnob!" A broader, bald-headed, ginger-bearded leprechaun demanded, "Give us back our gold, or taste the rainbow!" But the line of strippers had shifted laterally, making it difficult for the wee little man to see over their shoulders, so his glare instead fixated on a whole lot of bedazzled shifter vagina.

And that's when shit got weird.

CHAPTER 17 — QUINN MACKENNA, VEGAS

I spent a large portion of my life fearing for my immortal soul. As a child growing up Catholic in Southie, Hell was as real a place as the drugstore around the corner. I'd never dwelled on what the Inferno would look like, but then I hadn't really needed to; it's sort of in the name, and besides, there are far more pictures and descriptions out there of a fiery underworld than of the pearly gates. Marketing 101. Of course, in none of those pictures were there demented, blacklight-illuminated leprechauns with flaming fluorescent hair battling shapeshifting strippers beneath glimmering lights.

Because no one is that creative.

Then 'Crazy Bitch' by Buckcherry came on.

"This is the soundtrack of my life," Aria hooted, climbing up on top of the table in a low crouch, grinning from ear-to-ear at the growing tension in the room. I glanced back at her, cocking my head slightly. She wasn't remotely concerned about the epic bar fight facing us. Was she really that crazy or was it the booze talking?

I let it go, rose to my feet, and danced away from the rest of the group, trying to put some distance between myself and the raucous fighting. Leprechauns, or the Little People, as Paddy had called themselves, were launching themselves at the were-strippers. I watched as the first stripper we'd seen dancing used the stripper pole to perform a series of Neo-style kicks, each sweep of her heels booting a squealing leprechaun across the room. As she landed, one industrious leprechaun snatched her by the ankle and yanked, drawing her down into a waiting crowd of pissed off Little People.

Before I could see how that situation resolved itself, a half dozen leprechauns saw us and began climbing the rails towards us, gold teeth gleaming in their snarling mouths. "This is your fault," I said, turning to the Reds.

They glared up at me. "Is not," they replied, in unison.

Before I could argue with them, the leprechauns struck. Fortunately, so did Callie. My mouth hung open as I watched the woman wade into the crowd of approaching Little People. Silver light flashed as leprechauns fell, screaming, rolling on the ground clutching various parts of their anatomy. She had acquired some gleaming daggers of her own and wielded them between the fingers of her closed fists like wolverine claws.

She cackled as she danced through the swarm like an angel of death.

"Impressive, right?" Othello said, nudging me.

I'd seriously underestimated her. "She's like a ninja," I whispered, awed.

"With tits," Aria added.

"*Big* tits," Sonia offered.

We all nodded. Then ducked, as a weretiger came flying at us from across the club, blown back by a glass-headed hammer that was smoking with rainbow-colored fog wielded by none other than Paddy McKnob. A fucking rainbow hammer? Christ! The weretiger slammed into the wall behind us, then onto the table we'd been occupying. Glass shattered. The weretiger didn't move.

"Come on then," Paddy roared, impressively loud for his size. "I'll take ye all on!"

I glanced at my companions, minus Callie, who'd gone over the railing in pursuit of the leprechauns; apparently, they'd decided running was more conducive to their health. "Divide and conquer?" I asked.

The Reds grinned with razor sharp teeth. Othello shrugged and patted her briefcase. I flashed them a thumbs up, then leapt into the fray. It wasn't your typical bar fight, and it might have been someone's idea of Hell, but in the end it was still a brawl.

And I was a brawling kind of girl.

CHAPTER 18 — CALLIE PENROSE, VEGAS

I 'd finally reached my limit.
All the alcohol.
All the strippers.
Dorian Gray's mud-wrestling bar.
My failed Gateways.
Casino robbery.
The lollipop guild of leprechauns.
The Ninja Turtle thing.

I wasn't entirely sure which one of these had broken the last straw, or if it even mattered. But I had leapt up from our table, using my magic to create twin blades to extend from between the knuckles of each of my fists. My Edward Scissorhands impersonation. Then I was diving into the chaos, shoving hairy strippers out of my way as I bobbed and weaved, targeting the Little People with a sudden release of my pent-up frustration. I was careful not to touch any of the strippers directly.

One, you had to pay for that kind of thing. Two, they weren't my enemy. I slashed and stabbed hamstrings, thighs, biceps, forearms, and any other appendage that came into my whirlwind of pain—hoping to do as much damage as possible without actually murdering anyone. I used my knees freely since my targets were at perfect height for such tactics and it was harder to hamstring someone so low to the ground.

I was halfway through the chorus before I realized I was belting out 'Crazy Bitch' at the top of my lungs, laughing as I mowed down the Rainbow Riders. I slashed one forearm, making a grizzly old leprechaun drop his odd cane on his way down, and I quickly snatched it up.

Out of the corner of my eye, I saw one leprechaun crouch down and one of his pals race up his back like a ramp to throw himself at me. I swung the cane using the full strength of my hips and clocked him in the jaw, sending him flying into a fan on the ceiling, tearing it free. It crashed to the floor, taking out a few more leprechauns and I hooted. "Homerun!"

I swept my surroundings for any immediate threats and realized I had made it to the opposite side of the club, a clear path of groaning, whimpering leprechauns curled into different variations of fetal position on the floor, marking my warpath back to our original table and the Rainbow Slide.

I watched as two strippers picked up one of the leprechauns by an arm and a leg on either side and began swinging back and forth. On the count of three, they hurled him towards one of the stages where he struck the stripper pole, bending it slightly before he collapsed to the ground onto a pile of crumpled dollar bills gathered into a small pile.

The shifters were definitely winning, and I saw Quinn on one of the far stages taunting an opponent I couldn't see. I gripped my newfound cane and made my way over to her, batting down any leprechauns that got too close.

Any leprechaun that came too close simply ran away screaming upon seeing my face. I touched my cheek to realize that it was coated with a thin sheen of blood from all the leprechaun wounds I had inflicted. I knew I hadn't taken any hits, but if it scared away any more attackers I was fine with it.

And to be honest, I felt like having another drink.

Going berserk was hard work. No wonder Vikings had been such hard drinkers.

CHAPTER 19 — QUINN MACKENNA, VEGAS

I dropped into a crouch beneath the outstretched paw of yet another weretiger, this one fighting on its hind legs. Theoretically, I could have grabbed hold and allowed the shifter's human form to emerge, but I had bigger problems. Like a luck of pissed off leprechauns on my heels, trying to pound me into oblivion. That was the trick with bar fights: you had to be judicious with your punches. Provoking the drunk next to you into knocking out the woman talking shit behind your back was an artform. It required patience. Finesse. Which is why I let the leprechauns take the full brunt of the weretiger's attention as I scuttled away like a crab.

It wasn't nearly as graceful as what Callie was doing on her side of the club, but it had a remarkably similar effect: I was alive and unhurt, while my enemies suffered.

A win is a win.

I hopped up onto one of the stages to get a better vantage point and found a vast majority of the brawlers engaged in direct confrontations. A werepanda, pink thong stretched precariously across its fluffy ass, rolled around, dodging the descending shillelaghs. They cracked solidly into the tile floor, denting the surface. On the opposite side of the club, two leprechauns stood on the bar tossing back pints of frothing beer, guzzling it down until Othello—looking mildly amused— popped up from behind the bar itself and lit their trousers on fire with a Zippo. She ignited a cigarette off their squirming bodies, took a drag, and waved. Not far from there, two bouncers played a game of tug-o-war with a half dozen leprechauns, both sides trying to wrench free a length of velvet rope. I had no idea why.

At last, I spotted the leprechaun I'd been looking for.

"Paddy!" I yelled. I reached out to grab the stripper pole for balance, then yanked my hand back and shook any potential germs loose in a panicked, instinctive flailing motion. "Gross, gross, gross," I muttered under my breath.

"MacKenna!" the leprechaun yelled, still wielding his rainbow hammer. He'd taken off his jacket and torn free his bowtie, his bushy beard licking at his chest like tongues of flame. He marched forward, sweeping his path free with the hammer. Several were-animals fled immediately, having seen what kind of damage the hammer could do.

I grinned in anticipation. It wasn't like I had a deathwish or anything. And I'd recovered enough of my sobriety to realize there was every possibility that the bastard's hammer might blow right past my defenses—even without magic, weapons were weapons. A hammer would hurt something fierce.

But I had a plan.

"Reds!" I yelled, scouring the crowd. I spotted Aria repeatedly punching one of the leprechauns in the face, his head tucked under one arm, his eyes dazed but still trained on her boob pressed against his face. He was grinning, half his teeth missing. Sonia, nearby, was fending off two strippers who seemed as interested in her gold bar as the leprechauns had been. Greedy bitches. Both redheads swiveled to look at me, then broke free of their respective engagements, grinning maniacally.

I danced back to the other side of the stage, forcing Paddy to come up after me. He sauntered up to the raised dais, only the top of his head visible. "Come down and fight me, woman!" he called up to me.

"No, ye come to me, ye wee bastard," I replied.

I could hear Paddy muttering under his breath as he plopped the hammer down on the stage and tried to clamber up. He threw one leg over, trying to hoist himself using the hammer, and groaned. "D'ye need help?" I asked, hands perched on my hips.

"No, I've got it," he said, through clenched teeth. "Just gimme a moment."

I mimed checking my watch. The Reds hopped up behind me, on either side, while I waited. "You called?" Aria said.

"I need your gold," I said.

The two weredragons drew back from me, hissing.

I rolled my eyes. "I promise I'll give it back. And I always keep me promises." I held out either hand, trusting them to hand the gold bars over without a fuss. They did. The bars were extremely heavy, and by the time I had them held properly, Paddy had managed to find his feet.

He was breathing heavily but was able to speak. "T'ings might have been different between us, Quinn MacKenna."

"I'm not into short men," I quipped.

He growled and took hold of his hammer with both hands, then charged me. I could read the strike in his shoulders. That's the problem with hammers: the windup gives your opponent plenty of time to react. Basically, you're trusting that you'll hit with so much force that it won't matter. But to succeed, you have to land the blow.

Of course, I had no intention of letting that happen.

Instead, I lunged forward as far as I could, closing the distance between us by half. I brought both gold bars around, arms fully extended, and crashed them like cymbals around his ears with enough force to send shockwaves up my arms. Paddy stood stock still for a moment, then dropped his hammer. The tip of the rainbow hammer exploded into shards of light as he fell to his knees, showering the ground with shards that looked conspicuously like Skittles. I let my hands fall to my sides, the weight of the bars too much to hold upright for that long, and pressed my boot into Paddy's chest.

"Stay golden, Pony-bitch," I said.

I shoved him back off the stage with my foot.

CHAPTER 20 — CALLIE PENROSE, VEGAS

The bar fight had finally died down, the participants in various states of recovery after the fall of Paddy McKnob—who had been kicked off the center stage by Quinn. One of the leprechauns had tossed down his weapons, lifting his hands into the air, and yelled *Truce* at the top of his lungs. His pals immediately followed suit, and the shifters had promptly ceased beating the living hell out of them.

Surprisingly, we'd managed to end the skirmish without any fatalities.

Well, except for Lucky.

Many of the shifters were simply passed out now—either in animal form or naked human form—and the number of thongs, bras, skimpy lingerie, and stripper heels littering the floor was actually shocking. I made my way past a huddle of leprechauns sitting on the floor and smiled in satisfaction as they reeled away from me in terror.

I finally approached the bar to sit beside Quinn and the Reds. A leprechaun was passed out on the counter in front of me, his pants in shambles as if they'd been set on fire. I slapped his cheek lightly to wake him up, careful to avoid the drool pooling from his open mouth, but instead of stirring, he began snoring beer breath in my face. I scowled, and then shoved him off the bar. He fell to the ground and bounced once but didn't even crack an eye, just kept right on snoring. Quinn nodded in approval, leaning her back against the bar.

Othello was behind the bar, pouring drinks for us. The Reds were cozying up to their gold bars and showing off their Fetush leather lingerie to a trio of topless strippers who wanted to know where they could buy it. I noticed Paddy McKnob sitting on a stool on the other side of Quinn, clutching an ice pack to his temple and swinging his feet back and forth since they couldn't touch the ground. His eyes were locked onto the gold bars, and for once he looked thoughtful rather than possessive.

Othello set the fresh drinks before us, and our new uneasy alliance grew silent as everyone waited for someone else to talk, make a toast, apologize, or kick off round two.

Surprisingly, Paddy cleared his throat first, setting the icepack on the bar beside his drink. He met each of our eyes with a slightly embarrassed, but also impressed look. "I was ready to battle for our gold, but I wasn't ready for a fuckin' *war*. I'll admit, ye ladies sure know how to put up a fight. So I'm t'inkin' ye take these gold bars as a gift. But be careful with 'em. They have luck magic to 'em, and often cause more trouble than they're worth." The Reds grinned from ear to ear. Paddy then turned to the trio of strippers and realized that his face was at their nipple level. He grinned instinctively before looking up to meet their eyes. "We will cover the repairs for all the damage we caused and compensate ye lot however ye see fit."

The strippers nodded after a few moments. "A toast to honor the occasion?" Paddy asked, raising his own glass. As a symbol of good will, everyone followed suit, all the tension of the fight fading away.

I cleared my throat. "Rest in peace, Lucky?" I suggested.

Everyone nodded somberly, and we downed our drinks.

Sonia leaned in close to her sister, attempting to whisper, but failing. "Did she mean rest in *pieces*?"

I put my head in my hands.

Quinn quickly cleared her throat. "How 'bout another round?"

~

TURN THE PAGE TO READ COLLINS, *A PREQUEL NOVELLA TO* THE PHANTOM QUEEN DIARIES.

PART II

COLLINS

Phantom Queen Diaries #0—prequel novella

Every story has a beginning, but not every story has a happy ending. When you live in Boston, you make peace with that, or you find another town. A softer, gentler town. But Quinn MacKenna—a black magic arms dealer just coming into her own—isn't a soft, gentle person, and Boston suits her just fine. Which is why, after getting caught up in the middle of a kidnapping case, she sticks around for a night of blood and mayhem guaranteed to give her new nightmares.

Walk with Quinn as she and her old friend, Jimmy Collins, reconnect, forging a new bond of friendship under fire, even as their very beliefs are put to the test. Prepare yourself for wizardry and ritual, for victims and violence. For walking corpses and cleansing fire. Prepare yourself for the worst of what Quinn's world has to offer.

Because when the things that go bump in the night come out to play, sometimes you have to bump back..

CHAPTER 1

P olice raids are the worst.

It's not so much that I hate them as it is I find them incredibly inconvenient. I had a roommate once who used to employ the same shock-and-awe tactics—flipping on all the lights in the apartment as she prepared to work her night shift, including the light to her closet, where I was passed out on a shoddy air mattress—as if she'd catch me doing something other than sleeping, like I was some sort of sock-fondler. A Prada-phile. Thankfully, my nights sleeping in closets were long behind me. My current profession paid the bills and then some. Unfortunately, it was this profession which occasionally meant dodging uniformed officers intent on catching bad people doing bad things.

I guess that made me a bad girl.

The hotel lobby where this was all going down was extra swanky, far posher than any I'd stayed in; despite the money I made; I was definitely more Marriott than Ritz-Carlton. But, considering the man I'd been hoping to meet up with was a Honduran drug trafficker, the accommodations made sense. What's the point of taking advantage of thousands of people if you can't sleep in a room with a skyline view?

I did my best to look inconspicuous as I walked, trying to stay to the right as if pulling over for emergency vehicles on foot. I got a few looks from the cops watching the doors, but most were the leering sort I was used to; being six-foot-tall and reasonably fit tended to earn more male attention than it ought. Wearing a black pantsuit complete with heels, not to mention an eye-catching shade of lipstick that offset my naturally pale, freckled skin and deep red hair, were likely responsible for the rest. Still, my grip tightened on the bag I carried. The bag itself wasn't important, but what was inside would have interested the police very much.

After all, I doubted many of them had seen a hundred grand in cash before.

I angled for the exit, hoping to pass by unmolested. No such luck. The arm of a uniformed police officer shot out as I walked past, forcing me to stop. I considered doing the limbo and hightailing it out of there, but it would have looked suspicious, and the heels weren't that sensible. Instead, I gave the officer a startled look, as if I hadn't expected to be stopped. Play-acting was my least favorite part of the job, but I'd been practicing.

"Officer?" I said, turning the moniker into a question, my lilting Irish accent catching the cop off guard. His eyebrows shot up, climbing towards a high-and-tight haircut which drew too much attention to his comically large ears. Otherwise, he was handsome, albeit in the way most men are when they workout enough to have jawlines as opposed to jowls. Judging from what I could see, this guy worked out a lot; his uniform hung off his shoulders like it had been suspended from a coat hanger and his neck was as thick as my thigh. He retracted his arm.

"What's in the bag?" he said, voice gruff.

I pretended to be surprised. "Me bag?" I asked.

"Yes, ma'am," he said. He pointed down, as if I needed help locating the item in question.

I held the tote bag up for him to see, the Victoria Secret logo on display against a black background. I held my breath for a second, letting my face redden as if I were embarrassed before saying, quietly, "Panties."

The cop's eyes widened for a second time, and now it was his turn to blush. He coughed into his hand while I fought the urge to laugh in his face. I had no idea what it was about the word "panties" that made men so uncomfortable, but it did. And it was that discomfort I counted on. If he asked to search my bag and I refused, I'd look suspicious. But rifling through a woman's underwear on the pretense of a routine search? He'd never live it down.

He waved me through. "Go on."

I nodded, flashed him a thankful smile, and headed for the street. I made it about twenty feet before another uniformed officer approached. I felt my heart skip a beat. The odds of me surviving a second encounter were slim, especially if I got someone a little more professional this time around. They might not ask to go through my bag, but they might ask me to open it. Not good.

"Quinn!" the officer yelled, his voice rich and deep. "Quinn MacKenna!"

The sound of my name being called brought me up short. I lowered the hand I'd raised, hoping to hail one of the white Taxis that swarmed throughout Boston. From now on, I decided, I'd call one in advance. Quick getaways are a lot more efficient when you have a car running, after all. I turned, eyes narrowed. "Aye?"

"It's me, Jimmy. Jimmy Collins," the cop said. As he got closer, I was able to make out the man's freshly shaven face, his smooth, black skin a shade darker than I remembered. But then, the last time I'd seen Jimmy was the week before he shipped out to join the Marines, and that had been what, six, seven years ago? I shook my head in disbelief.

"What are ye doin' here, Jimmy?" I asked, surprised, but also relieved. A personal chat beat the hell out of an interrogation.

He grinned at me, his teeth a stark contrast to his dark, full lips. "I think that's my line," he said, traces of his Boston accent lingering, but not overwhelming. "What were you doing in that hotel?" he asked.

So maybe it was going to be an interrogation, after all. I rested one hand on my hip. "It's been over half a decade and that's the first t'ing ye say to me?" I asked, deflecting his question.

His smile widened as he eyed the bag in my hand. "A little liaison?" he said, flexing his eyebrows in a knowing gesture. I grunted, amused, but mostly glad to have an excuse; a clandestine meeting with a lover wouldn't get me hauled off to the nearest precinct. Concealing stacks of hard-earned drug money in a tote bag might.

"Ye caught me," I said, pursing my lips.

Jimmy settled his hands on his hips, looming over me. I realized that, while Jimmy had always been tall—six inches over six-foot by the time he graduated high school—he'd become large since I'd last seen him. Imposingly so, built like a linebacker, the service weapon holstered at his hip like a children's toy next to those massive hands. "Quinn MacKenna," he shook his head. "You look good."

The way he said it made a real blush creep up my cheeks. It wasn't so much the words as the tone; he'd dragged the last word down, his voice dropping an octave on the way. I frowned at him, trying to decide what to say. Thank you? Somehow that seemed lame in comparison. To be fair, I rarely knew how to respond when men hit on me. It's not like it was entirely unexpected, but it was rare. Between my height and the don't-fuck-with-me vibe I knew I gave off, few men were ever bold enough to approach me. And, of those that were, fewer still had what it took to keep me interested.

Fortunately, I was saved the trouble by Jimmy's walkie. It crackled, once, before a shrill voice cried out a series of numbers, followed by the words "all available officers." Jimmy and I exchanged glances, and I raised an eyebrow.

Cops began trickling out of the hotel, leaving the raid team to find their man alone, in favor of whatever was going on. A few rushed past, piling into their squad cars, many of which lined the valet parking section. Jimmy cursed. "Damn, I've got to go. Is it alright if I give you a call, later?" he said.

"D'ye have me number?" I asked, too thrown by the implication to debate whether or not I wanted him to have it.

He grinned. "I think Dez will give it to me."

Dez was my aunt in name only, though better known as the woman who'd raised me after my mother passed. She and Jimmy's grandmother were neighbors back in Southie, which meant matchmaking was a foregone conclusion. I thought about it, then nodded. "Fine, but don't ye let her go on and on about me," I said. Dez had a tendency to do that, and I didn't want Jimmy finding out how remarkably available, how remarkably unmarried, I was—something Dez would be sure to mention at least a half dozen times.

Jimmy laughed. "I know the drill," he said. He gave me a curt nod, flashed another smile, and took off past me. What happened next was probably just an accident—an eager, excited man rushing off into danger without paying close attention to his surroundings. But, when Jimmy Collins tore by, his thigh clipped the tote bag, sending it crashing to the pavement. Stacks of bills spilled out, poking out like mint green teeth from the mouth of the bag. Jimmy froze. I froze.

Well, shit.

CHAPTER 2

Sitting in the back of a squad car is a pain in the ass, both literally and figuratively. Unlike its civilian counterpart, the backseat of a patrol vehicle isn't designed for comfort; the seat was a sheeny black bench made of plastic, so slick that I ended up sprawled against either door every time Jimmy took a tight turn. Had I been handcuffed, the effect would have been doubled. But I wasn't handcuffed, and Jimmy didn't seem to care that I hadn't put a seatbelt on—he whipped us about, zipping through traffic like his life depended on it.

At least we wouldn't get pulled over.

"Tell me the truth, Quinn," Jimmy said as he blasted past SUVs and convertibles alike, his siren sounding somehow less loud inside the car than it had outside. "Whose money is this?"

I stiff-armed the nearest door, trying to keep from sliding from one end of the car to the other, glaring at the man through the thick Plexiglass that separated us. Jimmy had insisted I take a ride with him to clear things up—unless I'd have rather explained myself to his superiors at the nearby precinct. It wasn't the best deal I'd ever gotten, but I knew it was the best deal I was going to get. The problem was, I had no idea if I could trust Jimmy with the truth. Sure, we'd been friends on and off since we were kids, but he was still a cop. Looking the other way was practically an art form for some of

Boston's finest, but those days were fast fading, and Jimmy never struck me as the type of guy who'd take a bribe and be on his merry way. In fact, he struck me as the kind of guy to take a bullet in the back rather than go on the take.

Call it a hunch, but I didn't think he'd approve of who I'd done business with.

"Ye can't handle the truth, Jimmy," I intoned, reciting my favorite line from A Few Good Men, hoping it would earn me another flirtatious grin.

It didn't. Guess I wasn't as cute as I thought I was.

"It's Officer Collins," Jimmy drawled. "And try me."

I muttered a few obscenities under my breath. Now that flirting was off the table, there was little point pretending to be a lady. I was never very good at that, anyway. I tried to sit up straighter, but the ceiling of the car was too low, so I ended up hunched and glaring at the man. "First of all, it's me money," I clarified. "I deal in...antiquities. Artifacts. Rare stuff that people pay good money for."

The truth was a bit more complicated. Wasn't it always? Thing is, I did deal in antiquities. But they weren't your average, everyday museum pieces. Nothing I traded or sold belonged in a display case. What I dealt in were magical artifacts, items with enough juice to earn their own Wikipedia pages. Cursed totems, holy objects, you name it. Most people would have taken one look at my goods and written them off as superstitious junk or novelty items you could buy off SkyMall, but then most people were Regulars—men and women without an ounce of psychic or magical ability. People who wouldn't know the Golden Fleece from a fur coat. And yes, in case you were wondering, that meant I was not a Regular.

Which made me a Freak.

In more ways than one, if I was being honest with myself.

"Since when?" Jimmy asked, probably referring to my choice of profession, but my thoughts betrayed me and I blushed a little.

"For a couple years, now," I replied, looking away. Frankly, I'd been at it longer than that, though at the time I wasn't exactly running the show; I'd had an abusive boyfriend who'd inadvertently shown me the ropes. It'd been sort of like dating a drug dealer, except—instead of learning how to weigh and sort product—I'd learned how to avoid customs and network. You'd be surprised how much of my job relied on knowing the right people.

"And it pays this well?" Jimmy asked, pointing to the bag in his passenger seat. He'd refused to touch the money, unwilling to "contaminate evidence." Not a good sign, that.

"It can," I said, refusing to admit that I'd earned twice this much on at least two jobs in the last year. The first had paid for my apartment. The second, my car. I wasn't sure where this newest installment would land, but it never hurt to have excess cash on hand. I'd always considered myself fairly low maintenance, but I'd developed expensive tastes lately; you can never have too many pairs of shoes.

Or enough guns, for that matter.

"And what was it you sold tonight?" he asked, angling us northeast towards Massachusetts Bay.

I cringed, trying to figure out how best to answer that. So far, Jimmy had no reason to think I was anything more or less than I said I was, but a hundred grand was a lot of money. If I told him the truth, he'd balk at the exchange and call bullshit. But I didn't have a handy lie ready. As I tried to decide whether or not to tell him the truth, I realized we were working our way around Pleasure Bay, the water an inky pool of blackness for as far as the eye could see, illuminated only by the occasional vessel skimming across the otherwise placid surface. "Where the hell are we goin'?" I asked.

"Answer my question, and I'll answer yours," Jimmy said.

Since he was driving, it didn't seem entirely fair, but I didn't argue. I knew my response would be a sticking point, no matter what I said; Jimmy had never been the type to let things go, even before he'd started putting on uniforms. I cleared my throat and decided to tell the truth. Not because it would set me free, or any optimistic nonsense like that, but because I couldn't think of anything more plausible. "Me buyer wanted a pair of gloves," I said, at last.

Jimmy grunted. "You expect me to believe that someone paid a hundred grand for gloves?"

"They were uncommonly rare gloves," I replied.

"Made out of what? Diamonds?" he joked.

"Dragon scale, actually."

Jimmy's eyes met mine in the rearview mirror. He didn't look amused, but then I hadn't expected him to. See, I told you the truth wouldn't set me free. In fact, from the look on Jimmy's face, it seemed guaranteed to get me locked up. "It's not smart to lie to a cop, Quinn," he said.

I sighed. "I'm not lyin' to ye, Jimmy." And I wasn't. Honestly, I had no idea what a drug lord needed gloves covered in dragon scales for, but then it was my policy not to ask those sorts of questions. If he'd asked me for something a little more militant, maybe I'd have done some digging, but unless he planned to punch people to death, I doubted I'd lose any sleep over the exchange. Besides, there were easier ways to kill people, and I was betting the swarthy Honduran knew that. "I came across a few items last month from a shipment out of St. Louis," I went on. "Apparently, a couple of the more industrious hunters had harvested scales from some of the dead dragons. I went through their merchandise and picked up a few pieces I thought I could sell for a higher price." I shrugged.

"Jesus, Quinn, give me a break. We both know dragons aren't real." Jimmy's hand tightened on the steering wheel. "Look, I saw the St. Louis video like everyone else. I'll admit it made me wonder. But it was a prank. Somebody's idea of fun, that's all."

The video Jimmy was referring to was one of those highly publicized hoaxes that occasionally captured the public's attention—a grainy video of a dragon attacking a busy, car-laden bridge in the middle of the night. The whole thing was very Cloverfield, shaky and scary at the same time. Of course, public opinion was that the whole thing was a publicity stunt, a trailer for some nifty independent film. But I knew better. Granted, I'd never seen a dragon before, and hadn't believed they existed myself until a few months ago. But one look at the gloves was all it took to make me a believer; no metal on earth shined quite like those silver gloves had.

Besides, all metal melted at certain temperatures. These hadn't.

"T'ink what ye like, Jimmy," I said. "But I answered your question. Now it's your turn. Tell me where we're goin'." At this point, I might have preferred the precinct. I wasn't sure how long it would take my lawyer to get me out of this mess, but being stuck in an interrogation room sounded a hell of a lot better than sliding around in the back of a squad car until Jimmy decided I was too crazy to be let loose on society.

"I'm responding to the all call," Jimmy replied, still looking dubious. "They want additional officers re-directing traffic around Castle Island."

I cocked an eyebrow. "What traffic?" I asked. Castle Island was a popular destination for tourists and locals alike—one of those few places where adults can find some lively entertainment and kids can play to their heart's content. At its heart was Fort Independence, a granite edifice you could tour for a price. Usually, the island would be crawling with obnoxious couples walking arm-in-arm, spandex-coated bicyclists out for a ride, and yoga enthusiasts squatting over the lawns like double-jointed dogs. But at night, especially this late at night, traffic was unlikely.

"No clue. Apparently, they want to establish a perimeter," Jimmy said, sounding doubtful.

"Around the island?" I asked, blown away by the enormity of that request. Castle Island was huge. Something like twenty acres. I wasn't sure they could establish a perimeter if every officer in the state were available, let alone those who'd been called from their usual stomping grounds.

Jimmy shrugged. "I'll know more once I get there. Listen, I'll drop you off before we get there. But this money..." He shook his head, and for a moment I wondered if he'd insist on keeping it. Things wouldn't go well if he did; I wasn't about to let him run off with my hard earned cash. "Listen, you need to be more careful," he said, finally. "And come up with better lies."

I started to open my mouth, but Jimmy wasn't finished.

"No," he said, "I'm not stupid. I saw you come out of that hotel. And I don't know how many people out there run around with this much cash, but I can guess who you met with. Honestly, I don't know what kind of arrangement you made with the bastard, and I don't want to know. Just tell me this...will anyone get hurt because of what you did?"

I frowned, considering whether to protest and insist I'd told him the truth. In the end, however, I decided it was better to let Jimmy think whatever he wanted. As long as he didn't make life difficult for me in the process, I could handle him thinking I was in bed with a drug lord. Figuratively speaking. "No, as far as I know, they won't," I said at last.

Jimmy nodded. A tension I hadn't noticed left his body in a rush, as if he'd been fully prepared to arrest me if he thought I were a danger to society. I smirked a little, amused by the thought.

If only he knew.

CHAPTER 3

W e ended up parked among a swarm of squad cars, their lights flashing so bright and so frequently that everything in sight seemed like it had been painted by Uncle Sam. Jimmy had promised to drop me off, but had insisted on avoiding Marine Park at night. Something about it not being safe. I decided not to mention the fact that I was both armed and very capable of taking care of myself. Policemen never seemed to care much for the words "concealed carry," so I'd refrained from mentioning it to Jimmy when he'd asked me to go for a ride. Instead, Jimmy had swung west, into City Point, only to be swallowed by the blockade.

"Wait here," Jimmy said. He hopped out of the car, leaving me alone in the backseat. I tested the door. Locked. I sighed and settled back, relieved to not be moving anymore, at least. Now that I was alone, I was able to adjust the pistol riding my spine, easing some of the pressure that had built up while Jimmy drove. The P226 Sig Sauer wasn't a massive handgun, nothing like the .44 Magnums toted by Dirty Harry fanatics, but it was a bulky hunk of metal. If I'd been a man, I could have worn a shoulder holster and let the gun sit under my armpit beneath a jacket. But I wasn't, and while anyone who's ever had to carry a gun can tell you how difficult they are to conceal, even fewer are the women who manage to do so and look fashionable at the same time. I'd done what I could, but in my pantsuit it'd meant holstering the sidearm at the small of my back and buying a jacket that flared out enough to make sure the bulge was less than noticeable.

Unfortunately, it seemed I wasn't as alone as I'd initially thought; a finger rapped against the window as I adjusted the pistol, and I looked up to find a short Hispanic woman in a pantsuit of her own, her hair pulled back in a no-nonsense bun that left her face looking bare and severe. The cool expression on her face didn't help. "Let me see your hands," she barked.

I did as she asked. Ordinarily, I might have argued, but I knew how this looked. I was sitting in the back of a squad car, fidgeting with a firearm. Not exactly a winning combination. I held my hands up a little, though I was still ducked down thanks to the cramped backseat, my slouched back starting to ache from the pressure on my spine—probably a tactic used to fuck with alleged perpetrators.

I'll take Stress Positions for 100, Alex.

"Do you have a permit for that?" she asked, eyes dull and emotionless, lips turned down in a frown.

I nodded and carefully patted my jacket pocket where I'd stored my conceal carry permit. It was an unrestricted permit, which was actually a bitch to get; I'd had to submit proof that I was in danger often enough to need a gun on my person to apply for one. I'd fudged the details a bit, but made sure the licensing office knew how much money I made selling goods, and what some people out there were willing to do for that kind of money; I didn't mention that most of the offenders were greedy clients looking to score a two-for-one deal.

They hadn't asked.

The woman never took her eyes off me, and yet somehow seemed to be scanning the crowd. Cops could do that, I'd noticed—use their peripheral vision like a third eye. Until she did that, I hadn't really known for sure she was a cop; if she was wearing a badge, I couldn't see it. "Where's the officer who put you back here?" she asked, her voice sounding thin and reedy through the door, like I was in some sort of fish tank.

"I t'ink he's lookin' for someone to let us through so he can drop me off," I said, shrugging. Honestly, I had no idea what Jimmy was doing. All I knew was I wanted to get the hell out of here sooner rather than later.

"Well, that's a shame. No one is going anywhere right now," she said.

"Why?" I asked, yelling a little to make sure she heard me.

"Detective Machado," Jimmy said before she could respond, coming into sight from the front of the car, only a third of his body visible through the passenger window. I watched his hands move as he spoke. "I was trying to find someone to take this woman home," he explained, as if she'd asked.

"We got a tip about the Reynold's boy," Detective Machado replied. "They've cordoned off this side of things, and will have the bay entrance blocked off soon. I don't think we can spare anyone."

Jimmy's hands fell to his sides in resignation, but there was an excited edge to his voice I couldn't miss, even with the distortion of sound. "The Reynold's boy? Really? Here?"

The name brought with it a host of questions, but none I dared ask with the detective standing nearby. The fate of Lukas Reynolds, the twelve-year-old son of wealthy socialites Sofia and Peter Reynolds, was practically all anyone talked about since his abduction two days ago from a carnival. Not since the Lindbergh kidnapping had this much media attention been given to a missing person's report; the boy's cherubic face had been plastered on every news station, local and national alike, alongside a picture taken by an enterprising photojournalist of the scene Lukas had been abducted from—a high resolution image of a glistening red lollipop Lukas had been given melted partway on the ground in front of an out-of-focus carousel. The media had since dubbed the whole affair the Lollipop Case. No one knew who had taken him, or why, though a ransom seemed the likeliest motive. The Reynolds were descended from German aristocrats, and public speculation put their net worth in the millions.

Detective Machado shrugged. "I don't know the details. But this is coming from the top, so we're going to shut up and color."

Jimmy grunted. "I know something about that," he said, probably referring to his time in the Marines. I'd never enlisted, but after a series of failed career paths and financial struggles, I'd considered it; the military had seemed like a pretty viable option for someone who liked to fight and couldn't hold down a job. Of course, if getting dishonourably discharged for having a shitty attitude were a thing, I'd have been booted faster than you could say "drop and give me twenty."

The two cops flashed wry grins at one another, and I realized the detective was probably former military, herself—there was simply too much shared knowledge in that exchange. I also realized one other thing: Detective

Machado was attractive. Attractive, and into Officer Jimmy Collins. She leaned into him when she spoke and pressed a hand to her throat, probably unconsciously. Not that I could blame her. Between the muscles, the smile, and the uniform, there was a lot there to like. She jerked her chin towards me, letting the moment pass. "You should escort the civilian out of here and let her catch her own ride home. Especially before she flashes her gun a second time," she added, smirking.

"She did what?"

"Wait, she did tell you she was carrying, didn't she?" Machado asked, flicking her eyes at me, one hand settling on the butt of her gun as if worried I might draw on her at any moment. I wasn't planning on it, but I understood her concern. Her reaction was why I hadn't mentioned the gun to Jimmy; I hadn't wanted him treating me like I was a bomb that could go off at any moment.

Jimmy waved that off, trying to diffuse the situation. "No," he said, sounding far more calm than I'd expected after finding out I'd been armed during our little chat. Had he spotted the gun beforehand? Maybe I hadn't done as good a job hiding it as I'd thought. "But she didn't have to," Jimmy continued. "It was a social visit. I got the call while we were catching up."

"You brought a civilian to an active scene, Officer Collins?" Machado asked, her anger now directed at the much taller man.

"Not intentionally. I was hoping to drop her off somewhere more populated than the park at night, that's all. Dispatch didn't tell us what we were walking into."

Machado seemed to consider that, then folded her arms over her chest. "Listen, Collins," she said, her voice almost too low to catch, "I know you're good under pressure. You did well in the Academy. Good instincts. You have potential. You might even make detective, if you keep it up. But this? Shit like this will cost you. Set you back." She leaned back and searched his face, her expression surprisingly gentle.

"Yes ma'am," Jimmy said, sounding appropriately chastised. I considered interrupting to take the blame, but anything I said would only muck up the water further; better a dressing down for Jimmy than a prison cell for me. Selfish, I know, but if it meant I'd end up in my own bed tonight, cuddling a bag with a hundred grand in it, so be it.

Selfish was the new sexy.

Machado tapped his chest with her finger, but lightly. "Don't let it happen again. Now, get her out of here before—"

But that was as far as Machado got before something interrupted her. The two spun, facing back the way Jimmy had come, their backs to me. And that's when I heard what had both cops reaching for their guns, screams echoing through the night like a flock of birds being chased off by hounds. The sound made the hairs on the back of my neck stand up.

With that, any guilt I had leftover from getting caught flashing my gun fled in rush. Guilt was a luxury, and the only shit I paid for that I didn't need were designer clothes.

Fuck Machado.

I settled my hand on the butt of my gun.

CHAPTER 4

I banged on my side of the door. "What's goin' on?" I yelled, trying to see past the two cops. Neither responded, at first. Detective Machado ducked a bit, drawing her gun, and dipped between the squad cars like a wraith, swallowed by what few shadows were visible despite the sirens. It made me wonder just what branch of the military she'd been in.

Jimmy dropped down and spoke without taking his eyes off whatever he was seeing, "Stay in the car, Quinn. And stay low. I don't know what's happening, but you're surrounded by cops. You'll be safe here."

I opened my mouth to argue that I'd be a lot safer in a car that wasn't locked, but Jimmy was already taking off after Machado. He was a lot bigger than she was and had a harder time finding shadows thick enough to hide him, but he unholstered his gun and padded off stealthily enough to make me glad he was on our side. I scrambled to look around, but saw nothing out of the ordinary. Well, nothing out of the ordinary I hadn't expected to see. The screams, sounding more like cries of hysteria than people in pain, had died down, leaving an eerie quiet behind like a fog that swallowed the world outside the squad car. I considered drawing my gun, then thought better of it; if a cop found me with a drawn gun in the back of a squad car, I might never get it back.

The police were pretty particular about not drawing your gun in public without cause.

Instead, I did what Jimmy suggested. I got low, dropping to my knees, slipping between the seat and the wire mesh divider to kneel on the floorboards, peering out into the distance. I almost jumped when a uniformed cop popped up on the edges of my peripheral vision. He was a fairly muscular guy with broad shoulders and a beer gut—part beefcake, part donut. His back was ramrod straight, and he rested his hand on the butt of his gun like he'd never had to draw it before, like the threat alone had always been enough. He reminded me of a small town saloon sheriff, staring out into the night as if whatever was out there could be cowed by courage and grit.

Or maybe I was projecting.

Either way, I wished he'd draw his gun and stand ready. If there was something out there, I would have preferred a stouter line of defense. That's the thing with predicting the unpredictable: you either had imagination, or you didn't. I was betting Wyatt Derp had none, whereas I'd seen what was behind the curtain—and it hadn't all been pretty.

But when the cop finally did draw the gun, I had to admit even my wild imagination hadn't anticipated what had been lurking in the dark. The cop whirled, his gun lit by the sirens, blazing red one moment, burning blue the next. His hands shook, but his arms were steady. He was yelling something, probably a warning, but what came lurching out of the darkness didn't seem to hear him.

Of course, it's hard to hear without ears.

And this thing didn't have any.

What it did have were vaguely human characteristics. The creature was bipedal, shambling forward on two feet with the grace of a toddler on painkillers; it bumped into squad cars so frequently it seemed almost like a game. It wore no clothes, merely scraps wound around swathes of exposed bone. Something made me think female, even though there was no skin to speak of, no hair, and no distinguishable features. The hips maybe—too wide to be male. The first word that came to mind was the one you'd expect when you see an animated corpse: zombie. But it felt inadequate somehow, or perhaps inappropriate. I'd always thought zombies were fleshy things, covered in ichor, wearing clothes we wouldn't be caught dead in.

Pun intended.

Frankly, when I thought of zombies I pictured grotesque, fumbling things I used to cringe away from like Billy Butcherson in Hocus Pocus, Tar Man in Return of the Living Dead, or Michael Jackson in Thriller. Part of what had made them so horrifying was how human they looked, as if each were a walking, groaning reminder of what we all eventually become. But this creature wasn't horrifying, or at least not in that way. There was no flesh hanging in clumps on her skeletal remains like meat packed along the corners of a tuna can. In fact, she came forward on bones so dry and brittle I wondered what connected them; without cartilage, tendons, and flesh to hold them all together, bones alone should not have allowed for successful perambulation. Of course, compared to her very existence, the question seemed a bit silly.

The officer raised his gun, still shouting as the creature closed the distance between them. When she didn't move, he fired. The bullet tore through her sternum, blowing away a few ribs, sending shards of bone flying. But she didn't stop walking. The cop shouted again, but this time it sounded more like a curse than a warning, as if he couldn't believe what he was seeing. Still, he held his ground, sighting down the barrel once more.

Another shot.

This time, he took out the leg, blowing the knee off at the joint. The skeleton's shin bone and foot went flying, soaring off into the night. She collapsed and, for a moment, I thought that would be it. But then she started to crawl. It was almost comical in a way—so cliche I wasn't sure it was even real. Maybe I'd waited for Jimmy for so long I'd fallen asleep and was tucked away in my own private nightmare.

But it was real, because even in my nightmares, I'd have been able to run. I jerked the handle a few times to no avail, screaming, hoping the cop would see me and let me out. But the uniformed cop had already begun backpedaling, keeping his distance from the crawling skeleton, which is probably why he never saw the second skeleton come up behind him.

This one was freakishly tall and, unlike its counterpart, wore clothes—a faded red jacket and black leather boots, both littered with gaping holes. If the creature had been wearing pants when he died, he wasn't now. Of course, that didn't stop him from wrapping his arms around the officer, winding them around from behind like a lover. The officer jumped, startled, and glanced back at the skeleton with eyes full of primal terror. At first, I wondered why the cop didn't simply tear the thing off; skeletons had no muscle, after all. Bone was sturdy shit, but it wasn't like the creature could yank him down with force. Hell, without muscles lining the jaw, the thing couldn't even bite. At worst, the ossified creature was a disconcerting accessory, like a fanny pack or a man purse.

"Get him off ye!" I yelled, hoping he might hear me and stop staring. But then I realized what the creature was doing as the very flesh I'd been so fixated on began to knit along the creature's bones. Tendons sprung up like rubber bands, winding around muscles that glistened red like uncooked steak. The officer shrieked as his body began to shrink in direct proportion to the creature's growth, that beer gut sliding away like a punctured balloon, his broad, sloped shoulders squaring off to the point where his uniform hung off him the way it might a coat hanger. It was awful to watch, but I couldn't look away. Not until his eyes went; the sight of those fleshy orbs being swallowed back into their sockets like a flower curling in on itself made me want to throw up.

I ducked low, trying to catch my breath. What the fuck was going on? I drew my own gun, no longer the least bit concerned whether a cop saw it out or not; I doubted they'd be inclined to disarm a living, breathing woman when there were dead things out there to be, well, killed. I steeled myself and glanced up. The officer's clothes lay in a crumpled heap on the ground. Nothing, not even his bones, seemed to have survived. The zombies, or skeletons, or whatever they'd been, were nowhere in sight.

Not good.

Something clipped the window behind me and I spun, sighting down the line of my arm, worried that if I shot at something within the tight confines of the car I might not hear out of my ear for at least a week. But all I saw was darkness beyond the haphazard line of cop cars. I stared for a moment longer, then released the breath I'd been holding. Still, I knew better than to let my guard down. Something was out there, lurking. Waiting for something warm and fleshy to engorge itself upon, like a tick which swallowed bone as well as blood. I wondered what my clothes would look like in a pile on the ground and shivered, then gritted my teeth.

Not going to happen, I told myself.

If I was going to go out like that, I wasn't going to do it in a damn pantsuit.

A girl has to have some standards.

"Quinn!" Jimmy shouted. I spun back around, finger riding the trigger, safety off. Jimmy's face was pressed against the window, eyes so wide his dark pupils swam in pools of white. "Jesus, put the gun away!" Jimmy hissed and rose, shielding me from view with his body, which put his crotch in plain view through the window.

I lowered the gun, but didn't holster it. "Jimmy, ye need to be careful!" I yelled. "They're out there, and they got one of your people."

Jimmy sunk down again, staring at me. "What are you babbling about?" he asked.

I pointed past him, finger thudding into the window hard enough it made me wince. "Look!" I insisted. I could still see the cop's clothes in a pile. Jimmy followed my gaze and frowned. He held up a hand, the other clutching his gun.

"I'll be right back," he said.

"The fuck ye will," I said. "Let me the fuck out of this car, Jimmy Collins, or I will kill ye meself!" I probably sounded hysterical, but I didn't care. I didn't like tight spaces and hated being locked up. Add flesh-sucking zombies, and I deserved to have a meltdown. Jimmy flicked his eyes at me, then pulled on the handle from his side. The door opened, and I spilled out onto the pavement, pressing my back against the cruiser, prepared to shoot anything that came shambling out from the darkness beyond the streetlights.

"What is it, Quinn?" Jimmy asked, his voice a hushed whisper. Now that I was outside the car, I could hear other voices in the distance as more cops returned to their cars. The commotion, whatever it had been, seemed to have ended. I glanced at the much larger man still squatted beside me and realized I must have looked more than a little off; Jimmy's eyes spotted the gun and narrowed. "Something's got you spooked," he said. "But if you don't put that away, I'll have to take it from you."

"They sucked him dry," I muttered. I realized I didn't want to put the gun away, that I'd rather Jimmy try to take it from me than put it away. Which meant I was more scared than I thought.

"What did?" Jimmy asked, touching my arm lightly.

I jumped, surveyed our immediate surroundings, then holstered my gun. Jimmy was right. If I was this jumpy, there was no telling what would happen once more cops showed up. I wasn't sure if I could take the monsters without the gun, but I was damn sure I wouldn't be able to take the cops with one. I'd just have to pray the monsters were gone and had no plans of coming back. Of course, I wasn't sure my gun made me any safer, regardless.

It hadn't helped Wyatt Derp.

I waved Jimmy off. "Go look for yourself," I said. Jimmy searched my face then nodded and headed for the discarded uniform. He picked it up in pieces, raising the trousers with a look of concern, then the shirt. The pants hung awkwardly in places, weighed down by the cop's holster and belt. The top by his walkie. Jimmy held the material up as if unsure what to do with the mess. He finally tossed the clothes onto a nearby cruiser and gazed at the ground, and at last his puzzled expression gave way to something I recognized: worry. Jimmy stared down at the officer's boots, socks crumpled and lying half out like limp tongues. But what he picked up wasn't the boots.

It was a gun.

Jimmy swiveled his head around as if he might find the missing cop out there, prowling the edges of the barricade, buck naked and unarmed. Yet another prank. Another hoax to dismiss. Our eyes met, and for a moment I wondered if I could lie well enough to make Jimmy think that was all it was. But then I shook my head, feeling a little like a surgeon telling a family member that their loved one didn't make it. Except you could blame God for awful crap like that.

Being sucked into oblivion by a corpse like you were a fucking ramen noodle?

Let's just say I doubted God had anything to do with it.

CHAPTER 5

Wyatt Derp's real name was William O'Bannon. Bill to his friends, of which he seemed to have many. Bill had been one of those dependable lifers who rarely get the recognition they deserve, a cop good enough to stay in and survive it all—drug wars, gang violence, budget cuts—but not quite clever enough to make detective. I'd learned all this within only a few minutes after the rest of the cops showed up. A few of the younger officers joked that O'Bannon had run off with his mistress, in such a hurry he'd left everything behind, including his boxers. But the veterans were having none of it; Bill wasn't the kind of guy to leave his gun lying around for just anyone to find, no matter the circumstances.

In the end, they'd turned to me. Which was too bad, considering I had nothing to say. Now that my nerves had calmed down a little, I knew to keep my mouth shut; if I started raving about how they'd lost one of their own to flesh-sucking zombies, they'd probably toss me back into the squad car—with jewelry this time. If it had just been Jimmy and me, I might have said something. He hadn't believed me when I'd mentioned the dragonskin gloves, but at least he'd listened. Unfortunately, perhaps sensing I had more to say than I was letting on, Detective Machado had sent the man to go get her coffee while she interrogated me.

"What did you see?" Machado asked, probably for the third or fourth time. I tend to lose track of things when I'm ignoring someone.

"I didn't see anythin'," I replied, arms folded across my stomach. I wasn't as well endowed as some, but folding my arms over my chest usually meant hiking them up near my shoulders, which would have put my elbows directly in Machado's suspicious face. Of course, if she kept snapping at me, I'd do that anyway.

Another uniform approached from the darkness on the other side of the street, following a path which led past Marine Park towards Fort Independence. He flipped through the pages of a notebook, spotted us, and hurried over. I caught a bright, eager smile from him which might have been flirtatious, but reminded me more of a puppy wagging its tail. Some men, especially young men, were like that around women—as if you could ask them to do just about anything and expect to see it done. Machado noticed and grunted.

"What is it, Cassidy?" she barked.

Cassidy's smile disappeared so fast I wondered if I'd imagined it. "Reports from witnesses said they saw things coming from the Fort."

"Things?"

He thumbed through the notebook again. "Yeah, detective. Things. I asked them to tell me more, but most either couldn't, or wouldn't, give me a description."

"Wouldn't? Why not?" Machado asked, exasperated.

He glanced up, looking embarrassed. "Well, because they saw zombies, ma'am."

"Excuse me?"

Cassidy cleared his throat and read from the notebook. "One guy said, and I quote 'I know it's crazy, but I swear I saw skeletons come out of the fucking ground.' Another, 'they moved like they weren't human, and they didn't have any skin.' It goes on like that. What do you think, detective? A prank, maybe? College theater kids trying to scare the locals?"

Not likely, but I wouldn't be surprised if that's what it got chalked up to. While Machado mulled that over, I surreptitiously glanced at Cassidy's notebook, wondering how he'd managed to quote the witnesses verbatim. I saw a series of odd squiggles and lines. Shorthand, like what secretaries used for dictation. Nifty trick.

"If it was, we'd have found them." Machado shook her head. "What about Lukas Reynolds? Did anyone see him? Or a kid who could have matched his description?"

"Everyone I talked to said they were too busy running to notice," Cassidy admitted.

"Jesus, Cassidy, is that all you got?" Machado asked. She sounded pissed. I couldn't blame her. Despite copious evidence to the contrary, Regulars around the world refused to believe in the existence of the supernatural. According to them, magic amounted to sleight-of-hand tricks played on unsuspecting victims. Shapeshifters were exotic animals which had thus far avoided classification. Zombies were actors in gory makeup. The idea that the monsters out there were real wasn't something Machado could present to her superiors, not if she wanted to keep her job.

Cassidy shook his head, looking uncertain, then finally produced something from his back pocket. It was in a plastic evidence bag and took me a moment to identify. When I finally did, I took a step back, eyes wide. It was a hand. A skeletal hand so small and dainty it had to belong to a child.

Machado stared at me, gauging my reaction. "The hell is the matter with you?" she asked. "And what the hell is that, Cassidy?"

I answered before I could stop myself, too horrified to consider how crazy I'd sound. "The necromancer must have pulled them all up. The whole fort. Even the kids." My voice sounded breathy, and I realized I was babbling.

But it was true.

The only flavor of Freak I knew who could raise the dead were necromancers. Although I'd never met one, I knew what they were capable of, at least theoretically. Closer to witches than wizards, they used rituals to summon the undead to do their bidding. From what I understood, they formed a sort of contract with the souls they summoned, offering something in return. I had no idea what this necromancer had offered, but it must have been awfully tempting—raising as many zombies as this would have cost. A lot.

"Did you say necromancer?" Machado's voice was hushed but intense, which should have worried me, but at the moment she scared me a hell of a lot less than the idea that there were more skeletons out there waiting to drain us all dry.

I nodded.

Machado had her gun out and pointed at the ground before I could say more. "Cassidy, cuff this woman. She's coming with me."

The earnest beat cop hesitated, searching my face. I must have looked as surprised as he did, though, because he seemed poised to ask her to repeat herself. But Machado didn't give him that chance. "Now, Cassidy," she barked. "She's got a gun holstered at her lower back. Take it, hand it to me, and then cuff her."

The officer did as she asked. I kept my hands out to my sides, looking as non-threatening as possible. Part of me, a big part of me, considered drawing my gun and making a break for it. But I was surrounded by cops, and Machado had her gun out already, as if looking for an excuse to use it. If I so much as twitched, I knew she'd drop me. Of course, I still didn't know why. I frowned, but decided not to struggle; it wasn't often I got held at gunpoint and felt the warm glow of righteous indignation, after all.

"What the fuck am I bein' arrested for?" I asked.

Jimmy stepped through a growing crowd of onlookers gripping a styrofoam cup. He took in the scene with wide eyes. Not for the first time that night, I wished I'd never run into the bastard; I might have been in my comfy ass bed by now. Suddenly, it looked like I might be sleeping in a cell.

"You're being taken into custody for your insider knowledge regarding the Reynolds' case," Machado replied, holstering her gun the instant she held mine in her hands. Cassidy drew my hand back and latched a cuff into place, then the other. They pinched.

"Me what?" I asked, flabbergasted.

"Detective—" Jimmy began, stepping closer to us.

"Officer Collins, you're coming, too," Machado interjected. "You both need to answer some questions."

I glanced out at the pitch black darkness from whence Cassidy had come and cursed my shitty luck. I'd managed to seal a lucrative deal with a drug lord, avoid getting caught up in a police raid, and survived a run-in with flesh-sucking zombies, only to get hauled in for something I didn't do.

Figured.

CHAPTER 6

My lawyer was especially good at his job. But then, you get what you pay for, and Walter Sloan wasn't cheap. Although I was pretty sure Sloan represented the vast majority of Boston's lingering mob bosses, I'd graciously looked the other way and paid his hefty retainer without complaint. It was Sloan I'd asked for the minute Machado put me in the back of her car. And pretty much every minute after that; by the time they parked me in an interrogation room, it had practically become a game.

"Can I get you anything?" they'd ask.

"Ye can. Me lawyer."

"Soda?"

"Lawyer."

"Coffee?"

"Aye. And me lawyer."

I could never turn down coffee, not even the cheap, gritty brew cops drank.

Sloan had me out in less than ten minutes. In the process, I'd finally learned what had earned me Boston PD's hospitality. Turned out the term "necromancer" was what the kidnapper had called himself in the ransom note he'd sent the Reynolds—a ransom note which hadn't been reported to the news. Sloan argued that my using the term in front of Machado just outside the suspect's supposed location had simply been an unfortunate coincidence. Personally, I suspected the kidnapper's title might have been more than mere hyperbole, but I couldn't explain myself without getting into further trouble.

"Well, unless you plan on charging my client for saying a suspicious word, Ms. MacKenna and I are done here," Sloan said softly in an accent that reeked of the sort of upper crust upbringing which would have earned him a beating in my neighborhood. Sloan was a Harvard Law graduate—a short, thin man in his sixties with all the aggressiveness of a panda high on valium. Still, when he rose, he did so with an air of authority that no one questioned. "I suggest, in the future, you follow procedure and refrain from putting hand-cuffs on someone you simply wish to question. It smacks of police miscon-duct. And I'd hate to have to sue the department because of one overzealous detective." Sloan, who sounded like he'd be happy to do just that, gave Machado a condescending look and patted my shoulder. I flinched, but followed his lead. Truthfully, I've never been a fan of people touching me; letting Cassidy put the cuffs on had been especially grating. But when Sloan guided me out the door with his arm, I let him, ignoring Machado's steady glare.

Sloan and I headed out unmolested, winding our way through the busy precinct. If he had questions for me, he'd decided not to ask them. I was grateful; he wouldn't have believed me anymore than the cops would have. Times like these, I almost wish the whole world knew the truth about the things that went bump in the night. Sure would have saved me the trouble of having to lie all the time.

Almost immediately after leaving the interrogation room, I was reminded that it was a Friday night; drunks, hookers, and drifters took up most of the available seating. Sloan and I slipped through them with our eyes forward the way you might try to avoid agitating stray dogs at the pound. Eventually we reached the front desk, where we met an officer who handed over my Victoria Secret tote and my gun. The gun was sealed in a plastic bag, partially disassembled, the clip removed. The tote appeared untouched. The cop frowned at the weight as he passed it over, but didn't bother looking inside. I slid the strap over one shoulder and breathed a sigh of relief, wondering where Jimmy was and how he'd managed to sneak my bag inside without letting anyone rifle through it.

Maybe I'd let him take me for a drink, after all.

As long as he picked me up in something other than his squad car.

We turned to leave, but a commotion at the far end of the precinct snagged my attention. I watched as a man in a tan trench coat shook off one of the officers trying to talk to him, clearly upset about something. The man's eyes were hidden behind a pair of aviator sunglasses, head covered by a tan fedora. He looked ridiculously mysterious, as if he were trying twice as hard to conceal his identity than he needed to. "Why won't you listen to me?" he yelled, loud enough to be heard over the general racket.

A few officers rose from their desks, angling themselves in case the guy got out of control and needed to be restrained. The man's spidey-senses must have tingled, because he immediately balled his hands into fists and stomped off towards the exit. I thought one of the cops might stop him, maybe shake him down and look for drugs, but the only officer who reached for him immediately snatched her hand back, hissing as if she'd touched a stovetop.

I made room for the guy, but space was tight thanks to a fresh crop of drunks being hauled in for an overnight stay. He hesitated, then slid by, brushing only lightly up against me. I took a quick step back, bumping into Sloan in the process.

"Watch it," I said. I didn't care if he was on drugs, I wasn't about to let some asshole crowd me.

His eyes swung towards me, and I could see my angry face mirrored in his sunglasses. A smattering of freckles dotted my pale skin and my hair was a tousled mess that desperately needed to be brushed. "You were there," he said, suddenly. He snatched my hand. "You were there and you saw it!"

"Jesus!" I said, drawing my hand back. How crazy was this guy?

"Excuse me," Sloan said, "but we should be going." He slid an arm around my waist to guide me out, and—for the second time that night—I let him. I could handle being escorted if it kept the weirdo from grabbing me again.

"But you didn't find him. You never saw the necromancer in person, did you?" the man asked. He flicked his sunglasses down past the bridge of his nose, revealing hazel eyes in deep sockets, crow's feet running like jagged lines towards his ears.

I stiffened. "Excuse me?"

"You were there and saw the dead ones rise." His eyes narrowed. "But then how the hell did the Regulars miss it?"

That one word—Regulars—gave me goosebumps. Not that Regulars were particularly frightening, but the very fact that he'd used it meant he was probably a Freak, like me. A person or creature with abilities which made him unique and quite possibly dangerous. I gave him a long look. It was well past sundown, but he wasn't a vampire; no vampire would ever willingly walk into a police station. A shifter, maybe? But I didn't think so. Shifters tended to travel in packs, even in their human forms. Regardless, I couldn't let him keep babbling about dead ones and necromancers. All Machado needed was to find us out here chatting up a storm about zombies and she'd yank me right back into the interrogation room.

Sloan leaned in close. "Let's get you out of here, Ms. MacKenna."

"No," I said. I stepped out of the curve of Sloan's arm and patted his shoulder. "Ye go ahead. I'll be alright."

Sloan gave me a flat, level stare, but said nothing. Part of why I paid him as much as I did was that Sloan never asked questions. His discretion was what I counted on. In a way, he and I were kindred spirits; for the two of us, ignorance may not have been bliss, but it sure as hell beat going to prison for knowing too much. He shrugged. "Please be careful, Ms. MacKenna," he said. "And have a good evening."

I didn't bother promising to try; something told me my night had just gone from bad to worse. "Night," I replied, before turning back to the man in the trench coat. I jerked my head towards the exit, and he nodded, his aviators obscuring his eyes once more. I briefly considered mocking the outfit, but then thought better of it.

I could criticize his fashion sense, later.

Preferably after I figured out just how dangerous he was.

CHAPTER 7

Turned out the strangely dressed man wasn't all that dangerous, after all. Not unless you felt particularly threatened by heating pads or saunas. Technically, Bernie Wakowski—mid-fifties retiree and widower—was what we Freaks call a wizard. Wizards are a specific type of Freak who can bend the elements to their will. Sadly, the only element Bernie could manipulate was fire, and apparently that only manifested itself in an uncommonly high body temperature which occasionally spiked when he felt especially agitated.

"Wife used to say it was like sleeping next to a furnace," he joked as he poured me a cup of tea from a pot he'd set to boil using nothing but his hands. He'd lost the trench coat, hat, and glasses, leaving behind a reedy man in a denim jacket, shirt, and pants which—in combination—looked almost as ridiculous. A Canadian tuxedo, I'd once heard it called. On a beefy, bearded lumberjack, it might have passed for fashion. On the wiry wizard, not so much.

"Pretty sure that's a common complaint," I replied, smirking. At first, I had to admit I'd been wary of the older man. His manic behavior at the precinct hadn't given me the best first impression. But after a brief chat during which I'd reassembled my gun, I'd felt comfortable enough to accept his offer for tea. Frankly, I'd have preferred coffee, but after two cups at the precinct, I wasn't sure my nerves could have taken it.

And so here we were, tucked away in his tiny living room, exchanging pleasantries. "I'm sure it is," Bernie replied. "But every so often I'd have a nightmare, and she'd end up with first degree burns, so I let her bitch all she wanted," he said. Bernie had a funky Southern drawl I hadn't picked up on at first. It made him seem more earthy, somehow. Alternatively less pretentious and less thuggish than most of the East Coasters I'd grown up with.

"So," I said, getting down to business, "why were ye yellin' at the cops?"

He frowned, then sighed. "I used to know a guy back when I was serving. We were both airplane mechanics, but he switched career fields. Joined up with the military police. Got out, became a cop. Nowadays he's Deputy Superintendent of a Bureau. Nice guy. He and his wife used to get together with me and mine before Betty passed."

"I'm sorry for your loss, but does this story have a point, Bernie?" I asked, trying not to sound bitchy. I wasn't exactly a patient person by nature, and—if he was answering my question—he was taking his sweet time about it.

"Getting to it, miss," he replied. The "miss" made me smile. I waved him on before taking a sip of my tea. It was a chai blend, spiced so artfully it was the closest substitute to real coffee that I'd ever had, and I made an appreciative sound in the back of my throat. Bernie grinned and continued, "Anyway, it's been a while, but I know the man. So when I walked out by Fort Independence and saw the Reynolds boy the news keeps talking about, he's the guy I called."

"Wait, ye were the tip?" I asked, jaw dropping in surprise.

Bernie nodded. "The trouble was, the boy wasn't alone. As soon as I saw the kid, I knew something was up. I'm not powerful myself, but I'm sensitive. I can tell when something or someone isn't what they're supposed to be. I knew there was a necromancer nearby same as I know you're a null."

I nearly spat up my tea. "A what?"

"A null," he said. He waggled his hand. "Or whatever you want to call it. Magic doesn't work on you, am I right?"

He was right. My immunity to the various Freaks out there was, in a way, as abnormal an ability as any I'd come across, but I'd never heard anyone who'd had a name for what I could do. I guess it made sense. Null, as in null and void. "Aye, although it's not just magic," I replied.

"What do you mean?" he asked.

I considered whether to elaborate; I preferred my secrets. But it was also my policy to make friends in lowly places whenever possible. Networking 101. I knew having a wizard to consult, even a weak one, could prove useful down the line. "Nothin' works on me. If a vampire tries to bleed me, he has to do it without his fangs. Shifters that get too close in animal form turn back. Basically, nothin' gets through."

Bernie was nodding, slowly. "Well, that's useful. Although that's all still magic, one way or another. Magic animates vampires. Magic curses turn the shifters. But I can see what you're saying. I've never heard of anyone being able to cancel out all forms of magic."

"Well, I've never met a wizard before," I admitted.

Bernie laughed. "Yeah, you won't find many of us around Boston. The Academy cut ties to this city a long time ago, so most of us settle elsewhere. That was the appeal for me, though. I hated the politics, and I was a minor wizard, besides. No one cared where I ended up."

"The Academy?" I asked.

"Oh, right," Bernie said, taking a sip of his own cup, "It's a bit confusing for outsiders, but the Academy is the school wizards attend to learn how to harness their abilities. Of course, it's also the institution that governs us and upholds our laws."

I processed that, then nodded. "Aye, I can see how that works. But why haven't I heard of ye lot? And why would the Academy cut ties with Boston, specifically?"

"It's a long story. I'll tell you some other time, maybe. For now, just know that there's no one I can call in to take care of the necromancer on our end. And, for whatever reason, the powers that be in this city either haven't found out he's here, or haven't stepped in to stop him. I'm not sure which, and I don't care. The kid was scared, miss. Scared down to his toes. So I called up my old buddy and told him what I'd seen."

I sat back, frowning. There was a necromancer in town, and none of the local Freaks had stepped in to stop him from kidnapping a kid. Not even the Faerie Chancery—Boston's answer to supernatural law and order. Too high profile, maybe? Freaks and Fae alike preferred to stay under the radar whenever possible. Not everyone's abilities were as understated as mine, or as mild as Bernie's, and very few of the Fae could pass for human. "So when the cops got close, he raised some of the dead and sent the civilians runnin'," I reasoned, filling in the gaps. "Which gave him time to get away."

Bernie nodded. "Best as I can figure out. My buddy doesn't blame me, says it was a good tip, but nobody saw the kid. That true?"

I nodded. "All I saw were corpses. Skeletons, at least at first."

"At first?"

"Aye, one of 'em ended up suckin' a cop dry right in front of me. T'wasn't pretty." I shuddered at the memory and felt the cup jiggle a little in my hands. Usually, my nerves would have been better, but there was something especially grotesque about the dead rising which bothered me far more than the vast majority of shit I'd seen over the years.

"Shit," Bernie said, so loud it startled me. "Shit, shit, shit!"

"What is it?" I asked, eyes wide.

Bernie hopped to his feet and began pacing the room. "Raising skeletons is one thing, but the only way a zombie rises and gains flesh is if their master lets them. Zombies become harder to control the more human they look and feel, which he should have known. Hell, it's like asking for a mutiny. But if the necromancer is that desperate, the cops won't be able to stop him."

I frowned. "Why not?"

"Because if he loses control, the zombies will kill everyone they find, and he won't be able to reign them back in."

"Alright, but what's that got to do with why you're freakin' out?" I asked as I watched the man pace the room.

"I made another call while I was getting the tea together," Bernie explained, talking with his hands. Waves of heat radiated off his body, warping the air around him. "I used my senses to track the necromancer down after he left, but couldn't tell my buddy that. Spotting the kid in a crowd in a public place was plausible, right? But saying I'd tracked down the kidnapper after that would draw way too much attention. That's why I was at the precinct in disguise. I was trying to get them to go after him."

"I don't understand," I said. "Isn't that a good t'ing?"

His eyes met mine, and I could read the horror in them. "Not if they took my word for it. He's in the tunnels below the city. If they go after him, they could all wind up dead."

Ah. Well, that wasn't good.

CHAPTER 8

I don't know how I let myself get talked into these things. I'm not heroic. I'm not even altruistic. Honestly, the only reason I was tagging along was because I had a sneaking suspicion Bernie was right and—if we didn't at least warn them—some of Boston's finest were about to lose their lives. Ordinarily, I wouldn't have lost too much sleep over that, but—unless Jimmy had been forcibly benched for the night—that meant an old friend of mine might be in the line of fire. A friend who had gone out of his way to make sure I got my money even after I'd been arrested in association with a kidnapping.

I owed him.

And I always paid my debts.

I'd let Bernie drive while I considered whether or not to call in a few favors. Reinforcements were always good, but if we ended up running into the police, I worried my backup might draw unwanted attention. At this point, I was almost guaranteed a rematch with Machado in an interrogation room, but if it meant saving Jimmy's ass, I'd take it. Sadly, that also meant Bernie and I might end up taking a stroll through Boston's abandoned subterranean tunnels. At night. With zombies around every corner.

I wasn't excited.

We pulled up to Boston's City Hall Plaza, below which the tunnels could be accessed, but found maybe a quarter of the squad cars that had been parked at the last scene. After going all-in on the last response, it was likely they were reserving their manpower. Besides, the tunnels below the city were hard to navigate, and there were nearly two hundred miles of track to search through. This wasn't a scene from The Fugitive; we didn't have an army of searchers led by Federal Marshals to hunt the bastard down. In fact, I'd found out from Machado that the Feds weren't even part of the equation. Apparently, the Reynolds had insisted on no Federal interference, which the media had found especially suspicious. I agreed. Let the professionals do their job, I say. But then, he wasn't my kid to save.

"They've gone in already," Bernie said, hurriedly clambering out of his dingy Toyota, clutching a satchel. I'd been disappointed to learn that modern wizards used neither wands or staffs; apparently, my formative years were full of such lies.

Thanks, Tolkien.

"Aye, but what can they hope to find?" I asked as I followed, adjusting my holster, wishing I could simply draw the gun and be done with it. "The tunnels go on forever."

The answer came before Bernie had a chance to respond as a cacophony of barks and growls split the air. Dogs. They'd brought in the K-9 units. And it sounded suspiciously like they'd caught something.

Or been caught by something.

Suddenly, we were running towards the sound. It took us a couple minutes to work our way towards the City Hall garage, where a single rusted door allows entrance to the tunnels below, but it wasn't hard to find—the dogs were still barking. Two uniformed officers blocked the doorway, though they were turned towards the door, rather than guarding it. A rookie mistake, and one they could have paid dearly for had someone deadlier than us come upon them. As it was, neither saw Bernie reach into his satchel to draw out a slender glass flask, or to watch as it sailed into the door.

It shattered. In an instant, both cops were down, and a strange liquid dribbled down the length of the steel door. Bernie took one cop by the shoulders and slid him out of the way, grunting. "One of Betty's concoctions," he said, as if that explained everything. He patted the satchel. "I'm a shoddy wizard, but Betty was a damn fine witch." He grinned, then kicked open the door.

An eerie yellow light poured out of the tiny entrance. The sound of dogs braying and snarling grew louder. I swore I could hear people yelling. And we were about to wade into the mess. On purpose.

I drew my gun.

Fuck it.

CHAPTER 9

The first dead thing I saw was, mercifully, a rat. I wasn't fond of vermin or the possibility of contracting the plague while I was mucking about below the city, but at least it wasn't a zombie, or—Heaven forbid—a cop. I slid my finger reassuringly up and down the ridged slide of my fully enhanced P226. The gun had been a gift from an ex-boyfriend. A Navy Seal who'd known me well enough to buy me a military grade pistol for our six-month anniversary, but not well enough to know I'd point it at him when I'd learned he'd been seeing other women. Live and learn. To be honest, I liked the gun more than I'd liked him, anyway; the P226 may never have bought me a drink, but it'd never made me put up with mansplaining, either.

I realized I was trying to distract myself, thinking about the past rather than focusing on the present. I took a deep breath and let it out, still following Bernie, who seemed remarkably sure of himself now that we were in the thick of things. A military man, he'd said. It showed. "Everything alright?" he asked, softly, without turning to look back at me.

"Aye, everythin' is fine. Can ye tell which way they went?" I asked, trying to change the subject.

"Yeah. Down the tunnel to our left, then right, is my guess. It's hard to tell how far, though." He gestured towards the tunnel walls. Echoes of cries and howls cascaded around us, warping them into something manic and pain-filled. "If we hurry, we can catch up to them."

"What if they're trackin' the necromancer?" I asked. "Won't we be in the way?"

Bernie nodded. "Yeah. But what if they aren't? What if the zombies are chasing them, not the other way around?" This time he did look at me. "You don't have to come if you don't want to. If everything's good on their end, at worst I'll be picked up for trespassing. If you go and get detained," he eyed my gun, "I doubt you'll end up thanking me."

I ground my teeth. Bernie was right, but that didn't make things easier. The truth wasn't that I cared whether or not I ended up in Machado's crosshairs, or even that I wanted to ride to Jimmy's rescue. The truth was the flesh-sucker had scared the shit out of me, figuratively speaking, and I couldn't shake that feeling no matter how much I tried.

And I hated it.

Ever since I was a kid, I'd been fearless. At first recklessly so, but then—over time—it'd become a choice. I refused to let anyone or anything scare me. The minute a new fear had cropped up, I'd found a way to confront it. In a way, that's what I was doing, now. As much as I wanted to give in and let Bernie march into the tunnels alone, I would never have forgiven myself for being such a coward.

"Let's go rescue the cops," I said, finally.

Bernie grinned. "Anything you say, miss." He started to jog, his gait a little uneven, but easy enough to keep up with in flats. I clutched my gun two-handed and whispered a prayer to whoever, or whatever, was listening.

Don't let me be brave and die, please and thanks.

CHAPTER 10

We rounded the corner just in time to see a police dog leap towards a walking corpse. The German Shepherd's lean, muscular body coiled as it landed, snout covered in blood as it flashed its teeth. The ensuing snarl sent the hairs on the back of my neck standing straight up, and I took a quick step back. People tend to forget that dogs, while so often domesticated to the point of blind obedience, descended from something much fiercer, much deadlier. If you've ever seen an attack dog do its job, you'll know exactly what I'm talking about; never again will you casually reach out to pet a stranger's pooch for fear of losing an arm.

That, it seemed, was exactly what had happened to the corpse. His mangled arm, bloody and covered only by the barest sheen of muscle fibers, had torn free and flopped on the ground like a fish. I heard a shriek and turned in time to see one of the police officers slump over, unconscious against the wall of the tunnel. His skin was wan and thin, almost luminescent, like a white t-shirt stretched tight enough to see beneath. The zombie must have been sucking him dry, I realized, before the dog came to the rescue.

But that was as much time as I had to take in the scene before the zombie struck. It bum rushed the dog, charging towards it with one arm extended. Fortunately, the canine knew better than to let the thing get close; it hopped away, squirming between the creature's legs, only to turn and tear at the zombie's ankle. Bone crunched as the dog tugged, working its jaws back and forth, hind legs scrabbling at the ground.

The zombie turned and reached for the dog, its balance precarious, but close enough now to touch. I raised my gun without thinking, adopted a shooting stance, and fired. The hollow point bullet took the thing in the shoulder, the metal shell expanding on its way out, tearing through bone and cartilage to leave the arm hanging limp and useless. Ideally, hollow points would do exactly what Hollywood claimed they did: send the bad guy flying across the room like they'd been hit by a bus. But the reality was a lot less pronounced, although perhaps more cringeworthy; think of it like a metal shell passing through your body, then imagine a metal parachute being deployed almost as soon as it hits, allowing the bullet to tear through you as it slows.

That's a hollow point.

Of course, its effectiveness depends on the shooter. Typically, a kill shot is a kill shot, whether you use a full metal jacket or a hollow point round to do the trick. Which is why, immediately after I incapacitated the thing's arm, I adjusted my aim and put a bullet through the bastard's skull—such as it was. Shards of bone, blood, and flesh sprayed the tunnel wall. Far less of it than it might have if the thing had been a living, breathing human being, but still enough to contribute to a Jackson Pollock painting.

The body flopped to the ground in an oozing mass.

I started to look away, my ears were ringing from taking the shots indoors, but then caught the dog stalking towards me, muzzle dripping with gore. Too late, I realized that I'd blown away the animal's adversary, and that its owner likely lay passed out nearby, which meant there was nothing between it and us. I raised the barrel of my gun, but didn't take aim. Honestly, I had no desire to see what a hollow point did to a dog. I'd never liked the mangy bastards, but I wasn't a cruel person; I cried watching the Sarah McLaughlin commercials like everyone else.

"I've got this," Bernie said, reaching into his satchel. I took a deep breath, expecting him to throw another sleep potion down, but instead he fished out a grungy baseball. He held it up for the dog to see, like holding a coin up to the light, then tossed it back the way we came. "Go get it, boy!"

The dog snarled, looking more pissed off than it had before, but at least now it wanted to eat Bernie and not me. "That was dumb," I said. "Ye can't expect a police dog to play fetch, Bernie. They're too well trained."

Bernie fished out another ball.

"Seriously?" I asked, exasperated.

Bernie grunted and tossed the ball into the air, then took a step back, pulling me with him. The ball landed just in front of the dog, and—before I could so much as speak—the baseball burst. The gut which filled the ball began to spew out like Silly String, snaking out likes webs and snaring the pooch. Bound, the dog toppled, whimpering. Bernie flashed me a thumbs up. "Wanted to see how he'd react to the ball. If he tried to catch it in his mouth, he'd end up impaled," Bernie explained.

The image made me cringe. Alright, so Bernie wasn't completely useless in a pinch. Good to know. "How'd he get left out here alone?" I asked, half to myself.

"I was wondering the same thing," Bernie replied. "A straggler, maybe? Or maybe he got separated from the others?"

"I'll ask him," I replied. First, however, I checked to make sure the zombie was well and truly dead; I'd seen enough horror movies to know better. Once satisfied, I approached the cop against the wall. The canine growled. "Easy there, Fido," I said, hunkering down to get a closer look. "I won't hurt him." I frowned as I said it. There was something familiar about the man's face. Too late, I realized I was looking at Cassidy. But it wasn't Cassidy's face, it was as if the young cop had aged ten years, his skin tighter, thinner, somehow. His smile lines were deeper, the furrows of his brow more distinct. "Jesus, what happened to ye, Cassidy?" I whispered.

Cassidy's eyes fluttered open, like he'd woken up from a nap. He gazed drowsily at me, then his eyes went wide with fear. "Oh God, what was that thing? What's happening? Where am I? Oh Jesus, what happened to me?" He started to babble as he studied his hands, which were streaked with blackish stains, his mouth moving so fast I couldn't make out one question from another.

I slapped him across the face.

Not hard, mind you. But enough to get him to focus. I didn't have time to play therapist; I needed to know where the others were—fast. Cassidy could have a nervous breakdown later. After we survived. "Stop ramblin'," I said. "The others. Where are they?"

Cassidy blinked, shocked into silence. His mouth opened and closed like a guppy's before, at last, he responded. "They're up ahead. Past the turn. We found the boy...oh God, we found him, but he...he wasn't..." Cassidy began to hyperventilate.

"Calm down! Deep breaths," I commanded.

But it was too late. Cassidy passed out, which meant we were on our own.

"Let's go," Bernie said, studying the tunnel ahead.

I sighed, stood, and checked my gun to make sure everything was still working properly. We stepped over the fallen canine, ignoring its angry snarls, and prepared ourselves for what lay ahead, for whatever had sent Cassidy into a panic attack.

As if there were any way to prepare for what lay ahead.

CHAPTER 11

The carnage was unimaginable. It looked like I'd always imagined a war zone might: bodies strewn about like discarded dolls, their torn out stuffing oozing blood and other, more viscous fluids. For all that, however, it seemed the cops had fared well enough. All but two of the bodies on the ground belonged to risen corpses, many of them only half-formed. The other two had been torn apart, their clothes shredded and drained the way Cassidy almost had been. I took it all in as calmly as I could, knowing I'd have fresh material for my nightmares, as we followed the trail of broken bodies. The heads of the zombies had been blown to pieces, or were missing altogether in some places. I was guessing at least one of the cops had a shotgun; a bullet does plenty of damage, but taking a head clean off isn't that easy.

"Someone got smart," Bernie said, peering down at one such corpse. "Only way to break the necromancer's hold, damaging the head."

"Takin' out the brain?" I asked, mildly curious.

Bernie shook his head. "That's only in movies. The necromancer's ritual requires a focus point. Blood on the skull, usually. Destroy the mark, and you destroy the binding."

I nodded absentmindedly. It made sense. Otherwise the skeletal remains I'd seen would have been more or less invincible. Either way, Bernie was right: someone had known where to aim, and the other cops had followed suit. The low body count alone told us that much.

"What else can the necromancer do?" I asked, still listening for shots. They'd died down a few minutes before we arrived, leaving us little to go on but the obvious trail ahead.

"Besides wake the dead?" Bernie asked. "Depends. Some have training as wizards. Their abilities make it tough to differentiate between the two, early on. Once we know what they are, though, they tend to get kicked out, for one reason or another."

"Why's that?"

Bernie shook his head. "It isn't forbidden magic, but it is...frowned upon. Using magic that blurs the line between realms is considered unwise. There's a theory out there that doing so will bring back the old gods. The wilder magics. The legends." Bernie snorted. "Personally, I think that's a bit far-fetched. It'd take a whole lot more meddling to fuck things up that bad."

I shook my head. "None of that matters right now. I just need to know what to expect if we run into this bastard. If he's had wizard trainin', what's our plan?"

Bernie was quiet for a moment. The bodies thinned out considerably as we headed further down the tunnel. "I'll try and distract him, if he's alone. Throw everything I have into it. Maybe I'll get lucky and something'll stick."

"And me?"

"Put a bullet in him. Or a dozen. Whatever it takes."

I frowned. "And if the cops have him surrounded?"

Bernie shook his head. "They'll try to subdue him, probably. It won't go well. He won't be armed, and they won't have cause to shoot."

I cursed. "I hate this in-the-dark shit, sometimes."

"Me too. But it is what it is. The minute the Regulars start believing in the monsters is the minute they start hunting us down. We've seen it before." Bernie's eyes were haunted, and for a second I wondered if I'd guessed his age correctly. I'd heard wizards lived longer than most. Was Bernie really only middle-aged, or had he been around longer? Long enough to remember the age of torches and pitchforks?

Regardless, we didn't have time to get into it. Another dog barked down the tunnel and to the left. They'd found something. Bernie and I picked up the pace, still checking to make sure each corpse was well and truly dead before pressing on; we weren't about to get attacked from behind for being careless.

"Any idea for what we say to keep them from shooting us?" Bernie asked.

"Tell 'em we're civilians, and keep your hands where they can see 'em," I suggested. I didn't mention my reasons for joining him or my suspicion that Jimmy would be among the officers tasked with following up on Bernie's lead; I'd searched for the big man's body among the fallen as we walked, but mercifully hadn't found it.

Now it was Bernie's chance to frown. "Not the best idea, if we're about to get attacked."

"Best I can tell ye," I replied, the braying of the police dog getting louder and louder.

Bernie grunted, but didn't bitch about it.

I was beginning to like the guy.

CHAPTER 12

We found the cops nursing their wounds, an officer guarding either side of the tunnel. One held the dog's leash and had quieted the thing down, though its growls were still audible once we got within sight. I'd put my gun away. Bernie had slung his satchel around so it rode the small of his back, out of sight. We approached with our hands in the air.

"Who's there?" one of the guards asked. Two others joined him from the group on the floor, guns drawn and pointed at us. They were jumpy. Ready to shoot first and ask questions later. I didn't blame them.

"Civilians," I called back. "Is there an Officer Collins with ye?" I asked.

A fourth man rose to stand with the others, his shoulders well above their own. "Who's asking?" Jimmy asked. I let out a sigh of relief. He was alive, at least. As we neared, I could make out his perplexed frown.

"It's Quinn MacKenna. And this is Bernie." I didn't bother giving them Bernie's last name. If we made it out alive, they'd have plenty of questions for us both. But for now, his anonymity might as well remain intact.

"Quinn? What the fuck are you doing here?" Jimmy asked. I noticed he didn't tell the others to put down their guns. They noticed, too, because several of them adjusted for a better shot.

"Bernie here was the man who gave ye the tip to come down here," I said, sticking as close to the truth as I could. "When he told me ye were headed into the tunnels, I figured ye might be walkin' into a death trap. I came to warn ye."

"Little late for that," one of the uniforms quipped.

"We ran into Cassidy on our way here," I said. "He's headed back to the Plaza to call for backup. Said ye lost contact when ye got down here."

"Cassidy's alive?" Jimmy asked.

"He woke up a little older today than he was yesterday, but aye, he's alive."

Jimmy seemed to consider that, then nodded. "You can put your guns away, everyone," Jimmy said. "They're morons for coming down here, but I don't think they're here to kill us."

"And who put you in charge, Collins?" a cop, the same one who'd wise-cracked, asked. He was sitting with one other officer, a woman, conceivably the last of those who'd been sent down into the tunnels. He was bleeding from a gash on his forehead, his uniform torn along one arm, revealing a sleeve tattoo and more cuts.

"Sergeant Howard's dead, Sanchez," Jimmy said, staring down at the man. "If you want to run the show from here on out, I'm all ears."

"Collins kept us alive back there, Sanchez," the woman said, her hair pulled back into a ponytail so severe that it left the shape of her skull visible. "If he hadn't told us where to aim, we'd all be dead."

Sanchez spat onto the floor, and there was blood in it. "And just how did he know where to shoot, huh? Machado told us to keep an eye on you, you know," he said, jabbing a finger at Jimmy. "Said you might know more than you were letting on. And that one," Sanchez said, finger now jabbing at me, "was in custody not a couple hours ago."

Everyone's face turned towards me, and I shrugged. "Look, would ye have believed me if I'd told ye I saw those t'ings you've been huntin' down here? Because I sure as hell wouldn't have."

Jimmy grunted. "So that's what had you so freaked out."

I nodded. "Aye. One of 'em got O'Bannon while I was locked in the car."

Jimmy cursed.

"Don't tell me you're buying this shit, Collins?" Sanchez asked.

"You saw what they did to Sergeant Howard," the woman said. She had a haunted look in her eyes that I recognized. I'd seen it in the mirror often enough that I almost didn't say what had to be said next, if only to keep the horror on her face from spreading to everyone else's.

"Listen, ye lot don't have to believe a word I'm sayin', and if ye run back to your people blabbin', I'll deny everythin' I'm tellin' ye now. But these are the facts: the person who took Lukas Reynolds is probably behind this. Ye t'ink he wants to be called the necromancer to hide his identity, but I'm guessin' Necromancer is his identity. Which means what you've been fightin' are corpses."

"Bullshit," Sanchez said.

"Necromancers are real," Bernie chimed in, for the first time. "Magic is real. Make peace with that now, or get out while you still can. Because it's going to get uglier. I can feel it. He's preparing something worse." Bernie rubbed at his arms, and I noticed the hairs were standing on end.

"And who the fuck are you, old man?" Sanchez asked.

Jimmy held out a hand to cut Sanchez off. "Doesn't matter. Look, I appreciate you two coming down here to help us, but it's time for you to go. Civilians don't belong down here, and we can't protect you. I suggest you get out of here, then disappear." He gave me a knowing look. "If they find you sniffing around, they'll have just cause to pull you in for questioning." He didn't add the words "this time" because we both knew that Machado had overstepped. But he was right. I wouldn't walk away from this without another call to Sloan, if I didn't leave now. Hell, maybe even if I did.

Not that I gave a shit, either way.

"I'm not goin' anywhere," I said. "And I don't need your protection."

Jimmy opened his mouth to reply, his eyes dancing with frustration, but never got the chance to speak. Because that's when the dog lunged forward, barking so violently it made us all jump. The officers spun towards the opposite end of the tunnel, their guns raised. The uniform holding the leash cursed, straining to hold his canine companion back. Figures, far enough away to be little more than shadows, emerged from the mouth of the tunnel.

And they were running.

CHAPTER 13

Zombies should never be allowed to run. I wasn't sure what rules should dictate what flesh-sucking zombies were capable of, but their being able to chase you down and not simply overwhelm you with numbers or wait for you to make a classic blunder was really, really not fair. Apparently, the cops agreed, because all I could hear over the sound of their guns going off were their colorful curses on that very topic.

"Fucking die, you abominations!" Sanchez screamed, getting to his feet with difficulty, the cop beside him propping him up as best she could. I cocked an eyebrow at his choice of terminology before returning my attention to the oncoming zombies. Now that they were closer, I could see they were still skeletal, dressed in rags, animated by a power that defied logic.

The cops who could fight had formed a line in front of us, leaving Bernie and I with no openings unless we wanted to run around them. Jimmy held the center. He shot less frequently than his companions, many of whom were simply unloading their clips into the mass of bones, too freaked out to remember what the hell they were dealing with. In contrast, every time Jimmy fired, I saw a figure fall. Headshots, every one.

If we weren't about to get attacked by at least a dozen zombies, I'd have said it was sexy.

As it was, I didn't even have time to be impressed.

"Bernie, can ye lob somethin' at 'em?" I asked, leaning in so he could hear me over the roar of guns.

Bernie shook his head. "I could, but they're too close. We could all get caught up in whatever I use."

Well, damn. "Since when do these fuckers run?" I asked, mostly to myself.

"The necromancer has given them more power, somehow. I've never heard of anyone making that kind of contract. Not and survive." Bernie shook his head, fishing through his satchel for something he could use, clearly frustrated.

Before I could ask any more questions, they were on us. The first wave of runners broke through the line by leaping into the air at the cops like jungle cats, dessicated arms reaching out, bony fingers curled into claws. Jimmy went down to one knee and blew a hole in the jaw of the zombie who'd charged him, the bullet coming out the top of its skull. The other uniforms weren't so lucky. Two went down screaming, emptying their guns into half-formed bodies. One, the officer who'd held the dog's leash, managed to get away as his canine companion launched itself at the perambulatory fossil, meeting it in mid-air and chomping down on the creature's arm as if playing a game of fetch. The last officer rolled away, drawing a bead on his assailant and getting off at least one clean headshot.

Which left at least ten zombies for us to deal with.

Yippee.

I drew and rushed forward, going for the downed cops first. The zombies rode their bodies, draining them dry, skin growing over their faces like water filling an empty basin. I blew those faces away from close enough that I could see the whites of their freshly grown eyes.

Eight zombies.

I turned back and tried to search for Jimmy—hoping to keep track of his whereabouts—but I didn't have that kind of time; my actions hadn't gone unnoticed. I found two zombies gunning for me from opposite sides, like raptors from Jurassic Park. I cursed and picked the one closest to me, turned, and aimed. It left my back unprotected, but with only one gun, I knew I'd never take them both out. Better to take one with me and pray I could find a way to finish the other rather than to waste time deciding what to do.

I fired, twice. The first shot took out the zombie's lower jaw and half the maxilla, but missed the rounded skull. The second didn't; the zombie tumbled to the ground the instant I blew away the invisible mark that bound it, bones clattering across the gravel. Sadly, I didn't have time to congratulate myself. Instead, I dropped to one knee and spun, hoping to catch the other before it could wrap its arms around me and turn me into yet another victim. But I found Sanchez there instead. He stared down at me with hollow eyes, looming so large his shadow fell across my face.

A zombie rode his shoulder.

I leapt to my feet, put the barrel against its forehead, and pulled the trigger. It fell away, and Sanchez tumbled into my arms.

The female cop was suddenly there, trying to take him from me before his weight became too much to bear. "He jumped in the way before I could stop him," she said, eyes wide, shock written plain across her face. Bernie was suddenly there, too, looking concerned.

"See what ye can do for him," I insisted, handing the bulky man off to them as briskly as I could manage. Part of me wanted to say more, but I decided I could honor Sanchez's sacrifice later, if we survived. Bernie nodded and dragged Sanchez back towards the wall, the officer covering their retreat with her handgun drawn. As I turned to resume the fight, a shotgun blast drew my attention to the far side of the tunnel, and I finally found Jimmy. He had his boot pressed into a zombie's chest, sighting down the barrel of a tactical shotgun. The zombie's skull had been blown to smithereens, leaving nothing behind but a jagged stump of spine.

A quick glance revealed only two zombies remained, each emerging from their respective hosts covered in flesh, no longer mere skeletons. Which meant the other officers were probably as good as dead. I didn't want to think about what had happened to the dog; there was something crueler, less acceptable about an animal sacrificing itself for the rest of us. I watched as the two remaining corpses angled themselves to come at Jimmy the way the two had come at me, forcing him to choose one over the other. He did, whirling, the butt of the shotgun tucked neatly against one shoulder. I judged the distance, cursed, and rushed the other zombie, stepping in to save Jimmy just as Sanchez had to save me.

Except I didn't offer it my back.

I tackled the son of a bitch.

It might have been simpler to stand back and shoot, but landing a headshot at that angle would have been tough, and I couldn't risk missing if it meant Jimmy getting gobbled up. Besides, while wrestling with a zombie definitely wasn't on my to-do list, I knew what I had to do to win. All I needed was to land on top, put my gun into the bastard's face, and pull the trigger before it got me. Simple.

Only things didn't go as planned.

The instant I collided with the corpse, I felt its body give way, its flesh pouring over me with the sensation of water splashing across my back. Without the resistance I'd anticipated, I slid face first into the gravel, cutting my hands in the process, my gun skittering along the wooden rails. As soon as I slowed, I cursed and rolled onto my back, too full of adrenaline to take stock of my burning hands and forearms.

I found the corpse in pieces, divided neatly in two. Its legs twitched but—without a torso—had no leverage to stand. The zombie's upper body crawled forward on its elbows towards me, close enough I could see its jaw working overtime, teeth gnashing. If I hadn't known better, I'd have said the thing was pissed. I scrambled to my feet and searched for my gun, but it was too far away to snag and get a clean shot before the would-be ankle-biter reached me.

Looked like I'd have to do this the old fashioned way.

I stepped forward and brought my heel down on the zombie's head like you might an insect, preparing to stomp the fucker as many times as necessary to break its skull open. Of course, it turned out that wasn't required; the instant my foot touched the zombie's fleshy dome, the head burst in a spew of liquid, popping with all the resistance of a water balloon. I winced and hopped on one foot, clutching my aching heel where I'd slammed it forcefully into the ground, yelling obscenities.

Which is how Jimmy found me.

He stared down at the corpse, then looked up at me, his eyes wide.

"How did you do that?" he asked.

I grimaced as something wet slid down my back—the remains of the corpse's intestines, maybe, from when I'd tried to spear tackle it only to end up hitting the ground? I shook my head, took a deep breath, and tried not to gag. "I have no idea," I replied, once I felt I could speak without vomiting.

"I do," Bernie replied. He approached, Sanchez slung between the woman and himself, head lolling. "But first I think we should get away from here. I doubt he'll have enough power to send reinforcements, but we can't risk it."

Jimmy took a long look around at the various bodies, friend and foe alike, and nodded. "Alright, but then you fill me in on everything you've been holding back." He met my eyes. "Everything, you got it?"

I stared into those surprisingly calm eyes and nodded.

I wasn't sure if Jimmy could handle the truth, but— after seeing how he'd handled himself against the monsters, not to mention the fact that he'd lost more than a few of his fellow cops to this madness—I was sure he deserved it.

Besides, he wasn't the only one who wanted answers.

CHAPTER 14

We found a raised platform down one side tunnel, tucked into an alcove, and used it to get off the tracks and out of sight. Together we hoisted Sanchez, already wounded, up and over the side. The big man looked to have taken a dose of what Cassidy had experienced: he looked diminished, somehow. Less vibrant. It bothered me more than I cared to admit to see him like that; I hated having to be saved by anyone, least of all by someone I'd been content to hate only a few minutes before.

"Stupid fucker," I whispered.

"What was that?" Dawes—the female cop who'd stood up for Jimmy back in the tunnels—asked. She had Sanchez's head in her lap, brushing her fingers over the man's scalp as if her touch alone might bring his vitality back. I wondered if they were partners. Lovers, even.

"Nothin'," I said, then sighed, resting my back against the wall of the platform. While the tunnels had been lit well enough by overhead lights, the platform was brighter still, with a naked bulb shining above us. Beneath its unforgiving glare, I realized we looked as fucked up as we felt. Jimmy's uniform was covered in bone dust and thick, viscid liquids I didn't want to identify. Sanchez was unconscious, his breathing shallow, dried blood caking his face. Dawes looked like she'd been shoved into a horror movie as the sole female protagonist, her virginity a distant dream. Only Bernie looked relatively intact and unfazed.

"So, ye goin' to tell me what ye came up with?" I asked him.

Bernie glanced at the others. "You sure you want to talk about this here?"

"I meant it when I said I want to know everything," Jimmy interjected, moving to stand in front of us. His hands were balled into fists, and tension rode his shoulders. "I want to know what the fuck those things were back there, what we're up against, and why good cops had to die tonight."

Bernie sighed. "I don't have all the answers. Very little about this makes any more sense to me than it does to you. Those things back there were zombies. Old ones, probably pulled from these very tunnels. Beyond that, all I can say is I'm sorry. If I'd have known what you and your people were up against, I'd have never pointed you in this direction."

"What's that supposed to mean?" Jimmy asked, folding his arms across his chest.

"I'm the one who tipped the cops off about this place," Bernie said, staring down at his shoes, which is all that kept him from seeing the rage contorting Jimmy's face.

"T'wasn't his fault," I said, drawing Jimmy's attention to me. "He was tryin' to help, that's all. And he's down here now, the same as ye and yours, fightin'."

"That still doesn't explain why this is happening," Jimmy said, finally, his rage leaking away as quickly as it had come, although the tension was still there, lurking beneath the surface. "What does the kidnapping have to do with this Necromancer you keep talking about?"

Bernie shook his head. "Not a Goddamned clue. I'm fresh out of ideas. But, what happened to that creature back there? The one you curb-stomped?" Bernie met my eyes. "That was your ability. Your whatever you call it—your anti-magic field— cut right through the magic that animated that thing. First I've ever heard of anyone being able to do that, but it's all that makes sense, in theory."

"Anti-magic field?" Jimmy asked, cocking an eyebrow.

Bernie nodded.

"As in magic. Like real magic."

"It's not the fucking Easter Bunny," Bernie said, one side of his mouth curling upward. He held out a hand, let it hover just over Jimmy's chest, and a wave of heat radiated outward as if from a wood stove. Jimmy took a step back, eyes wide. For a moment, an expression crossed his face that I couldn't read. Not fear, exactly, which I would have expected. But something.

"And you?" Jimmy turned to me. "Since when?"

I sighed, knowing deep down what he was really asking. Jimmy and I had known each other for a long time, which meant—if I was a Freak—he should have known about it. Seen something. Felt something. Or at least that's what he assumed. I shook my head. "Whatever I am, what I can do, doesn't work like that. It isn't flashy or loud. Hell, I didn't realize what I was until after ye and I graduated high school. At first, it was runnin' into weird creatures around the city. Seein' t'ings I couldn't explain. But it got more obvious when I moved to New York. The Freaks were everywhere. Eventually, I found out I was immune to 'em." I shrugged, leaving out the more sordid details, like the vampire ex-boyfriend who'd recruited me because I rendered so many other Freaks powerless, including him.

Now wasn't the time.

Besides, if I was being honest with myself, I couldn't exactly fill Jimmy in on what I was capable of; I hardly knew, myself. I didn't rely on my nullification abilities. I relied on my wits and my reflexes. I relied on firepower. But it did give me an edge. An edge I could sometimes use to take down the monsters before they gobbled me up.

And for that I was pretty damn grateful.

"None of what you guys are saying makes any sense," Dawes said, her voice a little higher pitched than I remembered. "What were those things, really?"

"The risen dead," Bernie replied, as if he were talking to a child. "Zombies, if you want to call them that."

"That's not possible," Jimmy replied. "When people die, they don't come back."

Bernie cocked an eyebrow. "Is that right? Let me ask you a question: what made you think to shoot them in the head?"

Jimmy frowned. "Never seen anything or anyone survive having their head blown off. Seemed like the thing to do."

Bernie chuckled. "Pragmatic. But I don't think that's all there was to it. I think you knew, deep down, what you were dealing with. Regulars—your kind—walk around thinking the world of make-believe is just that, but when the lights go out, they have enough sense to fear the dark. Deep down, they remember. Trust me, the monsters are out there, officer. What you're up against now is simply one of many."

Jimmy seemed to consider that for a moment. He shook his head, the tension in his body easing as he uncrossed his arms. "Fine. Assuming I believe you, what's next?"

"What do you mean?" Bernie asked.

"How do we end it?" Jimmy replied, meeting the older man's gaze.

Bernie smiled and glanced at me. "Remember what I said before, about why we can never tell the world the truth about us?" Bernie jerked his chin towards Jimmy. "Guys like him? The pragmatic ones? They're the reason why."

Jimmy looked back and forth between us as if trying to figure out what he was missing.

"The enemy of me enemy?" I suggested, shrugging.

Bernie nodded. "Guess so."

"What are you two talking about?" Jimmy asked, finally.

"Nothing," Bernie replied. "Let's go kill us some monsters."

CHAPTER 15

W e left Dawes behind with Sanchez, promising we'd come back for them both if the backup Cassidy had gone for didn't arrive first. She hadn't wanted us to leave without her, but someone had to keep an eye on the unconscious man, and we couldn't risk dragging him along with us. Besides, I knew shell-shocked when I saw it, and so did Jimmy; Dawes would be a liability if she came, and we all knew it.

It wasn't until we left the relative safety of the platform that I realized we had no way of knowing where the necromancer was any more than we had when we first came down into the tunnels. Without the dogs to track down scents, we were basically back to square one. But when I brought it up, Bernie claimed he knew exactly where the Necromancer was.

"Like I told you," he explained, "I don't have a lot of magical talent. But my senses are good. I knew when he raised the runners. Knew where the ritual was taking place. It's not far up ahead."

"And the boy?" Jimmy asked.

Bernie cocked an eyebrow. "What about him?"

"Did you, I don't know, sense him, too?"

Bernie shook his head. "My senses aren't as precise as that. If I could use it to track down random kids who've gone missing, trust me, I'd have joined up with the Feds a long time ago. We practitioners aren't evil by nature, offi-cer. Our abilities don't determine who we are, any more than you being a big, buff guy determines who you are."

"Call me Jimmy," Jimmy replied. As we headed further down the tracks, he spoke up again. "I don't think it's that simple, you know."

"What do you mean?" Bernie asked.

Jimmy shrugged. "Being bigger than most guys didn't make me who I am, but it sure as hell defined my life in a lot of ways. For that matter, who's to say what Quinn calls her 'ability' isn't something she picked up from pushing people away her whole life?"

"Oy, I can hear ye," I hissed, trailing behind the two men, gun drawn. I briefly considered popping Jimmy in the spine for putting me on blast like that, but decided against it; he'd be far less useful to me as a paraplegic.

Bernie chuckled. "You might have a point. But that's above my pay grade. All I know is that it wouldn't be fair to hunt you down for being a physical specimen, and it isn't fair to hate us because we can do things you can't."

I grunted. Bernie had a point, but it was a moot one. People had always despised what they couldn't understand. Desired what they couldn't achieve themselves. Idealists could spin the world whichever direction they wanted, it wouldn't keep gravity from yanking us all down. I almost said as much, but Bernie held up a hand before I could wax philosophical.

"He's close. Just up ahead." Bernie inched forward. "Remember, let me distract him. Then you two take him out."

"We have to give him a chance to surrender," Jimmy said, matter-of-factly, like he was reading from a manual.

"Officer—" Bernie began.

"Jimmy. Jimmy Collins." The big man halted and met Bernie's eyes. "Look, I'm here to save the kid. That's my priority. Killing the bad guy is the part of this job I'm least interested in."

Bernie sighed, then nodded. "Fine. Quinn and I will take care of the necromancer. You find the kid. Keep out of the line of fire as much as you can. From here on out, I can't make any promises."

Jimmy smirked. "You'd have made a decent cop, old man."

Bernie grunted. "I was a soldier, once."

"Me too," Jimmy said.

"Ye two can get married later," I said, nudging them both. "Right now we've got shit to do."

They both glared at me.

And, just like that, we had our game faces on.

CHAPTER 16

The tunnel darkened around the next bend, the overhead lights blown out by some force, leaving shards of glass underfoot. We tried to avoid them, to avoid making noise at all, but there was no point; three people shuffling around in the near darkness on gravel and glass are bound to cause a ruckus. Which is why I wasn't surprised to hear someone call out to us, demanding we stop. What surprised me, however, was the voice itself.

It was the voice of a child.

"That's close enough!" it said. A single light remained above, leaving a single section of track illuminated, and it was into this light that the child, Lukas Reynolds, stepped. He had curly blonde hair, cut short on the sides, leaving a mop of unruly locks draped across his forehead. He flicked them away from his face, revealing eyes tight with worry and fear.

Jimmy let out a deep breath, still searching the darkness, holding his arm out to stop us from moving any further forward. "Lukas, we've come to save you," he said, voice entirely too reasonable, as if he were trying to talk a man off a ledge. "Please come with us, and we can take you home."

Lukas narrowed his eyes. "Save me? Save me from what?"

I frowned. Something was wrong. I searched the darkness for the kidnapper, but saw no one. Bernie cursed, and even without seeing his face I knew what he was thinking. Likely the very thing I was thinking: we'd made a mistake, somehow. But what? And how?

"From the man who took you," Jimmy replied, as if saying the words might jog the boy's memory, ignoring Bernie's outburst.

"No one took me, you idiot. I left."

"You were the one," Bernie said, and I realized he had his eyes closed, one hand reaching out slightly as if feeling for the child's aura. "The one behind it all. I can sense it. But why?"

Lukas cocked his head. "Step into the light."

Bernie opened his eyes and edged forward, walking around Jimmy's outstretched arm. The minute he became visible, the boy recoiled in fear. "You! I remember you. You're with them. I knew it from the second I saw you at the park. You're with the ones who wanted to take me away," Lukas said, voice thready with fear. A figure emerged from behind the boy—one I recognized. He still wore the long red coat with brass buttons, although it seemed he'd found pants since I'd last seen him sucking O'Bannon's flesh from his bones. Of all the zombies I'd seen thus far, he looked the most life-like, if a bit waxen. His eyes, a murky blue, flicked from Bernie to Jimmy before finally settling on me.

"She is the one, Master," he said, voice slithering out of his pale lips as if being forced out of a tube. "The one who stole from you."

Lukas pointed at us. "You're all with them, then!" He sounded hysterical. "I won't let you take my friends away. I won't, I won't, I won't!" He stomped with each word, and bursts of power split the earth, revealing cracks of green light that gave off a haunting glow.

"The Academy sought you out," Bernie said, hands held out in a calming gesture. "They tried to recruit you. Is that it?"

"As if you don't know!" Lukas spat. "They came and they tried to take me, but I already knew what they wanted. I know what they do to my kind. I saw it."

"What's he talkin' about, Bernie?" I whispered.

Bernie shook his head. "Someone's been filling the boy's head with lies."

"Not lies," the Redcoat said, resting a hand on Lukas' shoulder. The boy immediately gripped the hand with his own for comfort, giving the dead man's fingers a generous squeeze. "The boy was shown truths. He was shown the culling. He was shown what the wizards did, so long ago, to keep death from overtaking life."

"That was centuries ago," Bernie said. "Hell, maybe even longer. Wizards haven't hunted down their own like that since the Dark Ages."

The Redcoat laughed, and the hissing sound sent shivers up my spine. "Do they not? I think you overestimate your people. What do you think they would do with this boy? With his power? If they could not control it. Would they let him live?"

To his credit, Bernie didn't answer immediately. Instead, he seemed to consider the question. Lukas, still looking terrified, glanced up at his companion, then back to the old man. "Honestly," Bernie said, looking tired, shoulders slumped, "I don't know. I wish I could say they'd have tried to help him. But I just don't know for sure."

"Honesty...you are a rare wizard," the Redcoat said. "But it is too late for that, now. The boy belongs to us, and we to him. Our covenant has been made."

Bernie hung his head. "Is there anything you'll trade for the boy?"

"It is too late," the Redcoat said, sounding surprisingly sad. "He enlisted us, and so we serve. We did not try to take, but he offered us much. More than he should have. Now it will be up to you to stop us."

"Why does it sound like he wants us to stop him?" Jimmy asked, keeping his voice low enough that only Bernie and I could hear.

"Because even the dead know the concept of balance," Bernie replied. "Thanks to what the kid has done, they've gotten a taste of life. But that's all it is. A taste. Usually, that's all a Necromancer can offer. But this kid is strong enough to keep them, perhaps for as long as he lives. Problem is, to stay alive, they'll have to keep feeding. Keep killing. Eventually, the world will notice. Or worse, their watchers will."

"The gods below would punish us," the Redcoat agreed. "And, although we were eager to remember our bodies, we long to sleep."

"No," Lukas said, gripping the Redcoat's fingers. "No, you must stay with me. You have to protect me until I can get the book."

The Redcoat stared down at the child, eyes cloudy with death. "We do as you command, Master." But he sounded forlorn, as if he knew exactly how terribly this would end.

"What book?" Bernie asked.

"The Grimm book," Lukas replied. "The man in my dreams told me about it. About how whoever had it could rule the world. My dad knows where it is, I know it. But he wouldn't tell me."

"The man in your dreams?" Jimmy said.

"Silver Tongue," the Redcoat replied. In that title, I heard something like true abhorrence, the way some people curse dictators or fascists, as if the very title itself was despicable.

"He said if I get the book, I can bring back the Grimms and use them to stop anyone who wants to hurt me," Lukas said, oblivious to the Redcoat's tone. "The Grimms will be mine and they'll have to do whatever I tell them. Just like the rest." Lukas waved a hand, and two more figures stepped forward beside him. Both incredibly lifelike, as Redcoat was. Then three more behind them. Then four.

In an instant, we were staring down a small army of corpses, each looking remarkably alive. Meaning they must have fed on someone, at some point. I wondered how many vagabonds would be written off as having picked up and left town, never to be seen or heard from again. How many of Boston's fine, upstanding citizens would be reported missing, a pile of their clothes all that remained? I shuddered, then offered up a brief prayer that I wouldn't end up one of them.

My face was too pale for milk cartons.

CHAPTER 17

The final showdown, if you could call it that, began the instant Lukas retreated into the darkness. The zombies—soulless eyes locked, not on us, but some distant horizon we couldn't comprehend—took a collective step forward as if yanked by the string of some cosmic puppeteer, lunging in total unison. Then another. And another. Like automatons, they marched inexorably towards us.

It was creepy in every sense of the word.

"Same rules apply?" Bernie asked, looking at me. His gaze was intense. Pained.

I grimaced, but nodded. "Aye, same rules. Distract 'em, and I'll take care of the rest."

"You can't mean that," Jimmy said. "He's just a kid."

Bernie and I shared a glance. Jimmy was right. Lukas was just a kid. But he was also dangerous. He'd killed people. Maybe not with his own two hands, but the body count he'd tallied up would leave other children without mothers or fathers, not to mention widowed spouses. What happened next wasn't a question of right or wrong. Killing Lukas would be wrong. I'd lose sleep over it. A lot of sleep. But letting him live to terrorize more people would be worse. And Bernie and I knew it.

"I won't let you kill a kid," Jimmy growled, watching us.

Bernie sighed, shoulders sagging. "Fine, we'll do it your way. But keep in mind that, once this is all over, you'll have to give him over to my people. Your justice system isn't designed for shit like this, and the kid will have to answer for what he's done."

Jimmy looked like he wanted to argue, but there was no time. The zombies were closing in. Not fast, but fast enough. "We'll sort it out. What's the plan?"

Bernie herded us back. "I'm going to throw a few curveballs at these things. Draw them into the tunnel behind us. You two double-back and find another way around. The only way you're going to bring the kid down is if you sneak up on him from behind and knock him out." Something flashed across his face.

"What is it?" I asked, studying the older man.

"Nothing. We'll talk about it later."

I frowned.

"Go, now. And hurry. I don't know how long I can keep them busy." Bernie reached into his sack, drawing out a strangely shaped vial. The glass was tinted blue and spiraled in on itself like a nautilus shell. He grinned. "This was one of my favorites," he said, then tossed the vial into the air. It landed in the midst of the approaching zombies and burst, shattering forcefully against the ground. A wave of briny air washed over us, laden with the odor of sea and salt. Suddenly, the zombies were moving slower. Much slower. I squinted, eyes still adjusting to the dark, and realized they were wading through thick, murky liquid up to their torsos. A patch of water that filled a thirty-foot-long stretch of tunnel. "Betty and I used to crack one of these open in the summer, whenever it broke a hundred degrees, just to cool down," Bernie said, grinning.

"That's impossible," Jimmy said, staring wide-eyed at the mass of figures as they slogged pathetically through the water.

"Ye get over it," I said, although truthfully I was pretty impressed, myself. I snagged Jimmy's arm and pulled him away. "Come on, I saw a side tunnel we can try. Hopefully it'll take us far enough down." Jimmy followed on leaden legs before finally shaking his head and jogging alongside me. He was muttering things under his breath, but keeping up, which was good enough for me. We left Bernie calmly facing a horde of zombies, fumbling through his satchel.

"Can you do stuff like that?" Jimmy asked between breaths, his long legs keeping up with my own as we backtracked, searching for the side tunnel I'd spotted earlier.

I found it, wheeled right, and sped up, keeping track of our progress using a mini-map in my head, doing my best to make sure we didn't end up turned around. It was tough, but I seemed to have developed a knack for shit like this; I blamed my brief stint living in New York, where navigating on a grid had become a way of life. "Stuff like what? Make a lake appear out of thin air?" I asked.

"Sure."

I laughed, or would have, were I not breathing so hard from our pace. "Not a chance."

"Do you know other people who can?"

"Tell ye what, Jimmy. When this is all over, I'll let ye buy me that drink, and ye can grill me all ye want about the Freaks in this town. Hell, maybe I'll introduce ye to a Faelin' or two. But right now, I need ye to focus." I managed to say all this between breaths, eyes still scanning the tunnel for openings. If we didn't find a way to turn right again soon, we'd have to head back and take our chances with facing Lukas head on.

Jimmy grunted. "There," he said, pointing to an opening that joined the main branch we'd come from. Perfect. He bolted for it, but I held out an arm, slowing us both in the process. He gave me a funny look. "What?"

"Bernie said sneak, remember? We can't go runnin' in," I said.

"You're right." Jimmy took a deep, soothing breath, trying to get his heart rate under control. I mimicked him, letting my pulse slow as we padded towards the opening, quiet as church mice. Ordinarily, I'd have been happy to charge in, guns blazing, but if we really were going to save the kid, Bernie's plan had the most merit; my idea of problem-solving typically included spent shell casings and body bags.

Here was hoping we wouldn't need either one.

CHAPTER 18

We emerged into a lit section of tunnel, but not terribly far beyond the darkened stretch where we'd first encountered Lukas. In fact, I could make out faint sounds and strange lights playing beyond the bend. Probably Bernie, keeping the zombies at bay. For a moment, I worried Lukas might have gone deeper into the tunnel, but then I saw him. He was facing the darkness.

And he wasn't alone.

The Redcoat must have doubled-back for some reason, because we found him standing not twenty feet ahead of us, like a rear guard, arms folded neatly behind his back. He'd spotted us the moment we stepped into the light, but had said nothing. I noticed his lower half was soaked, the base of his coat stained a deeper, more vibrant shade red. He turned to glance at Lukas, then back to us, his expression placid. Unreadable.

We stayed like that for a moment, merely staring at each other, then I inched forward. Jimmy followed suit. Together, the two of us approached, stepping along the railway's wooden slats to avoid disturbing the gravel. I recognized all our sneaking around would make little difference if the zombie guard decided to raise the alarm, but so far he hadn't seemed inclined to give us up. So—at least until I suspected otherwise—we were going to keep pretending this would work.

The Redcoat tracked us with his eyes but said nothing, not even as we passed by him. Jimmy, prepared for a fight, walked sideways as we continued on, keeping an eye on both the zombie and the boy. But there was no need. The Redcoat merely turned and continued watching us. It was eerie and made no sense. But I wasn't complaining.

Not yet.

It wasn't until we stood not four feet from the boy, holding our breaths, that I realized I had no idea what to do next. Put him in a chokehold, maybe? But what if I accidentally snapped his neck? I'd been training in martial arts since I was a kid, but I'd always picked bigger, stronger opponents to fight. It's what set me apart from most fighters; I always anticipated being the underdog. But even a simple rear naked choke could do all sorts of damage if you weren't careful. Still, it seemed like the best option; I wasn't about to clout the kid over the head and have to explain why he had permanent brain damage. I started to step forward.

"I figured you'd come," Lukas said, spinning around, hands in his pockets.

I shuffled back, heart pounding. It made me feel ridiculous, being startled by a little kid. In fact, I had to stop myself from punching the little fucker in the nose on principle. Instead, I gritted my teeth. "Sorry, boyo, but we can't let ye keep doin' whatever ye like. This has to end."

"I don't think so," Lukas said. He flicked his hand, and the Redcoat was suddenly there, arms wrapped around Jimmy's torso, lifting the man in the air with inhuman strength. Jimmy struggled and squirmed, striking the zombie's face with his elbows, the zombie's legs with savage kicks. But nothing worked.

"Put him down," I demanded.

"I cannot," the Redcoat replied. "I am bound to serve." He looked past Jimmy's flailing body, meeting my eyes, and I saw the same sadness I'd seen reflected in them earlier. But there was something else there, too. Hope.

But why? Why look at me with hope?

"He saw through what you were trying to do," Lukas said, his voice petulant. Spoiled. "And now you're mine, too. Unless you want us to kill him." He pointed at Jimmy, whose struggles were quickly diminishing. He wasn't being drained, I realized, but he was being squeezed to death, his lungs crushed by the strength in those monstrous arms.

"Don't do it," I hissed, glaring at the zombie.

"I must, for the child is my Master," the Redcoat replied. "I am bound to him."

I frowned. There was that word again. Bound. Suddenly, I realized what the zombie was trying to tell me. What he'd been trying to tell me from the very start. I stared into those dead eyes and knew exactly what he wanted me to do.

I reached out, past Jimmy, and pressed a single finger between the Redcoat's furrowed brows. He sighed, the sound emerging from his throat like a death rattle, then collapsed into so much liquid. Jimmy fell to the ground, gasping for air like a drowning man plucked from still waters.

"No!" Lukas screamed. He reached out, and that eerie green light spread across the ground, but the liquid remained just that—a black ichor that stained Jimmy's backside like tar. "No! How? How could you?!" Lukas shrieked.

I didn't bother telling Lukas the truth: that the Redcoat had known this would happen. That he'd mentioned it purposefully in my presence the first time we met, hoping I would use my ability to free him and his brethren. That I'd simply been too dumb to realize I could stop them, could remove the bonds Lukas had so wantonly constructed. Instead, I reached out and crushed the boy to me, pinning his face against my shoulder as he sobbed.

"Deep breaths," I murmured. I felt the boy's power snap the instant I held him to me, like taut strings being snipped in two. The tendrils of power that connected him to the other zombies fell away like torn strands of a spider's web. The boy shuddered, then passed out, too exhausted by the abrupt departure of his power to stay upright a moment longer.

Jimmy was almost instantly beside me, wincing, but alive. "So," he wheezed, "you use maternal magic. That's a surprise."

I reached out and punched him in the stomach.

"Never could take a joke," Jimmy gasped, clutching his gut.

But I didn't get a chance to respond.

Because that's when the screams began.

CHAPTER 19

I handed Lukas off to Jimmy. "Take him," I insisted, then rose. The screams were coming from down the tunnel, where Bernie had been taking on the zombies. I took off at a dead sprint, drawing my gun in the process. My heart hammered in my chest, and a bad feeling churned in my gut. Something was wrong. Lukas, the necromancer, was unconscious. The danger should have passed. And yet, somehow, I knew it hadn't. If anything, it felt like things had gotten worse.

I raced through the darkness, trying to see what was happening around the bend, but couldn't. The clamor grew louder, and I realized they were more like howls—the sounds crazy people make when they're throwing their own shit against the walls, or breaking everything in sight. The instant I turned the corner, I realized what I was hearing: the zombies had gone insane.

No longer tied to Lukas, they had reverted to something ghoulish and awful—too animalistic, too vicious to have ever been considered human. Many had taken to wrestling with each other, tearing at their companions with wild abandon. I froze and scoured the scene for Bernie, praying I wouldn't find his limbs being used as clubs. When I finally found him, I let out a breath I hadn't realized I was holding.

He was holding what I assumed was another vial, although this one had a more familiar shape, dodging the zombies as best he could. As I watched, he poured a thick yellow liquid onto two zombies tearing into each other with their teeth. He jostled the vial. No, not a vial, I realized. A can. Gasoline. He was pouring gasoline on the zombies. Now that I knew what it was he was carrying, the stench was obvious. Acrid and bitter, it filled the tunnel with a sickly sweet odor which clung to the back of my throat. A quick glance around revealed the remaining zombies had been similarly doused.

He tossed the can to the side and caught me looking. He waved, then winked, and suddenly I knew what he was planning to do. But before I could stop him, he began beating his foot against a rail. It echoed through the tunnel, loud enough to draw the attention of the remaining zombies. Their wild eyes spun to the man, and they began slinking towards him like feral cats. "That's right," Bernie yelled. "Come on then!"

"What the fuck d'ye t'ink you're doin'?!" I screamed.

Bernie kept slamming his foot down on the rail, but he spoke to me. "I thought this might happen. The boy gave them too much power. Now that they have no one to tell them what to do, they'll be like beasts. Flesh-sucking beasts." He chuckled to himself. "You know, if I was a better wizard, I could just burn them all to ashes and be done with it." He shrugged. "But this'll have to do."

I raised my gun, aiming for one of the corpses. "Get the hell out of there and we'll burn 'em the old fashioned way," I called. I wasn't sure if they'd catch right away, but at least none of us would have to be bait.

Bernie shook his head and stomped once more. Nearly all of the zombies were within striking distance now, a seething mass of flesh encircling the older man. I doubted he'd be able to make it out, even if he wanted to. "Normal fire won't work. They'd survive it. If even one of them makes it out of these tunnels, the whole world will know the truth." He met my eyes, and I knew in that moment he was ready to go. Ready to give up his life if it meant saving others. That, perhaps, he'd been waiting to do something like this for a long time. "They aren't ready, Quinn. Not yet. One day, maybe, but not yet."

Jimmy came puffing up beside me, the boy cradled in his arms. Bernie saw them approach and smiled wide. "I'm glad you saved him. You did the right thing. Now it's my turn."

I opened my mouth to say something, anything, but it was too late. The closest zombie reached out and wound a hand around Bernie's arm, dragging him to one knee. The old man grunted, and I saw the big vein in his forehead pulse as his cheeks went red. His power surged, and the zombie's hand erupted in green flame. But it didn't draw back. Instead, the zombies crowded closer, like moths drawn to the light.

As each corpse touched Bernie, the flames spread. They licked up arms, along torsos, and across faces. The resulting heat was intense and immediate —a scalding wave that made me take a step back. Bernie knelt in the middle of it all, a furnace in truth now, emotions warring across his face. Anger, resentment, sorrow, and—finally—peace. The fire began to spread, spilling beyond the circle of the zombies, and soon he was lost to sight within the inferno.

"We have to go," Jimmy said. "If this continues, this whole section of tunnel could go up." He hiked Lukas up a bit, then took off down the tunnel. I watched the flames rise a moment longer, then turned and followed, never looking back.

CHAPTER 20

I avoided jail time, but it was a close thing. Detective Maria Machado was practically frothing at the mouth by the time Sloan escorted me out of the precinct for the second time that night, but she didn't have a leg to stand on; both Dawes and Cassidy had corroborated Jimmy's story: I'd followed the cops down into the tunnel because I was worried about Jimmy. It made me look dumb and girly, but I could handle that if it meant sleeping in my own bed. When she'd asked what we'd found down there, I'd been surprised to discover Jimmy was a very capable liar when he felt so inclined.

A man of many talents.

"Drug users," Jimmy had said. "High as hell on meth. We barely made it out alive before their lab blew up."

The rest of us had gone along with it, especially since no one would believe us if we told the truth. Besides which, the tunnels had been cordoned off by HazMat units; the fire Bernie started had spread much further than it should have, filling the whole subterranean infrastructure with smoke. I wondered how much evidence would be left over when things were said and done. My guess: this one would leave the cops scratching their heads forever.

Still, I doubt I'd have ever gotten out of the interrogation room were it not for the fact that we'd saved the kid. Cops had died in the process, but no one could pin that on me. They couldn't pin it on Jimmy, either. What they could pin on him was a fucking medal; he'd managed to drag out a few survivors, a well-meaning civilian, and a kidnapped child.

The media was already dubbing it Boston P.D.'s finest hour.

When I left the precinct, the other uniforms were already whispering things like "key to the city" and "detective material." Personally, I was happy for him. He deserved the praise, even if it was for all the wrong reasons. Sloan left me outside the precinct with a cool goodbye, making me promise not to get into any more trouble before dawn, at the earliest. I solemnly swore and caught a ride to the Plaza.

Breaking into Bernie's car was a little harder than I would have liked. I'd have smashed the window, but the cops were still swarming the area, and I meant to keep my promise to Sloan. Instead, I managed to force the lock; Bernie's ride was one of those older models, the kind car thieves practice on. I fetched my tote from the floorboards, then briskly wiped the interior down. Everyone who'd been in the tunnels had agreed to leave Bernie out of our statements. He'd sacrificed himself to save us and to keep our worlds separate, and it would have been harder to explain away the presence of a second civilian. Besides, somehow I knew they wouldn't find him down there. He'd used every ounce of power he had to destroy the zombies, and that much power would have consumed him completely.

Before I left, I fished through the car, making sure not to touch anything with my bare hands. After less than a minute of searching, I found what I was looking for in the middle console: his wallet. In it, I found a picture of Bernie and his wife, Betty, smiling. Happy. I slid the photo into my pocket. The wallet I'd chuck in the nearest trash bin before returning home. Let the world wonder what happened to Bernie Wakowski, the low-level wizard who'd stepped up for his kind when nobody was looking.

He'd probably prefer it that way.

JIMMY MET me the next night, at a bar. He bought the first round. I bought the second. He told me Lukas Reynolds had been moved to a hospital in Philadelphia. I wondered if the mysterious Academy had anything to do with it, but then decided it didn't matter. If the kid went nuts again, it'd be someone else's problem. I was done hunting zombies, and told Jimmy as much. I also told him about the seedy underworld I inhabited. He didn't believe most of it, but he made me promise to stay in touch, in case he ran into any more weird shit on the job. I promised him I would.

Truth is, once you know the monsters are out there, they're all you see.

∾

*TURN THE PAGE TO READ **BEERLYMPIAN**, A FUN NOVELLA ABOUT GUNNAR'S BACHELOR PARTY IN NEW ORLEANS*

PART III

BEERLYMPIAN

Nate Temple Series #5.5

There comes a moment in every man's life when he chooses to settle down with the love of his life. To put all those childish games and hobbies away to focus on building the rock-solid foundations of a true, everlasting, committed relationship—marriage.

Gunnar Randulf, the Alpha werewolf of St. Louis and Nate Temple's best friend is ready to make that plunge. But before the wedding bells chime...

It's bachelor party time.

Join Nate, Alucard, Achilles, and the Minotaur as they rip through New Orleans on a last-ditch effort to ruin Gunnar's life—erm, remind him why he loves his fiancée so much—with a Stag Night scavenger hunt marathon that introduces them to ungodly amounts of alcohol, mermaids, major felonies, Nicolas Flamel, ridiculous drinking rules, Valkyries, and a slew of other local supernaturals. And you thought you knew just how crazy the boys could get when left unattended.

It's cute, really, your naivety...

CHAPTER 1

My unicorn gang stalked through the woods like malevolent ghosts, the twilight masking our approach. A campfire flared in the near distance, filling the woods with the pungent scent of burning wood—which was good because it meant we were downwind. Still, we kept our profiles low as we crept closer to our target, slowly easing branches out of our way and paying meticulous attention to where we placed our feet. Our target was hyper aware of his surroundings at all times, and even the slightest disturbance could alert him.

My unicorn gang was bound by blood—united in our undertaking, dedicated to our descent into destruction, satisfied to sacrifice what little remained of our stained souls in order to succeed in this sinister, singular moment. We weren't just a *gang*. We were unicorn *demons*, and we'd toiled away our allotted slice of eternity waiting for this exact moment—but now we finally had the chance to break the chains of morality that bound us. Nothing would stop—

"Fucking *ridiculous!*" I heard a deep basso voice curse in an annoyed whisper, but Asterion's whisper could have been mistaken for a passing locomotive.

I turned to hiss at him, whipping my finger to my lips in the universal *shut the fuck up before I skin you alive* gesture every child learns from the first near-retirement, grade-school teacher they encounter on their long perilous journey through the public education system. But my finger hit the long snout of the rubber mask covering my face, knocking the eyeholes out of alignment. I quickly readjusted it to cast my glare at the Minotaur—only to find him also struggling with his own XXXL rubber unicorn mask. Since it had been designed for a human, his massive bull-head was simply too large for it; we'd been forced to cut relief slits into the neck so he could even put it on, and we'd had to extend those slits all the way up past his temples to accommodate his huge horns. Essentially, Asterion looked like a newly proposed dinosaur concept for the next Jurassic Park movie—the Tricera-corn.

He finally got it situated properly and noticed my intent glare. Below the mask, he was a giant, hairy, humanoid figure, wearing massive leather boots, a leather warrior's kilt, and a heavy set of prayer beads that hung below his muscular chest. He was a self-proclaimed Buddhist but wasn't too pushy about it. The first time I'd met him, I'd cow-tipped him because I thought it was a unique way to introduce myself to an immortal, legendary, human-eating monster. Our friendship had blossomed since, so I'd considered writing a book about my relationship-building tactics. I doubted he would give me a blurb, though.

I scowled at him one last time for good measure and then pointed at the campfire ahead, lifting my fingers—more carefully this time—to my lips to remind him silence was paramount.

The other half of my gang—Alucard and Achilles—fanned out on my other side so that we made a crescent-shaped arc as we continued towards the campfire.

Achilles needed no introduction—the legendary Greek warrior who had helped take down the city of Troy in his glory days. These days he owned a bar in St. Louis called *Achilles' Heel* and was somewhat of a new friend to my crew. He was buff in a natural-looking way, sported long blonde hair, and was covered in scars from his life as a brawler. His bar was also known for its dangerous patrons who spilled blood more often than they did their beer.

We'd had a rocky start to our relationship, too—trying to beat the hell out of each other a few times—but I'd done him a solid by helping him out of a pretty intricate legal contract, so tonight was kind of an olive branch between us.

Alucard was a Master Vampire—recently upgraded to Daywalker status thanks to drinking some blood he probably shouldn't have tried to sample. Luckily, it had only made him uniquely stronger instead of killing him outright. Our first encounter had been as enemies, but circumstances and a shared enemy had quickly convinced him to team up with me rather than fight against me. He'd moved to St. Louis and abandoned his vampire coven in New Orleans without batting an eye—a solid display of where his new loyalties rested.

He was tall, dark, and handsome—as many would say—and he naturally spoke in a thick southern drawl but often tried to mask the accent since we gave him so much grief about it.

All in all, my gang was comprised of enemies-turned-friends—a dysfunctional Band of Brothers. I also realized I was bringing the Triple-A team: Asterion, Achilles, and Alucard. I hoped that wasn't a sign of how the night was going to turn out—injuries and a whole lot of disappointment at shattered prospects.

If all went according to plan, we had an inside person—an accomplice—waiting for us at the camp. If they had failed to do their part of the job, things were about to get very messy.

I took a deep breath, the smell of scented rubber sticking in my nose since the designer had attempted to make it fragrant rather than pungent, but they'd simply succeeded in making it so strong I felt like I was huffing a Febreze canister.

We finally neared the edge of the camp and found two werewolves lounging in lawn chairs. One was a gorgeous, reddish-brown haired woman with her legs crossed on a log before her. She was sipping a beer and smirking directly at me. Ashley Belmont.

The other figure was a great giant of a man with long, blonde hair and a bushy, golden beard. He wore a black eyepatch that he somehow managed to pull off with a roguish look. Gunnar Randulf, the Alpha werewolf of St. Louis, was snoring loudly. My mask had restricted the sounds of the woods around us, hiding the now obvious snoring. I cursed, standing from my crouch to glare at Ashley. Out of pride, I didn't take off my mask.

"Do you have any idea how much time we put into our plan? How care-fully we snuck up on you?" I demanded, folding my arms.

Asterion stood from his own crouch, cautiously walking up to Gunnar before poking him with a sausage-sized finger. Gunnar snorted louder but didn't stir. Asterion tore off his mutilated unicorn mask and flung it on the ground, stomping on it as he snorted loudly, the thick ring in his massive nostrils swinging at the infuriated motion.

CHAPTER 2

A shley chuckled at Asterion's temper and then turned back to me, studying my face with a crooked grin. "Unicorns. Terrifying," she finally said, glancing back at the Minotaur again.

"You could have called to tell us we didn't have to creep the last mile to your campsite," I muttered.

Alucard and Achilles finally walked into the clearing to stand beside the fire, talking to each other softly—which was all the more hilarious because they still wore their giant unicorn rubber masks. That was the best part of costumes—when the wearers forgot they were wearing them and began to do normal, everyday things.

Like when you go to a cosplay event and see Darth Maul smoking a cigarette, Superman chugging a beer, or Deadpool at the urinal beside you.

Ashley rolled her eyes at my complaint. "He smelled something and started to get suspicious. I had to drug him sooner than we planned. Maybe a little stronger than I intended. But I have this handy epinephrine stick you can use," she said, brandishing the medical dagger colloquially known as an epi-pen. Many incorrectly knew it as an adrenaline shot.

I blinked at her, then studied my best friend since childhood. He was drooling into his beard, now. "How much did you dope him with? And don't you think it's a horrible idea to give an Alpha werewolf an epinephrine shot after we kidnap him?" I asked. "You're supposed to be the logical one in this situation," I reminded her. "If he wakes up in a strange place surrounded by four unicorn men holding something stabbed into his thigh...he'll have questions. Loud, violent, irrational questions like *why did you stab me, where am I, where is my fiancée?*"

"It's *Stag Night*," Ashley said dismissively. "If you four scoundrels don't know how to show him the wildest night of his life then maybe he needs to find some new friends," she teased, ticking off her fingers as she continued. "The big bad wizard, the Minotaur, fucking Achilles, and a Master vampire can't handle my little puppy?" she cooed in the voice one typically uses to talk to their pets. When none of us responded and she noticed me still staring at the epi-pen, she rolled her eyes. "He's a *werewolf*. This is nothing compared to a *shift*. It barely even qualifies as an energy drink. Werewolves have very strong hearts."

I scowled at her and my unicorn gang mirrored me, ruining the seriousness of the situation. Seeing three fake unicorns glare at someone really makes it impossible to maintain anger.

I attempted to rake my fingers through my hair and cursed when I knocked my mask askew again. I straightened it, muttering under my breath. She was probably right. He'd understand. He wouldn't freak out.

Yeah, right. Luckily, my mask concealed my unease from my gang. I would just make sure someone else stabbed Gunnar with the damned pen. Someone big and strong, able to take an alpha werewolf punch fueled by adrenaline.

"You guys ready?" I asked my crew. The bastards actually neighed in response as they circled Gunnar.

Ashley grinned, studying us. "What do gay horses eat?" she finally asked, biting her lip.

"Hey!" I snapped. "We're not—"

"Heeeeeeeeeeyyyyyyyy!" my gang sang out in an overly effeminate cheer. Ashley burst out laughing, clapping her hands delightedly as she nodded her head up and down upon hearing the correct answer. I sighed, overly ready for that first drink.

"Return him in more or less one piece and call me if you need bail money, or accidentally start a war in New Orleans."

"Ashley, you're the best kind of fiancée," I told her honestly, my excitement budding now that we were officially starting the bachelor party shenanigans.

She curtsied dramatically, then glanced down at the epi-pen in her hand. She looked up at me, a very devious grin on her face. "Mind if I do this part? That way he doesn't think I'm in danger as soon as he wakes up."

I glanced at my crew and they nodded in relief. I noticed Asterion hadn't picked his mask up so I pointed at it eagerly. "Put your mask back on, man! Otherwise he'll recognize us." He hurriedly scooped it up off the ground, struggling to line it up properly on his head.

Achilles cleared his throat. "I bet he only needs one guess with you," he offered helpfully, pointing at the Minotaur and his horns.

I ignored the bickering and turned to Ashley, rubbing my hands together excitedly. Alucard, Asterion, and Achilles loomed over Gunnar's chair, forming a circle with me at the front. I finally gave her a thumbs up, knowing she would never do anything that would actually put Gunnar in any real danger so she must have been very confident on the potential side-effects of using an epi-pen on an unconscious werewolf.

Ashley chuckled, popped the top off the pen, and then stabbed her fiancée in the thigh. Gunnar woke with a roar, his lone eye—he'd lost the other in a fight with the Brothers Grimm—shooting wide open to find his wife leaning over him.

"Have fun tonight, sweetie," she said, snapping him out of his chemically-induced sleep, before planting a wet kiss on his lips.

He blinked back at her, then noticed the four unicorns surrounding him. His lone eye narrowed, his chest still panting rapidly from the epinephrine. "What..." he began, jerking his head first one way and then another.

"Hold your breath," I told him, turning to open a Gateway—a nifty way for wizards to travel great distances in a single step—in the air before us. "It's Stag Night!" The Gateway was essentially an open doorway to another place —in this case a shimmering pool full of naked women in New Orleans.

Mermaids.

Ashley began to cackle uproariously as Gunnar struggled to get out of his chair, but my three companions pinned his arms down and then hoisted the entire chair high up into the air.

"Let there be BOOBS!" Ashley roared. The naked mermaids on the other end of the Gateway erupted with cheers and laughter.

Gunnar spun his head around, torn between horror, anxiety, and excitement—his emotions likely even more out of whack as he struggled to process the drugs coursing through his veins.

Without hesitation, my unicorns hurled him and the chair through the open Gateway and straight into the pool of topless women who were bouncing up and down in excitement. They'd been waiting on us for about thirty minutes now since we'd had to tailor Asterion's unicorn mask to fit him.

Gunnar bellowed before splashing into the pool.

I gave Ashley a high-five and she pulled me in for a hug. "Take care of the hairy lummox for me, but make sure he has a truly unforgettable time. It's his last chance to cut loose."

I chuckled and squeezed her back before leaning away to meet her eyes. "You really are the coolest fiancée ever," I told her, pointing my thumb back at the pool full of mermaids.

She grunted. "Just keep him away from any werewolf bitches and you can have at it."

I chuckled and locked eyes with my crew. "Let's ride, uni-squad." I threw the extra unicorn mask intended for Gunnar ahead of me as we leapt through the Gateway and into the pool.

Although it was night, the air was warm and muggy, so the pool felt refreshing. Also, with as many breastacular women as were swimming around us, I'm not sure any of us would have noticed the water temperature if it had been in the Arctic Circle.

We didn't last more than thirty seconds before our clothes were forcefully removed from our bodies by the school of mermaids giggling and laughing as they tossed them out of the pool for another nude mer-person to hang to dry.

Because this was a ritzy hotel with an optional nude swimming pool. And it was only our first stop. We waved one last time at Ashley with all the excitement of kids waving goodbye to their mother on the first day of school. Then I released the Gateway.

CHAPTER 3

unnar was sputtering, shouting, and laughing as he tried to stop the mermaids from unclothing him; realizing everyone else was naked, he gave up on being prudish. Achilles and Alucard were hooting with laughter as they were stripped to their skins by the mermaidens, but Asterion looked extremely uncomfortable with that many strange hands on him at one time. This party was all about breaking boundaries, though, so he would be a new bull by the end of the night.

Gunnar spun to shoot me a mock scowl, shaking his head in wonder. "What's up with the unicorn masks?" he asked in bewilderment, glancing down at his hands where he held the mask I had thrown in for him.

I grunted as I glanced down at the floating rubber mask beside me. I'd almost drowned to death after jumping in the pool when the damned thing had filled with water. Luckily, an overzealous white-haired, caramel-skinned mermaid had saved me with excessive concerned touching and patting on the back. It didn't stop her from stripping me as efficiently as one cleaned a fish.

"We thought we were going to have to kidnap you and wanted disguises to surprise you." I admitted, shrugging. "And I'm sure we'll find plenty more opportunities to use them as the night unfolds."

He slowly shook his head, grinning from ear-to-ear. "I can't believe

Ashley was in on it. Wait..." he said slowly, thinking. "She... drugged me? Is that why my heart is racing?"

"Better than a stripper making your heart race, right?"

"Stripper? I don't need any strippers."

"I hate to break it to you, but tonight isn't only about you. Stag Nights are group events. You're the focus, sure, but you're not the only one looking to have a good time."

Gunnar scowled at me. "I think it *is* supposed to be about me."

"Ashley said we could get strippers. We're getting strippers," I said in a final tone. The mermaids cheered their agreement with Achilles and Alucard—still in their unicorn masks—splashing water at a few of them playfully. Asterion just stood there uncomfortably, trying to avert his eyes. Finally, he slapped his own mask on to hide his embarrassment.

He was quiet for a moment. "She did say *let there be boobs...*" he said, trailing off thoughtfully.

I nodded. "No *werewolf* boobs, though. Pretty generous of her, really."

Abruptly, I realized we were being surrounded by a half-dozen of the topless mermaids, and they were grinning at us with their razor-sharp teeth —which kind of killed the sexy factor—but they didn't look like they wanted to murder us or anything. It wasn't like they could help how they looked.

"You boys ready to play?" a red-headed mermaid said, looking as if she had seaweed dreadlocks woven into her thick tresses. "You've got a long night ahead of you."

Alucard finally ceased his splash fight and waded closer with Achilles and Asterion—who still looked positively mortified. Maybe that was because he was taller, and his nudity was more revealing unless he crouched down a bit in the pool.

"The Alcochemist is ready whenever we finish up here," Alucard said mysteriously.

"Oh, nice choice," a mermaid with blonde cornrows said, licking her lips. "We better get started. I call the big one."

Achilles stepped forward proudly. "Hop on up, my fair mermaiden—"

"I said the *big* one," she interrupted with emphasis on the word. Then she locked eyes with Asterion. He stiffened like a board and I could almost see his blush through the mask. He was doing everything he could to not stare at the assorted breasts around us, even though I'd warned him that it was totally natural for mermaids to be nude and that if we wanted their help in our planned activities, we needed to give them something in return. They rarely got to play with others the way they wanted, and bachelor parties were a mysterious, exciting rite of passage that people, and mermaids, generally wanted to participate in when they saw one shambling down a street.

Every girl wanted to become a vague, half-formed memory in some poor guy's mind on his 'last hoorah' journey before marriage. Even if it was just to be part of the soirée, hidden back in the crowd. Like a public hanging back in the old days, one was compelled to attend. Something about bachelor and bachelorette parties simply required everyone to lower their inhibitions as if they were behind some cosmic curtain where no one could see what truly happened and you could cut loose for a few hours.

Asterion hadn't believed everything we'd told him about our plans, but if he was balking at our first stop...

"Asterion..." I warned in a low tone, speaking for only him to hear. "You're coming across as disrespectful, even though you don't mean to be. And..." I held out my arms invitingly, turning back to our hosts to openly appreciate the naked display before us, "what's good for the goose is good for the gander."

The mermaids tittered—pun intended—demurely, but Gunnar rolled his eye at me. "Gander puns? Really?"

"Don't be a tit, Gunnar," Alucard grinned.

"I'm plenty *big*," Achilles muttered, still hung up on the earlier dismissal.

"Oh, I want to ride those shoulders, don't worry." Another voluptuous, red-headed mermaid with alabaster skin, minus the seaweed dreads, promptly climbed onto his shoulders, nipping at his ears on her way up, her human legs hanging free over his chest. He gripped them to support her balance, grinning as she readjusted the unicorn mask on his head. "You're plenty big, my Greek stallion," she cooed, stroking his horn suggestively. "My name is Atlantia." He patted her rump with a chuckle and she beamed.

Alucard burst out laughing as a lithe, copper-skinned brunette climbed onto his shoulders. "This will be fun. Alucard, right?" she purred. He nodded his stupid horse head. "Good. My name is Isla. Instead of *Chicken*, we will play *Seahorse*! Your masks will make this much more fun!" She had a good point, and I found myself grinning at the mental image of our drunk, visually-impaired bachelor party playing chicken—*seahorse*—with mermaids.

With a resigned sigh, Asterion lowered his great big horns so the blonde mermaid could climb up his back. She straddled his shoulders with one leg on either side of his massive neck and promptly used his horns like handlebars. "Tactical advantage," she giggled. "My name is Chloe."

Gunnar stared at me, dumbfounded. "We're playing... chicke—" he cut off, remembering Isla had changed the name of the game, "Seahorse? For what reason, exactly?" he asked, not sounding upset, but baffled.

Alucard chimed in, gripping Isla's pale legs. "You don't get to ask questions tonight, Gunnar," he said, turning his unicorn mask towards the bachelor, his voice echoing slightly. "Your job is to simply comply."

I met Gunnar's eye and nodded. Then I pointed past his shoulder at a ridiculously well-developed, blonde-haired mermaid who was eyeing him from behind like he was a piece of sushi all wrapped up and ready to gobble down. "There's your handler," I indicated.

He spun to stare at her with a crooked grin. The sides of her head were shaved, but she had a mohawk with seashells woven into the hair on the top of her head. She also wore fat coral earrings that pulled at her earlobes. "My name is Manta, and you are mine," she told him with a dark grin.

My own rider climbed atop my shoulders, her warm flesh pressed against the back of my neck and shoulders. It was the white-haired, caramel-skinned mermaid who had saved me from drowning and stripped me to my skins. Now that I thought about it, I was pretty sure that we had each wound up with the one who had gotten us party ready—like it had been them staking their claim. She giggled, and I patted her shins to let her know I had her. "Call me Echo," she purred in a smoky voice, squeezing my neck in introduction.

I had assumed I would be struggling to support a fishtail or something, but the mermaids had made it easier on us by shifting to their human forms. Still, I noticed gills on the sides of their necks below their ears, and they had seashells for fingernails, so they weren't entirely human even when they tried.

I scanned the party to find all my unicorns now had a mermaid on their shoulders and were staring at each other anxiously. I also noticed that several mermen at the other end of the large pool also had mermaids on their shoulders. One of the mermaids was tossing a large beach ball eagerly in her hands as she straddled a beast of a merman. I grinned through my mask.

"The rules are simple," Gunnar's mermaid—Manta—called out. "Each team takes turns trying to get the ball into the goal at either end of the pool, like your game of basketball. Except full-contact." She then pointed out a massive coral horn at the edge of the pool. "Join me at the sacred conch."

She steered Gunnar towards the coral horn, and the rest of us followed suit. A trio of mermaids lounging on the land beside the conch had a case of cheap beer beside them and were each holding a few cans at the ready. They poured the beer at the wide opening near the top of the shell and it spiraled down to the funnel extending out over the pool, like a giant beer bong. "You first, bachelor," she demanded, forcefully pushing Gunnar's unicorn head towards the tip.

Alucard burst out laughing as Gunnar was forced to beer bong two cans of cheap beer through his unicorn mask or drown. He finished, gasping and spluttering, as he struggled to keep his rider on his shoulders through the process. Luckily, it was high enough that he didn't have to crouch too low. Also, our riders were forced to drink, but they were simply tossed cans of beer that they had to chug; they were shockingly efficient at it, using their coral fingernails to stab into the can as they popped the top to make their own impromptu beer bongs—or as I knew of it, shotgunning a beer. I wondered where mermaids had learned that trick.

Next it was my turn. I think I also got a double, because I felt like I was being waterboarded through the unicorn mask, half of it going up my nose.

I was laughing and choking as I teetered slightly, but somehow managed to keep Echo upright as she shotgunned her own beer.

One by one, we each did our introductory beer bong, the mermaids cackling as they watched us flounder with the added difficulty of drinking through our masks. Finally finished, we watched as our mermen opponents did the same, although with much more skill since they were obviously practiced and weren't drinking through a rubber horse's snout.

Gunnar's mount clapped her hands, getting our attention again. "When one team scores, the other team drinks from the conch. You lose a rider, you both drink from the conch. Halfway through the game, everyone pauses to drink from the conch."

My unicorns were all shaking their heads left and right, but I knew they were grinning beneath. Well, maybe not Asterion. Party pooper. A distant part of me was simply excited to hang out with some mermaids and play their games. Something that was, ironically, less crazy than my typical day.

I thought about that. Uniquely crazy was probably more accurate.

"There will also be random objects hurled at you from the spectators," Gunnar's mount continued, grinning wide. I noticed lines of naked mer-people in human form standing on the pool deck while others were lounging in their natural, half-human form; there were piles of starfish next to them. "You or your rider gets hit, you drink from the conch. You exit the pool, you drink."

"What do we *win*?" Gunnar asked, his voice muffled from his mask.

She patted his head. "You get to proceed to your next engagement. If you lose, you play *again*, but the more you drink the harder the game becomes, so I recommend you don't lose."

Before any of us could react, someone blew the fucking conch horn, and everything went crazy.

CHAPTER 4

In the first few minutes, I had been tagged three times by the damned starfish projectiles, and they were more ninja star than soft and squishy. Which meant I was totally useless to my team, spending most of my time with my lips around the tip of the conch.

Add to that, our opponents had been scoring points, so I'd had to drink even more. We had knocked down a few of their team, so they'd been forced to drink as well, but we were definitely trailing by the obligatory halfway drinking point.

After that, we ratcheted up our game and were currently tied at eight points each—mainly because we resorted to excessive violence.

The conch horn blew three times in rapid succession and everyone stopped. My mount leaned down to speak in my ear, finding it necessary to rest her hot palms on my chest and squeeze in the process. "Two points left, and we're tied so we must all drink a triple beer," she said, giggling as she explained the rule.

I grinned, squeezing her shins to let her know I'd heard her. In response, she squeezed my pecs one last time and then squeezed her thighs as she straightened. Part of me was slightly horrified at how much beer we'd been chugging. I was definitely feeling it but knew the full effect hadn't hit me yet. Which meant we had to win or we would be playing this drinking game for hours. We drank and then took a short breather, having ingested more beer and pool water than air, it seemed. Our riders rallied us into a huddle. "Tie game. Coran must not be allowed to win. I thought you would be much better at this."

She openly pointed at the largest merman on the opposing team. He was staring right back at us with a face I didn't like very much.

Asterion snorted beneath his water-logged mask. "Time to take off the floaties," he said, looking directly at Alucard and Achilles. Throughout the game, the two had frequently lost focus on their objective to openly ogle the topless mermaidens at the worst possible moments. Of course, the mermaidens had caught onto this weakness and had begun to go out of their way to fondle themselves or stretch and pose in order to *really* distract Achilles and Alucard throughout the game.

It also didn't help that the other team was much better at maneuvering in the water, obviously. "We need an edge," I said, brandishing a few starfish I had scooped up from my last foray underwater.

I saw Gunnar's mount grin wickedly. "I was wondering how long it would take for you to realize you could cheat. Coran's been doing it since almost the very beginning," Manta admitted. "I wasn't allowed to say anything until one of you actually cheated or suggested it. It's like an unwritten rule—win by any means necessary."

I stared at her in disbelief. "You're shitting me..." The rest of the bachelor party growled beneath their masks, not finding it nearly as funny. They looked as if the new purpose of the game was to see how many rules they could break—and how fast they could do it. I agreed.

She shook her head slowly, using a free hand to wipe her soaked hair from her brow. "Two of your drinks are courtesy of him throwing his own starfish at you."

I turned to glare at the beast of a man. He was staring right at me. I narrowed my eyes, but all he saw was an angry unicorn staring at him. "Let's filet these fuckers." I winced almost instantly, glancing up as I realized that half of our team were mermaids as well. "No offense."

"Let's hook, gut, and fry these fuckers," Gunnar's mount corrected with a feral snarl.

I let out a relieved breath, glad I hadn't offended them. "We're good at cheating," I said.

"Well, you might be," Asterion grumbled. But he was also glaring point-edly at one of the larger opponents who had taken an interest in him.

Before we could formulate a plan, the beach ball was tossed into the center of the pool and someone blew the horn. In a frenzied splash, we swarmed after the ball. Knowing that my relative strength compared to my allies wouldn't help keep our opponents back, I went for the ball, leaving defense to my bigger, stronger friends. Echo leaned down over my shoulders to scoop up the ball and I began to haul ass, pointing to my left and right to indicate Achilles and Alucard who had fanned out ahead of us, their riders waving their hands that they were open for a pass.

I twisted just as one of the mermen dove for me, but I used the motion to hurl one of my starfish at the merman guarding Alucard. It struck him in the chest and he cursed, but he didn't catch that I had been the one to throw it. Echo didn't even hesitate as she tossed the ball at Alucard's rider—I forgot her name. A merman launched up out of the water and speared Alucard the moment his mermaid reached to catch the ball, sending them both crashing into the water where Alucard lost his unicorn mask.

But Achilles leapt up into the air impossibly high, using his knee to clock another merman in the face who had been diving for the ball. His mermaid caught the ball and hurled it into the goal, scoring us a point.

We were ahead for the first time, even if only by a single point.

I lifted my fists in victory and felt Echo grasp my wrists as she gyrated rather vigorously against my neck with a triumphant shriek.

Which was when Coran struck us like a torpedo. My mask flew off as I crashed underwater, but I jumped up, reflexively helping Echo clamber back up onto my shoulders even though I knew she didn't need any time to catch her breath, being able to swim underwater and everything.

I glared at Coran as he stood from the water—having sacrificed himself to take me down for the sheer spite of it since the ball hadn't been in play. He sniffed pointedly and turned to wade hurriedly over to the conch since we now both had to drink. I saw those on the edge of the pool toss cans of beer to our lovely passengers and heard the *snikt* sound of them shotgunning them as fast as possible so we could get back into the game.

Coran was already finished when I reached the conch, so I splashed some water onto the tip to get rid of his fish mouth saliva before chugging my own penalty beers.

I spun to jump back into the fray just as Asterion literally tackled one of the opponents trying to shoot at our goal. He struck him like a killer whale, knocking the mermaid clear off the merman's shoulders as they all went under. But the ball still went into the goal, so I spun around to take my double beer from the conch as fast as possible, my head spinning slightly.

I made my way to the center of the pool waiting for a teammate to join me against the waiting horde. Achilles joined me, straightening his unicorn mask. He saw me staring at him and nodded. Then he reached up and gave his rider a loud slap on the ass. "Game time!" he roared.

She gasped in surprise and then burst out laughing. "The rider is supposed to slap the horse's ass!" she shouted between chuckles. In response, Achilles reached up to slap her other ass cheek even harder than the first, sending her into a giggling fit. Two hand-shaped red welts were already visible on her pale rear.

I felt my own companion wiggling suggestively on my shoulders. "I'm waiting..." she purred.

I grinned. "What the hell," I muttered, as I reached up to slap her on the ass. Because I always thought about others before myself and didn't want her to be embarrassed in front of her friends with only one handprint on her ass, I gave her a wet slap on the other side.

"That's what I'm talking about, magic man! Good horsey!" she hooted, patting my head.

I rolled my eyes, but I was laughing. I scooped up the ball, staring down Coran as he squared off against me. "Let's do this."

I tossed the ball at Achilles and Coran took off in hot pursuit. The moment his back turned, I flung my last starfish at him, striking his partner in the ass-cheek before it ricocheted into his back, actually drawing blood.

I lifted my fist in victory, but quickly realized he hadn't stopped to go get his drink. He was... cheating—ignoring the projectile.

"I wouldn't do that, Coran!" I shouted. He ignored that, too.

"You should probably teach him a lesson," Echo cooed in my ears, bending down to tweak my nipples playfully.

I jolted, slapping her hands away. "Hey! Easy, Edna Shellhands! I have sensitive nipples!" She roared with her smoky laughter and I resumed my glare at Coran's back as he made his way after Achilles—who was running with the ball to the goal.

Gunnar suddenly roared beside me and fucking hurled his mermaid at another opponent attempting to plant himself in Achilles' path. She laughed loudly as she sailed through the air, but his drunken aim was slightly off. His mermaid more than made up for it by stretching out with her hands to grapple the mermaid on the merman's shoulders, sending them both splashing into the pool and clearing a path for Achilles.

But Coran was going to cut him off.

I took a deep breath and patted Chloe on the ass. "Feel like flying?"

"Oh, absolutely."

I didn't even wait, dropping into a crouch and hurling her as hard as I could. She flew through the air and tackled Coran into the water. He splashed down head-first, sending his rider flying. He came back up with a snarl, but my girl simply straddled him and began making out with him. Then the mermaid who had been on his shoulders joined in, distracting him entirely.

Achilles scored, and I hooted with a fist in the air.

"I'm a winner!" I shouted at the top of my lungs. "I told you, mom!" I added without really thinking first.

Alucard turned to me, cocking his head at my specific choice of words. "What?" he asked in a muffled voice.

"Forget about it. We've got somewhere to go," I told him.

Our team lowered their mounts and we gathered in a small circle at the conch, those on the sidelines cheering us on.

Asterion glanced up at them. "Shouldn't they be cheering for their home team?" he asked, tearing off his shredded unicorn mask.

His mermaid flicked his massive nose ring playfully. "Winners drink!" she hooted.

"Sweet gods," he said, shaking his head. "Do you guys always drink like this?" he asked no one in particular.

I sighed, wading over to the conch. "Let's do it. We have more to do after this."

Everyone drank, and we said our goodbyes—well, Coran and his two groupies were occupied on the edge of the pool, not bothering to hide their amorous activities from the rest of the group. Then again, it was a nudist pool, and apparently that meant whatever could be seen could be fondled. I didn't object to that but would have been interested in experiencing it first-hand—just to make sure it was fair.

Achilles' mermaid planted a long, wet kiss on his lips and then pulled away. "Come back soon. And don't forget your new drinking rule."

I leaned forward, wondering what they had chosen. Gunnar and the rest were frowning. Achilles was frowning for entirely different reasons, of course, as if considering abandoning us already.

She skipped back from his reach. "When someone says *Shark Attack*, you all have to get your feet off the ground. Last one to do so drinks."

One of the mermaids from the other team had backstroked over to us, her goods on full display as she floated near us on her back. Her entire torso was also covered in intricate ocean-themed tattoos that looked so sharp and clear they could have been real. Part of it was even what looked to be an authentic treasure map rendition. The detail led me to believe it was either real or meticulously designed prior to her putting it on her skin.

We obviously ogled her and her tattoos since she was swimming like that only to get a rise out of us. "Don't accept any test tube shots on Bourbon Street. They're a rip off, for one, but they're also a great way to get drugged... unless you're into that kind of thing, I guess." Then she was floating past us, humming softly to herself. The moonlight hitting the pale wet canvas of her tattooed body was—in all seriousness—so beautiful that I knew I would remember it forever. All dirty jokes about treasure-hunting aside.

We nodded, climbing out of the pool unsteadily, the effects of our drinking much more noticeable on dry land. This is also when we were reminded that we, too, were naked. Which resulted in a whole lot of awkward facing away from each other and hands over our goods. The mermaids rolled their eyes and decided this obligated them to play keep-away with our now dry clothes, which produced a flopping, hopping game of tag that left us breathless and laughing despite our indecency.

Especially since everyone laughing at the game was also as naked as the day is long.

They kept our masks as mementos, but we didn't really put up a fight to keep them. They had served their purpose.

CHAPTER 5

I rolled my eyes at the repetitive debate behind me, likely fueled by the alcohol in our bloodstreams, making our mental capacities fuzzy.

"For the third time," Alucard reminded the Minotaur. "We're visiting Freaks-only locations, so you don't have to worry about any humans recognizing that you're a giant fucking bull." The two of them were weaving back and forth between the tables of the rickety bar where I had made a Gateway from the mermaids' pool.

The Alcochemist. I'd heard rumors about this place, but only that it was a fun bar for us supernatural folk to have a unique, custom-made drink while in New Orleans, which seemed obvious based on the clever name. Not just Alchemist—those who meddled in magical chemistry—but Alco-chemist, a play on words combining alcohol and alchemist.

The old bar was full of patrons from all walks of life. I saw a few witches —I think—a handful of shifters, some vampires, and a few other flavors I didn't dare bother asking about. There was even a man in stereotypical voodoo priest attire. Judging by the wide berth everyone gave him, I presumed he was the real deal. The patrons watched—our progression through the bar resembling nothing more than a drunken stampede on our way to the watering hole. It would have been even more appropriate if we'd kept our unicorn masks.

"Shark attack," I said loudly, grinning as I hopped up onto a barstool and lifted my feet.

Asterion leapt for one of the stools, but it shattered under his enthusiasm and he dropped to his ass with a loud crash. The rest of our party scrambled up onto barstools, laughing at Asterion who was mumbling as he climbed to his feet. The rest of the bar chuckled when it was apparent we weren't purposely causing problems, but merely playing shenanigans.

I glanced up at the bartender, and instantly leaned away from the intensity of his eyes. He was a middle-aged man with luxurious silver hair and a pregnant caterpillar of an oiled and curled mustache, but he looked at me as if I was an ingredient rather than a person. He slid a large glass of dark beer towards Asterion, and the liquid was emitting vapor of some kind like smoke or steam, but I could tell it wasn't hot. "They got you, old friend," he said to the Minotaur, smiling slightly.

Asterion grunted and then sniffed at the drink warily. He looked up sharply at the barman. "What is it this time, Flamel?" he asked. "And it's nice to see you, too. Bastard."

I looked from one to the other. "*The* Nicolas Flamel?" I asked, fangirling a little.

The two nodded, not looking at me. I really should have guessed that one from the name of the bar, the Alcochemist. Nicolas Flamel was the fabled alchemist who had figured out how to turn substances into gold. I wondered if his wife was kicking around somewhere—Perenelle Flamel.

Asterion scooped up the strange brew and downed it surprisingly fast. I say surprisingly, because it smoked out of his nose as he did, looking as if it was burning his insides. He set the empty mug down, eyes widening and pupils dilating instantaneously. He finally looked back up, shaking his head. "Much better than turning things into gold."

I frowned at a distant thought, remembering that Asterion was also pals with King Midas, the man who could turn items into gold with his touch. I wondered if the Minotaur had realized his tendency for making goldsmiths his friends, or if he was entirely aware and had a specific motive behind it. Maybe it was so he could order replacement nose rings on call?

"What's the game here?" I asked the immortal alchemist.

"A bull-riding contest and to protect your voodoo bride," Flamel said, grinning through perfectly, pearly white teeth. I blinked in confusion, but he was already pulling out a human-sized, female plush doll like a large stuffed animal. She wore a bridal veil and tasteful lingerie, but she was way too anatomically correct, making her inappropriate to carry around town.

Flamel handed the doll to Gunnar who took it with a frown. "Am I supposed to carry it around with me? Who's to say I don't toss it in a dumpster or take it back to our hotel?"

"Firstly, I'm not telling you where our hotel is," I said, grinning. "Secondly, he's got a suspicious twinkle in his eyes..." I said, eyeing Flamel.

Nicolas grinned with his teeth. Then he reached out and poked the voodoo bride with a toothpick. Gunnar grunted in surprise, slapping at his own forearm where a tiny droplet of blood had welled up—the same spot Nicolas had stabbed on the doll. "Voodoo," he reminded us. "And at some point tonight, you'll have people trying to take it from you, but I'm not privy to the details of that escapade."

My mouth was hanging open. I hadn't been privy to details on what we would encounter either. I had merely worked with Alucard on setting up the contacts for various hangout spots in town and where we could go for a fun game and a new drinking rule at each destination. The only stipulation was that the hosts swore on their blood to act in good faith. That way we knew we weren't walking into a trap, or that we accidentally killed a group of creatures simply trying to play a prank on us. In exchange for their cooperation, we had promised not to ask them for forewarning. That way it was a surprise for all of us, not only Gunnar.

I knew only the vaguest of details on where we were going after each encounter, but our hosts could easily change the destinations if they saw fit. But this... was getting interesting. There was actually a bit of danger to this one.

"How do we know this isn't a trap?" Gunnar asked, wobbling slightly on his stool.

Nicolas waved a hand. "We don't want to start a war, that's why. We've all heard about the craziness your crew causes up in St. Louis. The doll can hurt you, definitely, but nothing permanent or serious. Just a little pain." He said this with an eyeroll, as if asking if Gunnar needed a Band-Aid or a kiss for his owie.

Gunnar looked slightly doubtful, but I slapped him on the shoulder.

"They all made blood oaths. We're fine. Like the mermaids. Fun and pain, but nothing serious."

"I want to hear more about this other bullshit," Achilles grinned, reminding us of Flamel's other admission.

Alucard was snoring on the bar-top, so I glanced up at Nicolas with a questioning look. He smiled with a slow nod. I leaned over to shove Alucard off his chair, depositing him to the floor. "Shark attack," I said once he jumped to his feet with a surprised grunt.

His eyes narrowed, but Nicolas was already pouring him one of those smoking beers. To be honest, I was inclined to simply ask for one, but that might have been alcohol-induced bravery. "Ah, Betty," Nicolas said reverently, pointing at an enclosed ring in the far corner of the bar where a pristine, golden mechanical bull was currently being ridden by a vampire. Nicolas slid Alucard his penalty beer as the rest of us watched the bull hurl the vampire into the low wall surrounding the ring. He jumped back to his feet a moment later, chuckling as he shook his head at his fellow vampire pals. Then Betty emitted the angriest *mooing* sound I had ever heard—much scarier than any *moo* I'd ever heard Asterion bellow.

From the look on Asterion's face, he realized he needed to step up his mooing game.

Alucard pounded his beer in one pull, gasping at the end as he stared down at the empty mug, his eyes also instantly dilating like Asterion's had. What was in that stuff?

Alucard extended his fingers, inspecting them with an incredulous look. "I think I can feel my cells vibrating."

Nicolas nodded matter-of-factly. "Infused with more vitamins than a human body can process, but with supernatural beings it's practically an energy drink for your soul. Kills colds in their tracks, helps increase your alcohol tolerance, and often obliterates the chance at a hangover in the morning." He met my eyes. "But with this being a bachelor party, I'm not making any promises. You five look like you're ready to set some new records in the Alcolympics."

I grinned eagerly. "We're Beerlympians," I said, agreeing with him.

Nicolas cocked his head, scratching at his chin. "That's... actually not a bad name for this beer..." he said thoughtfully, eyeing the empty stein. He promptly licked his finger and wrote *Beerlympian* on the tap for the keg where he had pulled our beers. I blinked in astonishment to find the word permanently etched into the handle, but the rest of my friends were busy staring at the bull. Nicolas noticed my attention and winked at me.

Alchemists were pretty damned cool. Maybe I would hire him for a few side projects...

"That's it?" Alucard drawled, turning back to Nicolas. "We just have to ride the bull?" I frowned at the gleaming mechanical bull that was wildly rocking back and forth, tossing a shifter to the pads below. Gunnar was poking a finger at his voodoo bride's boobs, chuckling every time he felt the same sensation on his own pecs. It was kind of masturbatory in a way.

I reached over and grabbed a tight fistful of the voodoo bride's boob and he almost fell off his stool with a shout. I burst out laughing. "Quit fondling your doll or we'll start fondling her, too," I told him.

Nicolas cleared his throat to get our attention; we turned to find him grinning at us like a loon, leaning over the bar. "It looks like the other team is running late, so you have a few minutes to get a practice run or two in. Your top three members will form a team to compete with your challengers, and whichever group has the most cumulative seconds astride Betty wins. The losing team has to fulfill a dare from the victors." We frowned thoughtfully, sharing long looks at his sinister smile. "If anyone lasts eight seconds or longer, every member on the other team has to drink one of these...Beerlympians," he added with a low laugh. "And every time one of your teammates falls *before* the eight second mark, each of you must drink a Beerlympian. Even those *not* competing," he clarified.

I realized that he had placed fresh Beerlympians before each of us, and that none of us had noticed him do it. "I think what he's trying to say is that we are going to be hammered in about eight seconds," I told my friends, neatly summarizing Flamel's game.

Gunnar grinned competitively. "Cheers, gents," he slurred slightly, lifting his mug. "This one should be a piece of cake after the mermaids. I think it's obvious I should be on the team. Me and my voodoo bride will last longer than eight seconds. Easy."

"Famous last words," I muttered, grinning. Alucard burst out laughing at the double entendre.

Nicolas pointed at Betty and we all turned to watch a shifter climb onto her back. He was a large, strong son-of-a-bitch, his back about as wide as a billboard. He lasted about two seconds before being thrown entirely from the ring. I blinked in disbelief. Betty hadn't thrown the vampire *that* hard. Nicolas chuckled. "Betty matches her rider's strengths, otherwise any big son-of-a-bitch could just walk in and outmuscle her."

I eyed the bull doubtfully, and then lifted my glass to the others. "Slowest chugger goes first?" I asked. Everyone shook their heads, all pointing at Asterion in unison.

"I think it's fairly obvious who should go first," Achilles said with a grin.

Asterion simply downed his beer. "Let me show you how it's done," he growled, wiping his Minotaur goatee—which was smoking from the Beerlympian foam, making him look menacing.

We grinned excitedly, pounding back our own beers as we watched Asterion make his way over to dominate Betty. I stared down at my Beerlympian in awe, licking my lips and waving at the vapor drifting out of my mouth. Alucard was blowing smoke rings with his, giggling gleefully.

I felt like crying.

It was so delicious I didn't quite know what to do with my hands. I realized I was rubbing at my lips, marveling at the sensory overload like I had just popped ecstasy. That's when I really took stock of the strange feeling Alucard had mentioned—the slight tingle to my skin as if I had recently chugged a pre-workout drink and felt strong enough to take on the world or lift every weight at the gym.

Nicolas was already pouring us another round, obviously having no faith in Asterion. I frowned at that. Nicolas apparently knew him from back in the day, so should have been a believer. After all, what kind of mechanical bull was a match for the Minotaur?

Nicolas sensed me watching him and glanced over his shoulder. "Just watch. Daedalus made Betty. Asterion doesn't stand a chance."

My eyes widened. The man who had made the labyrinth that had trapped Asterion in the first place had resorted to making mechanical bulls? It was well-known in the supernatural community that to say Daedalus made something was akin to saying it was the most structurally sound creation ever erected.

Which meant...

I turned to check on Asterion.

He was already lying on his back, staring up at the ceiling with incredulous eyes. I checked the timer on the wall.

He hadn't lasted even two seconds. Betty let out a triumphant *moo*, mocking the big bull god.

"Shit," I said, accepting the new drink Nicolas slid my way. "Betty made the Minotaur her bitch."

Achilles grunted, staring at his fallen friend with disbelief. "I have a feeling she's about to make us all her bitch. Who did you say we were competing against again?" he asked distractedly, scanning the patrons as if to scout out our challengers.

Nicolas smiled. "You'll know when they arrive."

I frowned at his tone, not liking it one bit. "You guys want to double down on Asterion or give Betty a slap and tickle yourselves? We still need to pick our top three before our...challengers show up, and I think a few practice runs will do us some good."

Their lack of confidence was overwhelming. As was the laughter of those in the bar.

None were louder than Nicolas Flamel as Asterion tried—and failed—again. Achilles rolled up his sleeves, storming off to give it a go.

CHAPTER 6

All in all, we got in three practice rides each before returning to the bar, surprisingly drunk and ridiculously thirsty—yet fully functional, thanks to Flamel's Alchemy beer. It really was a marvel. I felt ridiculously drunk but I wasn't a sobbing mess or anything—like the Beerlympian had given us all the benefits of being wasted without any of the consequences. My skin still tingled faintly, dancing with energy but not in a jittery over-caffeinated fashion.

Flamel had turned beer into the equivalent of liquid gold.

Despite that, none of us had performed even remotely as well as Asterion had on Big Bad Betty. We were hotly debating who was going to form our competitive bull-riding team—most of us angling to get *out* of the team—when the front door of the bar slammed into the wall with a concussive *bang*.

I turned to see a trio of leather-clad warrior princesses standing in the open door. Those patrons close to the door had wordlessly picked up their drinks and changed tables deeper into the bar. Some were even pressed up against the wall, averting their eyes.

I frowned, ignoring Nicolas' dark chuckle as I studied the three strange women.

"Where are our fuzzy little man-peaches?" the one in front demanded in a low, booming tone. It was still feminine, but tough like a drill sergeant.

Their dystopian-chic armor, and the many, many blades tucked into the little fun folds and curves of their bodysuits, definitely announced that they meant business. The two that hadn't spoken were taller than the leader, but very different from one another.

The woman on the left was the tallest and looked to be in her mid-thirties with wavy, golden-blonde hair, as thick as a goose-down comforter, that hung freely down her back. She had a single, thin braid down the left side of her jaw and wore a natural smirk on her narrow face. Her eyes reminded me of storm clouds.

The other barely looked to be in her mid-twenties and maybe weighed a hundred pounds, soaking wet. Her sandy-blonde hair hung in a short braid that cut off abruptly at the base of her neck, as if bunched together and then cut with a blade. Her features were more reserved and thoughtful—analytical rather than emotional.

The leader, who had introduced herself by asking for the man-peaches, had a spiked mohawk that ended in a blonde tail down the back of her neck and she had faint blue runes tattooed under her eyes. She was shorter and more heavily-muscled than her girlfriends. The chest of her armor was unfastened and tucked beneath the leather was a fan of throwing knife hilts that concealed most of her cleavage. I considered it a subtle hint that she didn't approve of peepers; the thought made me suddenly erupt with laughter. Her raptor gaze locked onto me and her eyes narrowed.

I glanced over upon hearing a breathy gasp from Achilles. He was staring at the trio like it was either the second coming of Zeus or as if Aphrodite herself had slid into the bar on velvet slippers and dental floss to ask if anyone wanted to maybe Netflix and definitely bone.

"I'll be her fuzzy little man-peach…" the legendary Greek warrior whispered reverently, his dilated eyes locked onto the leader. Alucard frowned over at him, noticed my equally surprised look, and finally shrugged with a bemused smirk.

Her friends were grinning expectantly at our squad, and then one of them pointed directly at us. They strode over, owning every single step along the way as if entering the gates of a smoldering city they had just vanquished. They stopped in front of Gunnar—who had placed his voodoo bride on his lap, wrapping one possessive arm around her shoulders while his other fist held his beer stein in a casual grip. He showed not one iota of concern, only revealing an expectant twinkle in his eye as he smirked in their general direction.

The leader's grin grew wider and she dipped her head respectfully.

Asterion folded his arms. "I feel like these princesses showed up to the wrong tea party." I held my breath, ready to go down swinging as his words registered.

But the leader belted out sudden laughter, her allies grinning from ear to ear as they nodded approvingly at Asterion. I let out a slow, relieved breath. I'd anticipated that the unexpected jibe from our most courteous member would have resulted in a lot more flames, screaming, and bloodshed.

She wiped at her eyes and slapped Asterion's beefy bicep good-naturedly. "Let's put these boys to sleep," she said, turning to Nicolas. "Pour us a round, Flamel."

Unsurprisingly, Nicolas was already sliding three mugs towards the women.

The three stepped up to the bar, and the scent of oiled leather, hot metal, and horseflesh was as thick as perfume around them. It wasn't necessarily a bad smell, but it was definitely pungent. Like a blacksmith. Achilles loomed over the top dog's shoulder, taking an indiscreet, big whiff like a creep. The warriors downed their beers in one pull, wiping their mouths with their sleeves, not even commenting on the vapor. Then the head bitch blindly flung her stein behind her, striking Achilles in the jaw.

It shattered over his face and he blinked rapidly. He managed to not lose his balance and didn't show any sign of pain, despite the fresh cuts on his face. The leader turned to look at him as if she had only just now noticed him.

He locked gazes with her, eyes as fiery as if he was challenging her to a duel. "I'm going to ride Betty like my life depends on it," he promised in a throaty growl. "And after *that* I'm going to kiss those plump lips of yours. Understood?"

She nodded very, very slowly.

He turned his back on her and began walking towards the bull, rolling up his sleeves in the process. "Get off your ass, then. I don't feel like waiting for that kiss," he growled from over his shoulder.

I raised my brows, literally speechless. I locked eyes with Alucard who was slowly shaking his head at Achilles' back, as amazed as I was. Gunnar and Asterion gave stiff nods and hopped off their stools to join Achilles—apparently volunteering for the remaining team openings.

The three women shared a significant look before following suit.

"Who are they?" Alucard asked, plopping down on the stool beside me.

Nicolas didn't turn to look at us, but he was smiling as he answered. "Valkyries..."

"Oh, man. That is not good," I breathed, rounding on Alucard. "You never mentioned that addition," I growled accusingly. "Ashley will kill me if anything happens to Gunnar."

Alucard was holding up his hands. "I didn't know either. I just reached out to *him!*" he said, pointing a finger at Flamel.

Nicolas grunted. "They swore the oath. Don't worry. Your friend is as safe as a babe..." but I caught a faint flicker of a frown on his face.

"You sure about that?" I asked him.

Instead of answering, he lifted up a tray of drinks and left the bar, passing them out among the crowd as recompense for all the hubbub. I grabbed my own beer—which Nicolas had magically refilled—and motioned for Alucard to do the same.

Then we made our way over to the ring like we were walking to the gallows. I saw Gunnar boldly mount Betty in front of the crowd now circling the ring. He tied his voodoo bride's arms in a knot and draped her over his neck like a cape before latching onto the handhold and signaling Asterion to hit the mysterious button that made Betty go so wild, so fast.

The irony wasn't lost on me, folks. The Minotaur knew how to find Betty's hot button.

Asterion slapped it and jumped back with a monstrous bellow of excitement.

CHAPTER 7

G unnar howled loudly as the gleaming bull tried to kill him. For the first two seconds, it seemed like he might stand a fighting chance, but then Betty jerked forward abruptly. He did a painful-looking front flip and landed flat on his back on the mat. Amazingly, his voodoo bride had flown free from his shoulders and got wrapped around the handhold where she stuck. The bride had lasted longer than the groom.

Probably typical for most newlyweds.

The Valkyries were cackling as Gunnar climbed to his feet, frowning. He scooped up his voodoo bride and made his way over to us. Nicolas Flamel appeared at my side as if by magic, extending a tray of three mugs brimming with more of the Beerlympian brew. Asterion, Achilles, and Gunnar each grabbed one and the five of us downed our drinks as we watched the Valkyries prep for their first ride.

Heh. Ride of the Valkyries...

To be honest, I didn't know much about Valkyries. I'll admit I never considered running into them at a bar, assuming they were too busy saving fallen heroes from the fields of battle to whisk souls off to Valhalla—the hall of the slain—otherwise known as Odin's buffet table.

There, the claimed souls were trained to be Einherjar—warriors for Ragnarok, the Norse version of the Apocalypse. I'd also heard that when they weren't training their Einherjar they were feeding them barrels of mead, so I was pretty sure they were open to a little hanky-panky—meaning that Achilles just might have a chance at that kiss he apparently wanted more than anything in the world.

The leader shot Achilles a sultry look as she prepared to mount Betty, some silent debate happening between the two warriors. Achilles grinned knowingly, and the leader hesitated. After a long pause, she stepped back and let the tall brunette take her place as first ride.

The crowd was silent as they watched the leader slap the button to get Betty a-bucking. The Valkyrie gritted her teeth and latched on with a familiar calm. Betty jerked back and forth, and the Valkyrie flowed with it easily, but then Betty snapped sideways and spun in a full circle, hurling the rider directly into Asterion's chest.

The Minotaur didn't even budge as the Valkyrie hit him with a grunt and fell to the mat. Asterion glanced down—not at the fallen rider, but at his own chest—and brushed his hand across his prayer beads as if wiping some crumbs from his fur. Then he simply walked past her and mounted Betty.

The Valkyrie climbed to her feet, her face a thunderhead, and we watched satisfactorily as the Valkyries drank their beers. Asterion took a deep breath, kissed his prayer beads, and Achilles slapped Betty's hot button.

Betty went buck-wild, faster and crazier than I'd seen her move so far. I heard the handle groan as Asterion gripped it tightly in one massive fist, but it was hopeless. He was tossed over the wall surrounding the bull ring— where he bowled over a group of bystanders who had been too busy drinking to notice the *Moo-teor*—a Minotaur meteor—hurtling their way like a hunk of alien rock in the darkest sections of deep space.

He jumped to his feet with a growl and I heard the Valkyrie he had snubbed chuckle mockingly. She mimed pounding a drink and folded her arms, staring back at him defiantly. Nicolas appeared with our beers and we all drank. I wobbled uncertainly as I tried to set the stein back on the tray, but I didn't feel sick or anything. Just tipsy as all hell. One quick look at my crew told me they weren't faring any better.

Even Achilles—for all his bravado—was weaving slightly, like a tall tree in the breeze, swaying left and right so subtly that he might not even realize he was doing it. The head Valkyrie seemed to notice, judging by the smile she was biting back. She motioned for the other Valkyrie to go, saving herself for last—like Achilles.

Long story short, she didn't fare much better than her fellow, but overall, the Valkyries were stomping our asses on the cumulative time-clock. If Achilles could last eight seconds, we might stand a chance. But if the lead Valkyrie matched *that*, we were screwed.

Achilles strolled up to the bull, trailing his hand across her flank as if she were a real beast he was trying to soothe and calm. He began climbing up onto Betty, but before he could get seated—while he was perched on her back on the balls of his feet—the lead Valkyrie slapped the button.

Betty immediately bucked back and forth, sending Achilles into a double backflip directly above the bull. Then he landed face-first onto her saddle with a sickening crunch of broken cartilage and flopped off to the side. He lay on his back, eyes wide as he panted in understandable bewilderment, likely wondering what the hell had just happened.

The lead Valkyrie leaned over him, grinning. She extended her hand to help him up and Achilles' eyes cleared long enough to accept the help. She pulled him to his feet, and at the last minute he leaned in for a kiss.

He managed to make contact before she reared back and headbutted him back to the mat.

Her forehead was bleeding as she climbed onto Betty with casual arrogance, held on with one hand, and nodded at one of her warriors to slap the button. Like she was a willow in the wind, she rode Betty as if born for it, not even remotely losing her balance or faltering.

And she stared at Achilles the entire time.

He had propped himself up with his hands, his face a mask of blood, and he grinned at her through bloody teeth, shaking his head in wonder. The timer hit eight seconds, but she rode it for a few more before kicking the button to shut Betty down.

The crowd burst into applause, catcalling and hooting loudly.

Nicolas cleared his throat beside us, proffering two drinks for each of us because we'd forgotten to drink after Achilles' ride was sabotaged. To be honest, I wasn't even upset that she had tricked him because with her performance, we would have lost anyway.

Achilles approached us with his arm wrapped around the lead Valkyrie's shoulders, totally unconcerned about his bloody face. "Totally worth it," he said, snatching up a stein, pounding it, and then doing the same with his second beer.

The rest of us double-fisted our beers as we made our way back to the bar, smiling and laughing with the Valkyries—who were suddenly much more conversational after the competition, as if it had forged bonds of friendship to get our asses handed to us so blatantly.

But we'd done it with class—which we humbly disguised as fumbling awkwardness for the crowd's sake.

CHAPTER 8

We settled back at the bar and I listened absently as the Valkyries began talking to Asterion, Gunnar, and Achilles, introducing themselves for the first time. I focused on remaining vertical, narrowing my eyes to improve my vision. At least it felt like it was helping. It probably just made me look standoffish, but it was better than looking comatose on the floor if I took a chance at walking around.

Herja was the lead Valkyrie—currently suffering Achilles' amorous affections. The Greek hero was following her around like her personal bodyguard, or perhaps a particularly aggressive guard-puppy. I heard her tell Achilles that her name meant *devastate*. That was either a not-so-subtle hint that she had reached her limit with him or a very honest warning he should probably heed before romanticizing their future relationship status.

The taller, wavy-haired Valkyrie was named Kara, and she was proudly telling Asterion that it meant *wild*. The Minotaur's face had the intense focus of someone who was so out-of-his-mind drunk that he was simply trying to catch every third or fourth word in order to guess whether he needed to nod or shake his head in response.

The last, and seemingly youngest, Valkyrie with the lopped-off hair was named Olrun, and although polite, she wasn't as talkative as the others, only giving Gunnar and his plush voodoo bride single syllable answers. I motioned for Nicolas to pour two more beers and slid one her way, smiling pleasantly. She looked suddenly relieved and pounded her beer in one go before plopping down on the seat beside me.

"Thank the gods," she breathed. "I needed that."

I frowned in amusement. "Why didn't you just ask for one, then?"

She pursed her lips as if debating on how to answer. "I'm not as comfortable talking to men. I always get tongue-tied."

I scoffed. "Well, look at you go! You're talking to a genuine manly man right now," I laughed, motioning at my body with my hands. "And you're not remotely tongue-tied."

She eyed me, looking abruptly hungry. I stiffened in my chair, wondering if I had missed a few minutes of the conversation or something. "We should talk," she murmured. "Later. When you're finished with your friends," she added in a huskier tone, practically panting as she leaned closer to me, licking her lips.

My eyes widened further, and I decided that either Nicolas had added a little something-something extra to her beer or that I had *definitely* missed major parts of our conversation. What had I *said* to flip her hormone switch so deftly? I realized that I really wanted to know the answer for future reference. But no matter how hard I tried, my mind only produced the sounds of crashing alcohol waves in my cranium.

Herja came to my rescue, swatting Olrun's arm with the back of her hand, snapping her out of a Valkyrie's equivalent of feline heat. "Easy, Olrun. He's just a mortal. They are quite breakable from what I've seen," Herja teased, but something in her eyes let me know she was slightly serious, and that the potential danger Olrun's flirting offered was very real.

Olrun pouted in disappointment and finally leaned back into her stool, muttering under her breath.

Rather than attempting to trade wits with Herja, I used the distraction to hop off my stool in search of Alucard. I found him down the bar openly glaring at a trio of vampires seated around a table-top a dozen paces away. The vampires shot me pleasant smiles and continued drinking. I turned back to Alucard. "What gives?" I asked him.

He grunted. "I don't trust the local vampires," he said in a low drawl. He didn't elaborate, and I knew I probably would have forgotten his answer in four minutes tops anyway, so I let it go.

Herja clapped her hands to catch our attention. My crew turned to face her, but I noticed the vampires get up from their table and casually make their way over as well. My shoulders tightened, expecting an attack, but they simply walked up to Herja, grinning wide enough to reveal their fangs.

"You princesses ready for your dare?" she asked us. We nodded, wondering what craziness could top the last two challenges. "I dare you all to go streaking around the block."

We stared at her as if we hadn't heard her correctly, our smiles faltering. "Um, that's the opposite of fun," I suggested. My friends instantly mumbled their agreement.

Herja shrugged piteously. "That's the dare. Refusal will result in a visit to the type of strip club none of you would *ever* want to visit...Cockodile Skins would eat you alive. Literally."

We put a lid on our protests so fast that the sudden silence was almost deafening, letting me realize that practically the entire bar was now listening. Herja nodded matter-of-factly and mimed brushing off her hands as she jerked her chin at the vampires standing beside her. "This is Julian."

"I don't think our streaking dare requires anymore dong on the roster," Alucard said, narrowing his eyes at Julian.

The vampire chuckled, shaking his head. "Don't worry. We won't be streaking."

And his lack of explanation seemed to imply a whole lot. Was this part of our bachelor party schedule or Valkyrie improv?

The rest of the bachelor party sighed in relief that Julian wasn't participating in the streaking, not picking up on the undertones, but Alucard cleared his throat. "What about our new drinking rule?" he asked Herja, eyes still fixated on Julian and his vampires.

Herja beamed. "An old one, but a good one. Anytime the bachelor mimes putting horns on his head like a Viking helmet," she began, holding up a finger on either side of her head like a bull, "any of you within earshot must pretend to row a boat. The last one to row has to drink."

Gunnar straightened happily. "This one is *much* better than the stupid shark thing."

Herja nodded and held out a hand for Julian to take over. The crowd around us was growing, especially at the mention of the Valkyrie's dare to streak around the block. I wondered if any of us were sober enough to survive it, decided we probably weren't, but that we had the sheer willpower to at least die trying.

That brief rational thought floated away like a puff of dandelion seeds as I turned to face the vampires to hear what they had to do with the dare, all the while keeping a close eye on Alucard—who looked ready to murder them all at the slightest provocation, real or imagined.

CHAPTER 9

Julian cleared his throat, smiling excitedly as he rubbed his hands together. Herja, Kara, and Olrun swaggered up to the bar to request more drinks, leaving us to the vampires.

"Your goal is to streak one lap around the block. You can't return to the bar until you all finish your drinks and have the voodoo bride safe in hand." I frowned at the last part and Julian grinned wider. "We'll be trying to take her from you," he explained, looking at my best friend—who was suddenly clutching his doll with a death-grip. "Gunnar, right?" he asked. "This is Javier and Renaldo," he said, pointing a thumb at the other vampires who could have been brothers straight from Italy. They merely smiled rather than speaking, making me wonder if they spoke English or not. Julian extended his pale hand towards Gunnar. "My name is Julian."

Gunnar took it uncertainly, twisting his body so that his wife was safe from the vampire. "The Regulars will notice vampires chasing us through the streets," he said dryly.

Flamel cleared his throat. "I put a little something extra into your last beer," he admitted without an ounce of shame. "It will disguise your powers as something believable. If you stepped outside and began throwing a few fireballs, the non-magical folk would see the fire, of course, but they'd also see something like you throwing a Molotov Cocktail or a streetlamp exploding and starting a fire." I frowned doubtfully as he turned to Gunnar. "If you shifted, they would simply see a drunk man freaking the fuck out like he had just overdosed on bath salts," he chuckled.

I blinked a few times, impressed. "That's...really cool," I finally admitted.

Alucard pointed at the massive Minotaur. "What about him?"

The bartender smiled. "Just a big son of a bitch who is so drunk he believes he's a bull. It's New Orleans. People are used to seeing the bizarre down here." Before we could ask any more questions, Nicolas waved a dismissive hand at us. "Give us a few minutes to set up and we can begin." With that, Julian and Nicolas huddled together with the Valkyries, speaking in low tones.

I squinted at them suspiciously, wondering what they were planning. He'd said something about us having to finish our drinks before the game was over so maybe they were filling up sippy cups for us to take on the road.

"That woman could start Ragnarok with a single twerk," Achilles commented, openly scrutinizing Herja's rear. Without considering the consequences, I realized I had turned to see what he was talking about and found myself openly inspecting the lead Valkyrie's ass. She'd spent a lot of time in the squat rack—or maybe she deadlifted cars in her daily warmup sessions.

I realized how it might look with both of us checking out Herja's ass and quickly averted my eyes. "Sure, man," I said hurriedly, still trying to process the fact that Achilles had used the word *twerk* with a straight face.

But Achilles wasn't quite finished. "Her booty is about to wake the world serpent," he chuckled, leering. I immediately tensed as Herja's shoulders stiffened. Had she overheard him?

"What are you two staring at?" Asterion asked from directly over my shoulder, making me flinch since I hadn't realized he was looming behind me. Then he snorted loudly as he caught on. "Oh. Wow. That woman is *thick*..." he murmured in an approving tone. Too approving.

I lifted my hands in an *I'm innocent* gesture and tried to extricate myself from the suicidal conversation before anyone overheard, but the two didn't budge, so my only exit was to approach Herja—which wasn't going to happen. That would only make me the first casualty when she finally decided to let us know how she felt about us leering at her.

I was pretty sure I would never call a girl *thick* and expect a positive response, even though it was technically a compliment. I was sure that certain other factors were involved that granted one the right to use the word, but for the life of me I couldn't gather my thoughts to recall what those requirements were.

"There's really only one thing to do about a booty like that..." Achilles said in a serious tone. "Marry it."

"No," I warned him, shaking my head adamantly. "Whatever you're thinking, don't—"

But he was already striding past me.

That's when he noticed that Julian had a pale hand on Herja's shoulder, laughing as the vampire spoke to her in low tones. Achilles' face darkened, and he lost his balance, bumping into a table. It fell over, spilling drinks to the floor and causing Julian and Herja to look over at him.

Achilles more-or-less composed himself, fixed a territorial glare upon Julian, and then abruptly began shadow boxing the air in what he obviously presumed to be an intimidating display of power, but to me it merely looked like a middle schooler showing off for a gaggle of cheerleaders. Julian and Herja frowned in confusion, cocking their heads. Achilles—none the wiser —began panting with exertion as he continued to box, his eyes closed now as if he was envisioning the ass-whooping in his mind.

"What is he doing?" Julian asked, risking a glance at me.

I watched Tae-bo Achilles go at it—beating the living hell out of the air. "How the hell should I know?" I finally said.

Julian nodded slowly. "Right. I think we'll just wait for you guys outside. Don't dawdle."

He and his vampires left the bar, eyeing Achilles out of the corner of their eyes, as if he was a rabid dog. Achilles finally spent the last of his reserves because he stopped boxing and opened his eyes. Seeing Julian had left, he grunted in triumph and strode right into Herja's personal space.

"Marry me," he told her in a low growl, more of a command than a request. I groaned, ignoring Asterion's rumbling chuckle behind me.

For an immortal, Achilles sure hadn't learned much about women over the years, because I was fairly confident that was not how one proposed. She blinked back at him.

Once.

Twice.

Then she side-stepped in a rapid blur and uppercut him in the jaw, knocking him clear off his feet so hard that he went horizontal. She grabbed onto him on his way back down and broke his fall with a raised knee beneath his spine in the infamous back-breaker move. Luckily, Achilles was immortal, or the bachelor party would have officially ended right there.

He slid off her knee to flop to the ground with a wheezing grunt, staring up at her with dazed eyes. He opened his mouth to speak but looked suddenly queasy.

Herja came to the same conclusion—that Achilles was about to hurl—and promptly picked him up by the belt buckle to throw him through the floor-to-ceiling window at the front of the bar, sending him out into the street amidst a shower of shattered glass. Nicolas sighed in weary resignation. Had Herja killed him?

My jaw was hanging open as I stared through the broken window in disbelief, wondering if someone should call a paramedic or something.

The bar grew very quiet—the air as tense as a bank robbery in progress.

Gunnar turned to the rest of the bachelor party and promptly lifted his fingers to his head like Viking horns.

Alucard and I managed to begin rowing a heartbeat before Asterion, forcing the Minotaur to pound another Beerlympian that Nicolas handed him from a tray, somehow having slipped out from behind the bar like a specter with no respect for the rules of time and space.

But since I was rowing, I followed Gunnar out the front door of the bar, hoping I was sober enough for a quick jog around the block. How bad could it be?

CHAPTER 10

A chilles stood on the sidewalk, palms on his knees as he puked the contents of his stomach onto the pavement. *So much for Flamel's wonder brew*, I thought to myself. His vomit smoked just like the Beerlympians we'd been pounding back, and he blinked down at the puddle several times as if contemplating whether it was really smoking or if he had reached some secret, heightened level of drunk and was about to transcend into some Dionysian-level of godly inebriation.

Generally, if your vomit smoked, you probably needed to get checked into a hospital.

But not Achilles.

He wiped his mouth and let out a chuckle. "I think I'm ready to party now."

But the weirdest thing was that he was entirely naked. Well, except for a utility belt around his waist that contained six beer cans—a utili-beer belt. He finally seemed to notice his state of undress and burst out laughing. Turning to us, his eyes widened further, and he began laughing even harder. "Looks like we're *all* ready to party now," he hooted. I glanced down to see that I was also naked with only a fully-stocked utili-beer belt around my hips.

We all were.

Nicolas stood in the doorway, curling the points of his mustache between two fingers as he grinned at us. "I'd start running if I were you," he warned. "I tailored my spell so that the moment you exited my bar your clothes would disappear, and they won't reappear until you finish the race, your beers, and then return with Gunnar's voodoo bride intact. Remember, it's only one lap."

The Valkyries were sitting on stools at the bar, watching us through the broken window. They looked overly pleased with themselves—especially Olrun, who tapped her belt and winked at me, subtly indicating that the belts had been her idea.

Julian and his pals, Renaldo and Javier, were leaning against the wall, struggling not to openly laugh at us. "Streaking is both celebrated and frowned upon, here," Julian said, grinning with his fangs.

That's when I heard the clicking of many cameras. I spun to see a bachelorette party cheering and snapping pictures a few doors down from us. They cat-called Asterion specifically but didn't seem to notice he was a Minotaur, so Nicolas' home brew must have been working as well as he'd claimed.

Or they'd have been running and screaming.

My anxiety grew as I found that the streets were surprisingly full of drunken revelers and wandering tourists all clutching neon yard-length tubes of green alcohol—probably hurricanes, a local favorite.

"Drink your beer quickly," Julian advised. "We will count to one minute and then chase you down to steal the hand of your lady wife." Julian spoke loud enough for us all to hear over the leering crowd. "Circle the block with your beers finished and bride safely underhand," he said, rubbing his hands together, "and you'll get your clothes back."

Unsurprisingly, Achilles seemed the most comfortable with his nudity.

He had his hands on his hips and was proudly posing for Herja through the broken window. Then he popped a tab on one of his beers and pounded it in one pull before tossing the can into a nearby trashcan. Herja was studying Achilles with a hint of a smile, so maybe his pimp game was stronger than it had looked.

True love survived such petty things as shattered windows and broken spines.

Gunnar was grinning competitively. He pounded a beer and then crushed the empty can with one fist. The rest of us followed suit and tossed our empties at the trashcan. None of us made it into the receptacle.

Gunnar let out a loud belch. "I can easily outrun you three," he said, sneering at Julian.

The vampire's grin split wider. "I'm sure you could... which is why the rest of my friends are hidden on the path ahead of you. You'll never know which bystander is a..." his gaze considered the crowd and he changed what he had been about to say, "a *gang-fanger* intent upon ravaging your bride. Consider it a trust exercise, but with no real harm involved. A husband must protect his wife above all else..."

I frowned thoughtfully at Julian, surprised by the unexpected romantic advice he had just dished out. Especially since the sentimental moment hit us as we stood ass-naked on the sidewalk with the bachelorette party hooting and hollering at us to *save the girl*—having apparently picked up on the general highlights of our game.

Gunnar grunted, let out another belch, and then tucked his bride under his arm like a football. I opened a second beer and began hauling ass. Only after a dozen steps did I hear my friends catching up. That's when I also realized that running with several full cans of beer strapped to your hips only managed to turn them into alcohol bombs—the constant jostling only managing to shake them up. I wondered if anyone was even watching to make sure we finished our beers or if we could simply toss them to the side. Figuring the hidden vampires would be watching us, I decided not to risk throwing them away. The punishment would likely be worse than our current game.

This bachelor party was going to be the death of me.

As we ran—flopping around in all our glory—we began to draw a lot of attention. Especially when the vampires screamed behind us, "Ready or not, here we coooooooome!"

"Are we allowed to kill them by accident?" Alucard snarled as he ran, beginning to outpace me as he tried to chug his beer while running at vampire speed.

Gunnar was already on his third beer, dumping it into his mouth and all over his face, still clutching his bride under his other arm, her arms, head, and legs flapping in the wind as he ran. Achilles was running in what he thought was a straight line—but clearly wasn't—with a very determined look on his face. Asterion was snorting and bellowing as he ran, threatening to stop traffic with his above average display of man-meat.

Then again, I wasn't sure how the non-magical folk saw him, so maybe it was just the fact that five guys were streaking through the streets of the *Big Sleazy*, pounding beers and carrying a life-sized plushy bride in lingerie.

I wondered what all the pointing, picture-taking, cat-calling onlookers thought of our bizarre procession. I also wondered which ones might actually be thieving vampires in disguise, waiting for their chance to abscond with Gunnar's voodoo bride.

The first stretch of our four-street race went by in a blur.

Then we rounded our first corner and stumbled directly into a huddle of policemen.

It was a strange collection of officers because one policeman was sitting in his car talking to the other three—one on a patrol horse, one on a bicycle, and another on a Segway.

We knocked them all over except for the one in the car, and the mounted horse began kicking and rearing angrily at the sudden mayhem. A vampire dove out of the nearby crowd, attempting to snatch Gunnar's bride in the confusion, but Gunnar instinctively tossed her at Alucard. The vampire struck Gunnar in the chest, sending him slamming into the policeman who had flung open his door in a desperate attempt to arrest one, or all, of the naked invaders.

Gunnar flew through the open driver's side door and knocked the cop into the passenger seat where his head struck the window, knocking him out cold. The vampire had careened off Gunnar and broken through the rear window of the police car with his face so that his upper body was inside the vehicle while his legs remained hanging outside of the car.

He began struggling to escape but Achilles lifted a booted foot in a dramatic pose. "This. Is. *N'awlins!*" he roared, kicking the vampire squarely in the rear to send him fully into the back of the patrol car.

Gunnar blinked, stared at the unconscious policeman next to him, then the steering wheel in front of him. The vampire raged in the backseat like a non-cooperative perpetrator.

Without further hesitation, Gunnar grinned, flipped the sirens on, and slammed the pedal to the floor. He hung his head out the window, cackling madly as the cop car peeled out with screeching tires. "Get my bride to the rendezvous!" he howled.

The policemen on the ground were climbing back to their feet, hands reaching for their service pistols as they decided enough was enough. Asterion immediately dogpiled on top of them, batting the guns away and shouting for the rest of us to run.

I saw Julian and one of his pals gaining on us as they rounded the corner. Achilles hopped onto the policeman's horse without hesitation, and slapped its flank, "Giddy'up!"

Except Alucard was directly behind the horse, and the horse didn't appreciate the slap or his new rider very much. Sensing his impending doom, Alucard had already lifted the plush bride before him as a defensive shield. I opened my mouth to shout a warning, but I couldn't quite recall what I wanted to warn Alucard about. The inbound horse hooves were obvious. No, it was something about the voodoo bride...

The horse bucked and kicked its back hooves in response to Achilles' sharp slap. The hooves struck the voodoo doll in the face before connecting with Alucard behind her. The force knocked the doll free from his hands and sent Alucard cartwheeling back into Julian and either Rinaldo or Javier, tossing them out into the street.

I heard a loud *crash* in the opposite direction and glanced up to see Achilles galloping down the street, screaming at the top of his lungs like a lunatic. Then I saw the crashed cop car wedged into the booth of a street vendor who had been selling Mardi Gras beads. The strobing lights from the car turned the surviving beads into mini disco balls.

Gunnar, looking dazed, was crawling out of the car. He was also chugging one of his beers and tossing strings of beads around his neck, the trooper.

Asterion had climbed off the pile of policemen and I heard them groaning as they tried to recover, but it didn't sound like they'd be vertical anytime soon. Watching Gunnar scoop up his beads and drink his beer in alternating hands, I finally remembered what I had been wanting to warn Alucard about.

"I tried to warn Alucard," I told Asterion. "It's a voodoo doll bride, right? Horse hoof to *doll* equals horse hoof to *werewolf*." I pointed an unsteady finger at Gunnar as proof. He had several cuts over his forearms and face, but

I knew they would heal fast since he was a shifter with incredible healing abilities.

Asterion snorted, shaking his head. Instead of talking, he popped the tab of a beer from his belt and began chugging. I did the same—down to three beers now. Sensing the policemen were getting back up, my eyes settled on the lonely Segway and I smiled.

CHAPTER 11

Alucard was wrestling the two vampires back the way we had come, looking ridiculous as he tried to finish his beer in the process. I righted the bicycle and rolled it in his direction. "Alucard! Get on the bike and drink, bitch!"

The third vampire from the bar suddenly dove out from the crowd that surrounded Asterion and I, trying to scoop up the doll in the confusion. I snagged her leg and yanked her out of the way just in time, letting the vampire tumble into the other side of the crowd. The people went down like dominos with phones, drinks, and purses flying up into the air. The bridal veil landed around my neck as I hopped onto the Segway and leaned the handlebar forward to get moving, draping the doll over the front like she was the prow of my pirate vessel. "Tally hoooo!" I roared, pointing my finger in the air like one of the great pirate captains of history. I wished I could have been wearing Gunnar's eyepatch to really get into character.

Asterion easily matched my stride, and we beelined for Gunnar who was still crawling away from the car, the physical abuse both he and the doll had been through turning him into a drunken, naked, hot-mess of a man. Asterion scooped him up—along with a fistful of beaded necklaces—and draped the collection over the back of his wide neck.

"Don't forget to drink!" I screamed, trying to keep the Segway steady since its steering was apparently faulty.

Gunnar was wheezing as he tried to crawl up onto Asterion's shoulders like he wanted one of those shoulder-rides dads give to their toddlers. Then he ruined that image by popping a beer and downing it as Asterion did the same. Even better, Gunnar lifted his fingers to his temples, and since Asterion was already swinging his arms as he ran, it really did look like the Minotaur was rowing his Viking king down the streets of New Orleans.

I very purposely made sure not to ride right behind them because the visual image of a hairy Minotaur ass and a hairy Viking king straddling his shoulders was something I never would have been able to burn from my memory, even with a back-alley lobotomy.

But Asterion was drunk, and weaving as he ran, making our low-speed chase very difficult indeed—me trying to keep them in sight while not getting too close of a look at the horrifying view. Add to that, Gunnar was howling at the top of his lungs as if to encourage himself onward and spur on his Minotaur mount.

Achilles was far ahead of us and had found his own beads at some point. He was prancing around in circles in the middle of the street, hurling beads at onlookers. Since he was naked, they were hurling just as many beads right back at him, pelting him in the face more often than not.

Which meant he didn't notice the vampire suddenly launch up at him, tackling him from the horse and into the crowd of onlookers. Achilles was roaring with laughter as he jumped to his feet, crushing his last beer as he bolted onward, not giving one shit about the rest of the bachelor party or the vampire still tangled up in the pile of drunken onlookers.

I had been paying too much attention to Achilles and abruptly lost control of my Segway, overcorrecting too violently and sending me flying off into Asterion and Gunnar, knocking us down into a terrible game of naked-man Twister.

"My wife!" Gunnar roared in a muffled shout.

"I got her!" A new voice cried out, and we all managed to disentangle ourselves fast enough to see Alucard pedaling past us like Lance Armstrong on the finishing stretch of the Tour De France, reaching out to grab the voodoo bride. He succeeded, but she instantly got tangled up in the wheel and Gunnar let out a sudden yelp of pain, crashing to his knees and rolling on the ground, clutching his goods.

Alucard skidded to a stop, wincing as he looked from Gunnar to the plush doll that was firmly wedged between the bicycle wheel and frame. He tried backing up, but Gunnar only began to howl louder until Asterion let out a loud belch, tossing his last empty can down on the ground and scooping up the bike with one hand.

"Follow me if you want to live!" he roared, tearing off down the street with the bicycle and bride in one hand.

"You got this, Gunnar. Do it for Ashley!" I encouraged him. He let out a groan and began to shamble after us, wincing with each step and gritting his teeth.

But he did this while also pounding his last beer. Like I said, a trooper.

I shared a look with Alucard and popped all of my remaining beers straight from the holster. Then I began pounding them as I ran after the hobbling Gunnar. Alucard did the same, so it probably looked like the Alcothon—like when those marathoners are spraying water all over their faces during certain stretches of the race.

I heard sirens and police cars in the distance, and a whole lot of shouting. Things like, *Stop resisting, you're under arrest, officer down*, and *we need backup!*

We brave bastards ignored it all as we poured on the speed. Either we had lost the vampires, or things had gotten too chaotic in the chase and they had given up at the arrival of the police, because we made it back to the Alco-chemist without incident, our beers empty and voodoo bride intact—kind of.

Luckily, the bar front seemed oddly deserted compared to the other streets, so there were no witnesses to conveniently point out where the naked man-meat parade had ended their show.

Alucard and I stumbled back into the bar, laughing loudly with our arms draped over each other's shoulders for balance. We looked up to see the Valkyries turning to look at us as Achilles loudly informed Herja that he had single-handedly saved the day.

Herja seemed a lot more interested in him than earlier, but the concealed smirk on her face told me she didn't buy a word of it. I think she was more impressed by the fact that he found it necessary to try and woo her with such a bold-faced lie. The fact that she was the first person Achilles had wanted to brag to about the chase meant something special to her, despite her tough demeanor.

Julian and his two vampires were sitting at the bar, cackling with laughter, rehashing the real story for everyone at the bar. Since they hadn't managed to see everything, it became a drunken game of one-up where we all began laughing and shouting over each other about our own private moments of glory.

Nicolas' cheeks were wet with tears as he poured more drinks, shaking his head in amazement. "The bar is veiled, thank god, or we would have a SWAT team on our ass any minute. I count at least five felonies in that story," he wheezed.

Gunnar had carefully detached his bride from the bicycle that Asterion had brought into the bar and was tugging his clothes back on like the rest of us.

Except for Achilles, who was still naked and had somehow maneuvered himself onto Herja's lap. She didn't seem to mind this time, and I wondered if we were about to lose our first man of the night. Oh well, he'd been next-to-useless anyway.

CHAPTER 12

Achilles had swindled a few smooches from Herja, but Nicolas had made her put on bright red lipstick first so that Achilles could remember it in the morning since he was so drunk it was unlikely he would remember even a hint of tonight's adventures.

The rest of us were in similar straits.

Then the other two Valkyries had taken the lipstick and slowly put it on their own lips in very artistic designs, revealing they hadn't learned to color inside the lines in Valkyrie school. They puckered their ruby-red mouths and convinced us to sing karaoke.

We sang way too many songs, but we each earned a cheek full of sloppy lipstick kisses and even convinced the Valkyries to flash us. They wore chain-mail bras underneath their leathers, which kind of killed the moment, but by the way they acted about even revealing that much in front of a crowd, I was pretty sure it was a first and that we better act very fucking appreciative.

We gave them all our beads, which ended up being a surprising stash.

I high-fived Julian, who was snorting with laughter as he watched us. His pals were shaking their heads incredulously at the shit-show that was the St. Louis crew. "You guys are hardcore," Julian said, bumping fists with each of us.

Then he motioned for us to gather around him, so he could point us towards our next adventure. Honestly, I felt like Odysseus—that we were on a never-ending adventure when all I really wanted to do was make it home.

I acknowledged this weakness in silence, reminded myself that this was a bachelor party, and promptly drowned the thought with the ocean of beer sloshing around inside me.

"Okay," Julian began. "Your next—and last—stop is the Foxies strip club. Head three blocks North and then two blocks West. The entrance is impossible to miss since it has a giant orange and white foxtail painted on the outside, but it's in an alley so the non-magical crowd doesn't accidentally stumble inside. And your new drinking rule is *Tinkle Time*. Anytime one of you needs to pee you have to sing *Tinkle Bell, Tinkle Bell, join me at the wishing well*." He waited to make sure we got it before nodding. "If you forget to sing, you drink."

We nodded, said our goodbyes, and forcefully dragged Achilles from Herja's embrace, ignoring his promises of undying love and that he would come back for her.

Now that we were clothed, the streets felt much different. The night had died down somewhat, probably a result of the heavy police presence searching for us. Thinking of that, I took the lead of our shambling group and decided to take to the alleys rather than the main streets.

That was our first mistake.

CHAPTER 13

e'd been walking for about twenty minutes and were now hopelessly lost, but we didn't dare risk going back out onto the main streets because we had spotted too many cruising police cars patrolling the streets for us.

The rest of the bachelor party was debating about where we had taken a wrong turn.

"Two blocks west and three blocks north," Gunnar said confidently.

I rolled my eyes. "No. You're wrong."

He eyed me, leaning like a drunken sailor. "Oh, yeah? What did he say then?"

I opened my mouth to reply but hiccupped instead. I finally raked my fingers through my hair. "I don't know," I admitted. "But it wasn't three blocks west and two blocks east," I argued.

"No, I think that *is* what he said..." Alucard murmured, frowning to himself. "It sounds right. I'm sure of it."

Achilles scoffed. "That doesn't even make *sense!*"

"Why?" Asterion asked. "Sounds logical to me. I think I remember Julian saying that."

Achilles scratched at his stubbled cheeks. "Maybe you're—" he cut off abruptly, eyes widening. "Tinkle Bell, Tinkle Bell, join me at the pissing well!" And he immediately darted for the alley wall, unfastening his jeans to take a leak.

I grunted. "I couldn't remember the damned song. I've needed to pee for like ten minutes."

The group burst out laughing. Then Achilles shouted loudly. We spun, ready to kick some ass, but Alucard lost his balance and toppled over a collection of trash cans loud enough to wake the dead.

No one helped him up, searching the darkness for Achilles instead. I spotted him talking to two shadowy silhouettes in hooded robes. Achilles was shouting at them. "Of course, I can pee here! Don't you know who I am?"

We made our way closer to them, our fists balled in case there was a fight. As we neared, I felt a tickling sensation at the base of my neck as if we were being watched. The hooded figures turned to face us, noticing our aggressive postures. Their shoulders relaxed and they each lifted their hands as if to tell us they meant no harm.

One of them slowly reached one of his hands back to politely knock on a door behind him. The surface of the door seemed to shine as if freshly painted. As I came closer, I realized it looked more like scales than paint.

"We found it," I said, letting out a breath of relief. "That door looks *exactly* like Jose described."

My crew murmured their agreement, sounding suddenly excited to find a strip club after our long walk through the dark, dirty alleys of New Orleans.

The two hooded figures shared a silent look but were interrupted by the door opening partway behind them. A hand emerged to extend a tray of fun-looking shots in test tubes. One of the hooded figures accepted it with a murmured thanks and the door closed again.

"Ooooh," Asterion murmured. "Those look delicious."

Achilles grunted. "What's this swill?" he asked in a suspicious tone.

"Don't worry," one of the hooded figures said in a low rasp. "It's not poison."

Achilles took a step back. "Who said anything about poison? I was going to say that it looks like pure *estrogen*," he said.

Asterion was already thundering towards the tray, shoving us out of the way as he skidded to a stop before the suddenly terrified hooded figures. The Minotaur didn't seem to notice their fear, despite the fact that the hooded figure's hands were shaking so much that the tray was rattling. Asterion scooped up three of the test tube shots and pounded them all in one go. For some strange reason I couldn't quite place, I had a brief thought that drinking from those tubes was a horrible idea, but it faded away almost immediately as Achilles and Alucard scooped up a fistful of their own and guzzled them down.

The hooded figures offered the tray towards Gunnar, but he shook his head. "My wife is a messy drinker," he said, rubbing his voodoo bride's head. The two hooded figures chuckled, but I didn't understand why. Gunnar didn't seem to find anything funny about it either because he didn't smile. The hooded figures' laughter cut off abruptly.

I waved away their offer as well. "I need to tinkle," I told the one with the tray. I found myself staring past him because Asterion was reaching a hand into the air and grasping at something I couldn't see. Alucard was giggling as if he couldn't quite recall how to stop.

And Achilles was resting his cheek against the scaly door. "It's so soft," he whispered incredulously, sliding his face back and forth as he hummed to himself.

Gunnar and I stared at the three of them, frowning. I finally waved my hand dismissively and turned to the hooded figures. "We came here for a job, and we're not leaving until that job is finished. We're gentlemen on a mission, you see." Gunnar cleared his throat pointedly and I glanced over to see him jerking his chin at the voodoo bride. I turned back to the hooded figures. "And my friend's lady wife, naturally."

The two hooded figures gave us another of those silent stares, but it was interrupted by Asterion who was now licking the dirty brick wall with a long tongue. "I can taste the flows of time itself..." he mumbled between licks.

I gagged instinctively, but Gunnar looked over at him curiously. "Really?" he asked.

I clapped my hands. "We're *gentlemen* on a *mission!*" I reminded my crew in a shout loud enough to catch their attention. Alucard was openly crying with laughter, kneeling in a puddle, and Achilles was still rubbing his cheek on the door, but they looked more attentive.

"If you will follow us, we have nudity inside," the hooded figures offered helpfully.

"Even better!" I cheered. "Much better than that other mission I mentioned."

"Absolutely," Gunnar agreed solemnly. "Let's go, honey," he told his voodoo bride, ever the gentleman. The hooded figures opened the doors and I—being the only responsible one left—managed to shove them all through ahead of me, after Gunnar helped pry Asterion off the wall.

We entered a long, narrow hallway that was illuminated with black lights, making us all glow, especially the voodoo bride's lingerie—even though it was now significantly stained, and she had tire marks from the bike across her panties.

A large figure loomed ahead of us, guarding a door. When he stood, I hissed, taking a step back instinctively. "No disrespect, but that's a hell of a nose you got there, pal," I said, smiling politely.

The slick-skinned bouncer studied me with narrowed eyes, his green snout easily a few feet long and full of razor-sharp teeth. Achilles was pressed against the wall and rolling across it like he was rolling down a hill in a field. Alucard was twisting his wrist back and forth, studying his hand in the glowing light as if it was the first time he'd ever seen it.

Asterion was smiling like a big idiot, trying to touch his nostril ring with his tongue and laughing with each failed attempt.

"I'm a crocodile," the bouncer finally said, frowning at us. "You guys do know where you are, right? Cockodile Skins..."

"Yep. That sounds right. We're here for a job, but we're going to need help. We should have a friend waiting for us inside to tell us what tonight's game is. We're just doing what we're told."

The bouncer's eyes widened, and he looked like—for the first time in his career—he wasn't quite sure how to respond.

He finally shrugged, opening the inner door for us. We stepped through and were immediately assaulted by strobing lights and some kind of electronic music with a lot of bass. The walls and floors were black marble, but all the decorations were an ivory tone—from rugs to couches to artwork on the walls.

As I accustomed myself to our new surroundings, I became more uncomfortable, but I wasn't quite sure why. I turned to scan the room in search of our contact. Had Julian given us a name or description?

Gunnar was frowning absently. "Something seems...different," he finally said.

Alucard froze suddenly, his laughter cutting off. I turned to find him staring at a naked male dancer standing directly before him. His costume consisted of a bow-tie around his neck. He gave Alucard a very friendly smile, but instead of smiling back, Alucard gave him an awkward high five and then turned around, steering us away.

"Hey," I snapped. "Who was your friend, Alucard?" I demanded. "That was very rude!"

Alucard shoved us into a booth and shushed us, glancing around quickly to make sure we were alone. Sensing his panic, we all focused on him, wondering if we were in danger.

"I don't know if you guys have noticed," Alucard began, "but I think we might be in the wrong place."

I frowned, turning to scan the dance club. I saw the stages and the stripper poles, a guy in a fox-tail thong and bow-tie giving a bachelorette party a lap-dance, and a bunch of other naked guys walking around with more of those test tubes shots—which looked pretty damned cool in the black lights. As I studied the rest of the room, I noticed many more naked guys with the fox-tail thongs and bow-ties lingering here and there.

I turned back to Alucard, shrugging.

He met my eyes, no longer giggling. "They're wearing bow-ties," he said in a very serious tone. "And we're not wearing bow-ties." He let us digest that epiphany for a moment or two.

Achilles grunted. "I'm not sure if that's what has my shoulders itching," he said. "Something is missing but I can't quite put my finger on it..."

Asterion was rubbing his horns on the back of the couch, moaning to himself. What the hell had been in those test tubes, and why hadn't I tried one?

Gunnar was whispering something into his voodoo bride's ear, not even pretending to pay attention to the conversation at our table.

I focused back on Alucard. "Do you think there's a dress code or something? Why are you so nervous right now?"

Alucard shuddered. "I don't know. Maybe it's just the crocodile thing," he said absently.

"What crocodile thing?" I asked, frowning.

"The bouncer. Definitely a crocodile."

I thought back, wondering how I had missed that. "The guy with the long nose and sharp teeth?" I asked, frowning.

He nodded. "That's the one."

"I'm sure he would have told us…" I said doubtfully.

"You're probably right," Alucard finally admitted. "It was just a guess, anyway."

"You guys want to head down to the stage and look for our next challenge?" I asked. Gunnar and Asterion were preoccupied so Achilles and Alucard joined me as we made our way to the stripper poles. That strange sensation kept nagging at me, but I brushed it off. No one was going to yell at us for not wearing bow-ties.

When we were about halfway across the room, the door we had entered the club from suddenly flew open and the long-nosed guy flew into the room, bowling over a few very distracted patrons. I turned to the door to see Herja and Julian glaring at the bouncer. "Where are they?" they shouted in unison, looking much angrier than the last time I had seen them.

I waved at them. "We're right—"

Just then, about a dozen naked women burst into the room from behind Herja and Julian. The naked women wore only crocodile skin cowgirl boots and they glared behind me where I suddenly heard hissing snarls. I spun to find a line of the mostly-naked men in the bow-ties and fox-tail thongs glaring and hissing back at the women in cowboy boots.

"Wait a minute…" I began, scratching my chin. "I think there might actually be a dress code, guys."

"My wife!" Achilles breathed, staring up at Herja.

"She's not your wife," Alucard mumbled. "You idiot."

"Get out of the way!" Herja shouted at us. "This is the wrong strip club! You were supposed to go to *Foxies*, not *Cockodile Skins*, you slobbering idiots!"

Before I could respond, the two lines of strippers attacked each other with us in the middle.

CHAPTER 14

Achilles snapped his eyes shut and began shadow-boxing in every direction. He clocked one of the women in the nose before he was knocked out of the way by one of the naked men behind us. Alucard tried to extricate himself from one of the male strippers, tearing his shirt clear off in the process. He spun, clocked the male stripper in the face and began shouting down at him. "Give me your bow-tie!"

The stripper blinked a few times before complying. Alucard snapped the elastic bow-tie around his neck and jumped back into the fight, leaving the male stripper on the ground.

I managed to slip out of the mob of screaming strippers to find Herja and Julian fighting a few more of the alleged 'crocodile' bouncers, so I left them to it, not wanting to get involved in that web of lies. I began walking around the strip club in search of one of those test tube waiters, but they all seemed busy fighting more of the naked women who had apparently entered the club while I was distracted.

A loud bellowing roar made me look up to find Gunnar sprinting through the strip club with his voodoo bride under one arm, knocking down anyone in his path. As I watched him mowing down those in his way, I realized that he was just running laps around the strip club, not actually going anywhere.

I saw the Minotaur pounding across the center stage with his head down like a battering ram. He struck one of the poles, ripping it entirely free of the bolts on the floor before he tripped, stumbled, and fell off the stage into what looked like a backroom VIP area.

I found one of the test tube trays and sat down on the empty couch beside it, propping my feet up on the table as I picked up one of the shots, sniffing it absently. I tasted it, licking my lips a few times as I watched the fighting continue. Gunnar ran past me for the second time, still roaring and running laps around the club. I downed the test tube and tossed it away, folding my hands behind my head as I watched the fight.

Things had escalated at one point or another because now there was a dozen or so shifter foxes battling an equal number of shifter crocodiles, no longer bothering with human forms. It looked like the naked men here had been crocodiles after all and had worn the fox-tail thongs as a mockery of the other shifter strip club in town.

Likewise, the foxes strip club had worn crocodile skin cowgirl boots to mock their competitors. It was all rather confusing, so I dismissed it from my mind.

Achilles jogged up to my table with an elastic headband around his forehead. A fox tail hung from the band and he shook his head to show me. "Look, I'm Davey Crockett!" he said, laughing.

I grinned. "More like Davey Cockett," I told him, laughing.

"What?"

I waved a hand, forgetting why that had been funny when I said it. "I don't know, man. I think I'm barely managing to keep my atoms together right now," I told him, pointing to the bucket of test tubes. "What the hell is in that stuff?" Because my vision was flashing with concentric light and my very soul was vibrating with energy like I was holding all the magic I could manage.

I blinked, slowly turning to Achilles who was reaching for one of the test tubes. "Dude, I think I know how to use *magic*..." I whispered, staring down at my hands, twisting them back and forth curiously.

He grunted, downing his drink. "You're just really high, man. It will pass."

"Oh, that's good. I'm probably the last person who should be given that kind of power," I admitted, feeling relieved. "I think I'm just going to hang here for a while. I think I finally figured this thing out."

"What thing?" he asked absently, watching the stripper fight below.

"Life, bro. Life."

He nodded. "Good luck with that. I'm going to try jumping off the stage to see how many crocodiles I can take down."

"Cool," I told him. "But wait just a minute," I said, holding up my hand. Achilles turned to frown at me, brushing the fox tail from his face.

Gunnar rounded the corner and ran past us, still yelling at the top of his lungs as he made another lap with his voodoo bride.

I waved Achilles on. "Okay, now it's safe to cross," I told him, closing my eyes.

"You're pretty deep, man," Achilles told me, but I didn't stay awake long enough to answer him.

CHAPTER 15

I woke up at a sudden noise. I was beside a strange campfire on a distant planet. I jumped to my feet in alarm.

"Easy, champ. Easy," Ashley chuckled from a lawn chair a few feet away.

"Oh, this is Earth," I said, letting out a relieved breath.

Ashley frowned at me but didn't comment.

Gunnar lay beside her in werewolf form, cuddling the voodoo bride doll. Achilles was leaning against a log with a strange elastic band around his head. A fake foxtail hung from the front of it, resting against his nose and lips so that when he snored it briefly rose, falling back down when he inhaled. It looked familiar for some reason.

Alucard was on his back staring up at the stars. He wasn't wearing a shirt, but he was wearing a cheap bow-tie for some reason. Although he was awake, he wouldn't make eye contact with me.

Asterion was face-down in the dirt, arms and legs spread-eagled as if he had swan dived on dry land and knocked himself out. He was missing one of his boots and snoring loudly.

I turned to Ashley, shaking my head. I felt surprisingly good—very confused, but not hungover. I sat in the chair next to her and let out a long breath. It was night, apparently.

"What happened last night?" I finally asked, wobbling slightly. I still felt kind of drunk, now that I thought about it.

She chuckled softly. "The Valkyrie who dropped you off said I wasn't allowed to talk about it unless you remembered first."

I nodded after a few moments. "That's probably smart."

The silence stretched between us as we watched the fire, wondering who in the group would wake up next.

"Hey, Ashley. Can I ask you a serious question?" I mumbled, my eyelids feeling too heavy to hold open much longer.

"Sure," she said in an amused tone.

"I can...use magic...right?" I mumbled, fading away from the campsite altogether.

I think I heard her laughing, but I was too busy sailing off into the furthest reaches of the galaxy on the USS Segway, the dread-space-pirate Nate Temple reporting for duty. Constellations of Valkyries, foxes, crocodiles, and mermaids zipped past my ship as I turned on warp speed, leaving a distant campfire far, far behind me.

To boldly go where no space-wizard had ever gone before...

～

MAKE A DIFFERENCE

Reviews are the most powerful tools in our arsenal when it comes to getting attention for our books. Much as we'd like to, we don't have the financial muscle of a New York publisher.

But we do have something much more powerful and effective than that, and it's something that those publishers would kill to get their hands on.

A committed and loyal bunch of readers.

Honest reviews of our books help bring them to the attention of other readers.

If you've enjoyed this book, we would be very grateful if you could spend just five minutes leaving a review on our book's Amazon page.

Thank you very much in advance.

ACKNOWLEDGMENTS

From Cameron:

I'd like to thank Shayne, for paving the way in style. Kori, for an introduction that would change my life. My three wonderful sisters, for showing me what a strong, independent woman looks and sounds like. And, above all, my parents, for—literally—everything.

From Shayne (the self-proclaimed prettiest one):

Team Temple and the Den of Freaks on Facebook have become family to me. I couldn't do it without die-hard readers like them.

I would also like to thank you, the reader. I hope you enjoyed reading *LAST CALL* as much as we enjoyed writing it.

And last, but definitely not least, I thank my wife, Lexy. Without your support, none of this would have been possible.

ABOUT SHAYNE SILVERS

Shayne is a man of mystery and power, whose power is exceeded only by his mystery...

Shayne holds two high-ranking black belts, and can be found writing in a coffee shop, cackling madly into his computer screen while pounding shots of espresso. He's hard at work on the newest books in the TempleVerse—You can find updates on new releases or chronological reading order on the next page, his website, or any of his social media accounts. **Follow him online for all sorts of groovy goodies, giveaways, and new release updates:**

Get Down with Shayne Online
www.shaynesilvers.com
info@shaynesilvers.com

facebook.com/shaynesilversfanpage

amazon.com/author/shaynesilvers

bookbub.com/profile/shayne-silvers

instagram.com/shaynesilversofficial

twitter.com/shaynesilvers

goodreads.com/ShayneSilvers

BOOKS BY SHAYNE & CAMERON

CHRONOLOGY: All stories in the TempleVerse are shown in chronological order on the following page

NATE TEMPLE SERIES

(Main series in the TempleVerse)

by Shayne Silvers

FAIRY TALE - FREE prequel novella #0 for my subscribers

OBSIDIAN SON

BLOOD DEBTS

GRIMM

SILVER TONGUE

BEAST MASTER

BEERLYMPIAN (Novella #5.5 in the 'LAST CALL' anthology)

TINY GODS

DADDY DUTY (Novella #6.5)

WILD SIDE

WAR HAMMER

NINE SOULS

HORSEMAN

LEGEND

KNIGHTMARE

ASCENSION

FEATHERS AND FIRE SERIES

(Also set in the TempleVerse)

by Shayne Silvers

UNCHAINED

RAGE

WHISPERS

ANGEL'S ROAR

MOTHERLUCKER (Novella #4.5 in the 'LAST CALL' anthology)

SINNER

BLACK SHEEP

GODLESS

PHANTOM QUEEN DIARIES

(Also set in the TempleVerse)

by Cameron O'Connell & Shayne Silvers

COLLINS (Prequel novella #0 in the 'LAST CALL' anthology)

WHISKEY GINGER

COSMOPOLITAN

OLD FASHIONED

MOTHERLUCKER (Novella #3.5 in the 'LAST CALL' anthology)

DARK AND STORMY

MOSCOW MULE

WITCHES BREW

SALTY DOG

SEA BREEZE

HURRICANE

CHRONOLOGICAL ORDER: TEMPLE VERSE

FAIRY TALE (TEMPLE PREQUEL)

OBSIDIAN SON (TEMPLE 1)

BLOOD DEBTS (TEMPLE 2)

GRIMM (TEMPLE 3)

SILVER TONGUE (TEMPLE 4)

SHADE OF DEVIL SERIES

(Not part of the TempleVerse)

by Shayne Silvers

DEVIL'S DREAM

DEVIL'S CRY

DEVIL'S BLOOD

NOTHING TO SEE HERE.

Thanks for reaching the last page of the book, you over-achiever. Sniff the spine. You've earned it. Or sniff your Kindle.

Now this has gotten weird.

Alright. I'm leaving.